As always, thank you to the many book retailers, distributors, author and marketing partners, and of course, my family who have been so supportive in the pursuit of these stories.

"Moonlight drowns out all but the brightest stars."

J.R.R. Tolkien

Also by Michael Lindley

The "Troubled Waters" Series

The "Hanna Walsh and Alex Frank Low Country Mystery and Suspense" Series

Amazon and Goodreads Five Star Reviews for Death On The New Moon

★★★★★

If you love mystery and suspense with twisting plots, compelling characters and settings that will sweep you away, find out why readers are raving about *Death On The New Moon*.

Chapter One

The man named Caine sat in the fighting chair mounted on the aft deck of the 35-foot fishing boat as it trolled slowly through the calm waters of the Atlantic ten miles off the coast of Charleston. He was dressed only in tan Bermuda shorts and a faded and stained fishing cap to shield his eyes from the hot sunny day. His upper body and legs were deeply tanned and glistening with sweat. He calmly watched the steady throbbing of two fishing rods set off the stern, pulling bait with lines trailing out far behind in the wake of the big boat.

It had been a good day, he thought. He felt at home on the water as far away from people as possible. When he was around people, someone was often going to die.

The sun was just above the far horizon to the west, glowing hot and reflecting back across the water. To the east, the first sliver of the new moon glowed bright in the darkening sky. No other boats were in sight. The low rumble of the twin engines below deck mixed with the cry of gulls hovering over the boat and screeching for more bait and chum to be thrown overboard.

The boat was on a slow auto-pilot course and needed no tending. A puff of wind came across the starboard rail. He leaned back and closed his eyes allowing all his senses to take in the serenity and peace of the moment.

He stood and reached down into a large white pail against the transom and grabbed a metal dipper hanging on the edge. He brought up a dripping scoop of bloody red fish chum and poured it overboard into the churning water behind him. Drops of blood and fish offal splashed on the white deck and rail of the boat. He flipped another scoop of the bloody slop out into the water and watched it mix with the green frothing wake. Reaching down for the bucket, he poured the rest of the chum over the side then turned and walked into the cabin of the boat. He pulled back the throttles for both engines and felt the boat slow and rock gently in the low swells of the ocean.

Within minutes he had both rods reeled in and secured in holders above the cabin.

A low muffled moan came from the hatch leading down into the cabin and galley below deck. The man scanned the horizon. Still no other boats or aircraft above. The moans became more urgent and frantic, as if the slowing of the boat had triggered some fearful response.

Caine went down the steps and then came back up carrying a woman in his arms. Her hands and feet were bound with plastic tie straps. A piece of gray tape was stretched tight across her mouth. She struggled in his arms, but his firm grip held her fast. He placed the woman down in the fighting chair and when she tried awkwardly to get up, he pulled a long-bladed knife from a scabbard on his belt and held it out an inch from her nose.

The woman's eyes grew large and she moaned again, trying to speak. Her hair was short and brown and clung to her face in sweaty curls. A dark purple bruise spread across her left cheek from the blow he'd delivered when she'd been abducted. She was dressed in tan slacks and a white blouse that was also wet from sweat. Her feet were bare and she tried to gain purchase on the foot rest of the heavy chair.

"Please...," she tried to cry out, but Caine ignored her and turned to look over the back of the boat. Two large sharks had come in to feed on the chum. Their long gray bodies turned quickly to stay behind the boat, large mouths open wide to take in the bloody feast. He grabbed another bucket of the chum and threw it all overboard. A third large fin raced through the red trail in the water.

That should do, he thought and turned back to the woman. He stood before her and in a calm voice said, "You had a job to do and you let everyone down."

She shook her head frantically and tried to stand from the chair again until the sharp point of the knife on her forehead pushed her back into the seat. The blade cut a small slice in her skin above one eyebrow. It began to bleed and flow down between her eyes and onto the white of her blouse. She screamed out in pain.

"So, the money wasn't enough? Is that it?"

"Nooo..." she cried out through the tape in a low moan.

He wiped a spot of blood off the end of the knife on her slacks, then held the blade up, examining the long sharp edge.

The woman was weeping now in gasping sobs. The blood from the cut on her forehead was streaming in a steady flow along her nose and dripping off her chin.

"You brought this on yourself," Caine said, his voice low and measured. "They weren't asking for much."

The woman thrust forward and fell onto the deck when her restraints prevented her from standing. Her blood mixed with the fish chum on the hard wet surface of the boat deck. She lay on her side breathing heavily and moaning.

Caine unhooked a clasp that held a door in the middle of the transom on the back rail of the boat. He swung it to the side and walked down onto a teak platform just above water level. The three big sharks were still feeding and churning the water below him. He turned and calmly walked back onto the deck. He grabbed the long wooden handle of a fish gaff hanging along the rail. It had a sharp steel hook on the end for gaffing fish and pulling them on-board.

With no warning, he swung the gaff hook hard into the thigh of the woman and she screamed out into the fading light of the day, no one but the man named Caine to hear. Almost effortlessly, he pulled her with the gaff through the opening and down onto the wooden platform.

She saw the sharks as their fins and long backs swept back and forth through the red water behind the boat. She began trembling and struggling to break free from the hook embedded in her leg. Caine placed a foot on her stomach to hold her in place.

A smile came across his face. "You picked the wrong people to let down, ma'am."

She shook her head violently trying to pull free.

He pulled the gaff savagely out of her thigh and she wailed again as more blood flowed.

Caine came around behind her and stood for a moment, taking in the vast scope of ocean and cloudless sky.

Without warning, he pushed her over the edge of the deck with his foot. "Bon appetit!" he whispered with a grin across his face. He watched as the woman splashed into the churning water. The sharks came quickly, and he saw the last frantic and helpless look in her eyes as she was pulled under and away. He was disappointed they hadn't torn her apart on the surface.

He calmly walked back on deck and got a hose to clean up the mess.

Chapter Two

"Good morning, Detective."

Alex Frank turned away from the ocean, almost knocking over the cup of coffee on the armrest of the weathered Adirondack chair on the deck of the old beach house. He smiled and made room for Hanna to sit beside him. He was dressed in wrinkled white shorts and a faded Clemson t-shirt. His short brown hair was mussed from sleep. Three days beard remained unshaven and showed traces of gray along the edges of his chin.

Hanna felt his hand on her shoulder as she looked out over the beach and the blinding glare on the water as the sun just made its way above the far horizon. A low bank of clouds far to the east of Pawleys Island was cast in deep crimson with yellow shafts of sunlight pushing through. A sliver of the new moon was just now fading as a freshening breeze from the south moved the sea oats along the dunes in a slow cadence. A school of dolphin broke the stillness of the water, rising effortlessly, over and over to take another breath and continue on their early morning migration toward the inlet.

"Why do we ever leave this place?" she heard him say behind her.

"Let's not." She turned and leaned back into him, feeling his arms come around her and pull her close.

"It's Monday," he said.

"Be late."

"I have to meet Lonnie at nine." Lonnie Smith was his long-time partner in the Charleston Police Detective Squad.

Hanna pulled her phone from the pocket of her robe. It was 6:30, and she had appointments ahead through the day as well as she looked down the scroll of her calendar. "I need to be back in Charleston mid-morning. Do you have time for some breakfast?"

He didn't answer.

She turned and saw him looking across the dunes and the long expanse of the Atlantic to the south. "Alex?"

"I'm sorry, just thinking about the call with my father last night."

"You really think his memory is starting to slip?"

He took a sip from his coffee. "He's been forgetful for years. The booze hasn't helped." He pulled her closer and rested his chin in her hair. "His new mate, Robbie, called the other day to tell me the Skipper couldn't find his way back to the inlet on Friday on their last shrimp run."

Alex's father, Jordan "Skipper" Frank, had owned and operated the *Maggie Mae* shrimp boat out of Dugganville, South Carolina for over forty years. Alex and his deceased brother, Bobby, had grown up on the boat running shrimp with their father. Bobby had been lost to the war in the Middle East. Alex had chosen law enforcement after his tour of duty in the Marines. The Skipper had carried on without them and still managed to make a decent living harvesting shrimp along the Carolina coast.

"He couldn't find the inlet to the bay?" Hanna asked, sitting up and reaching for his coffee cup.

"Robbie told me he nearly ran aground two miles south of the buoy, thinking he was coming into the river mouth."

"Did you ask him about it?"

Alex took a deep breath and looked away. "He laughed it off, said he was still hungover from the night before down at *Gilly's*. He also didn't remember what day it was when I wished him a Happy Birthday last night."

"He forgot his own birthday?" Hanna said, "You'd think after all the trouble with the murder charge last year and his blackouts, he'd cut back some on the drinking."

"I think it's getting even worse."

Skipper Frank had been arrested for the murder of Horton Bayes, a rival shrimper from Dugganville. The man had been found brutally beaten and killed on the deck of his own shrimp boat. All signs pointed to Alex's father who had been pulled apart from a fight at *Gilly's Bar* with Bayes earlier that same night. Alex and Hanna had helped to track down the real killer, a long-time friend of the family who had gotten sideways with Bayes and a drug ring operating in the area.

"Is it safe for him to even be out on the water anymore?" she asked.

"Robbie's a good man. He's keeping him out of trouble for now, but you know how damn stubborn my old man is."

Hanna handed the coffee back and leaned in to kiss him. He held her close and buried his face in the warm curve of her neck.

She whispered, "You hungry."

"Not so much."

"When do you have to leave?"

"Soon," he said. "I need to shower."

"Is there room for two?" she asked, pulling back and smiling.

Chapter Three

Alex decided at the last minute to take the turn to Dugganville on his way back to Charleston. He had called his partner to tell him he'd be late and would meet him down at the precinct closer to ten. He felt compelled to check on Skipper, as he'd called his father since he was in high school. The narrow two-lane off Highway 17, to the little fishing village on the banks of the Duggan River leading out to the Intracoastal and Bulls Bay on the Atlantic was lined with pine and live oak. Cattle farms and cotton fields with stately restored Antebellum homes from the old plantations were draped in a low mist that had yet to burn off in the heat of the coming day. The sun was just above the trees now, glowing gold and blinding as he headed east into town.

The old familiar Main Street in Dugganville was just coming to life with several cars parked in front of *Andrew's Diner* for breakfast and two pick-ups in front of the hardware store. He drove along the river and saw the tangle of docks and tall masts from the sailboats and the riggings from the few shrimp boats that still plied the local waters.

As he pulled up to their old family house on the hill above the river and the dock that held the *Maggie Mae*, he saw that his father's truck was not in the drive. On a hunch, he turned left at the first street and drove two blocks to Ella Moore's house, the mother of his ex-wife, Adrienne. His father and Ella had somehow survived an on again, off again relationship over the years after Alex's mother had been killed in a car accident. Ella usually drank even more than the Skipper and their public displays of drunkenness and screaming arguments were legendary in town. His father's truck was parked in front and he pulled in behind it on the dirt shoulder.

Alex hadn't seen or heard from his ex-wife since she had come back to town over a year ago with a young son who she at first had told Alex was theirs. Her deceit had eventually been revealed when the real father came up from Florida for her and their son. Adrienne's attempts to win him back were still an occasional sticking point between he and Hanna. Hanna's trust issues with men were certainly justified from past relationships, including a now deceased husband who was a serial cheater, including with her best friend at the time, Grace Holloway.

Hanna had every right to still be skeptical of Adrienne's intentions, but he assumed now that his ex had finally settled in with the new husband down in South Florida, that issue was behind them. He hoped that was the case.

His time together with Adrienne from high school through his years away in the service had been marked with her repeated betrayals and deceptions. She had almost convinced him to take her and the boy back when she had last returned to Dugganville during his father's murder investigation. He had almost lost Hanna in the process.

As he walked up the steps to his former mother-in-law's house, he thought about how fortunate he was to have found Hanna Walsh. They had worked through most of their issues and it had been good with the two of them together this past year. He smiled as he remembered their parting shower just a short time ago.

He was coming up on the porch when his father opened the door and looked up in surprise at the sight of his son. "What the hell you doing here?"

"I was about to ask you the same," Alex said, stepping aside so the Skipper could open the screen door and join him on the porch.

From inside, Alex heard, "Get your ass out of my house and don't come back!"

"I can see you and Ella are still hittin' it off," Alex said.

His father grumbled and pushed by, letting the screen slam behind him as he walked down the steps. Alex started to follow him down to his truck. He could smell the bourbon and sweat on the man. "Why do you do this, Pop? That woman is a train wreck."

"You think I'm not?" the old man snarled back over his shoulder.

Alex heard the door open again behind them and turned to see Ella coming out on the porch. She was pulling a rumpled old plaid robe around her plump bare body and was clearly surprised to see him there with his father.

"Alex," she said hesitantly, finishing with the tie on her robe. "How you been, boy?"

"Fine, Ella, just fine."

"Tell your old man he's a *sonovabitch*, and he's not welcome around here no more!"

"Zip it, woman!" the Skipper yelled back.

Alex watched as she reached for a cigarette and lighter in her pocket and lit up. Her dyed red hair was all askew and the bags under her eyes were dark and puffy. "You got time for a cup of coffee, Alex?" she asked. "We haven't caught-up in a long time."

"No, Ella. Need to get back to Charleston. Just checkin' in on the Old Man."

Her expression darkened again. "Skipper, I'm through with your ass!"

His father didn't respond to her and opened the door to his truck. "Meet me down at the diner," he said under his breath. He slammed the door and started the old rusted Chevy truck. As Alex started to walk down to his own car, he waved at Ella Moore. "Nice to see you, Ella."

The woman waved back. "Adrienne asked about you the other night."

Alex felt his stomach tighten. "She and Scottie doing okay?"

Ella shook her head. "Never know with that girl."

Alex nodded back as he got into his car. He yelled up to the house, "You take care, Ella and take it easy on the Skipper. He can't help himself." He watched as she shook her head in disgust.

Skipper Frank had already found an empty booth at *Andrew's*. The proprietor, Lucy, was placing two cups of steaming coffee down in front of him as Alex walked up.

"Morning, Lucy," Alex said. "How about a couple scrambled and that whole wheat bread you bake toasted?"

"Coming right up, Alex," she said and gave him a hug. "Nice to see you." She and her husband had run the diner in Dugganville for over two decades and she had treated Alex and his brother like her own sons as they'd grown up here. She turned to his father. "Skipper?"

"Same," the old man growled back. "Throw some fried taters on there, too."

She walked away shaking her head and Alex sat down across from his father. He obviously hadn't shaved in days. His eyes were bloodshot, and his gray hair pushed out in stray clumps from a worn and dirty Atlanta Braves ball cap. "What's the latest with you and Ella?"

The Skipper shook his head in disgust. "The old woman must think I'm twenty years old. She wanted to do the nasty again this morning. I got about one in me a week these days, for *chrissakes*."

"Aren't the two of you a bit old for that nonsense," Alex said, not able to hide a smile.

"Damn woman's insatiable!"

"I swear you two together is worse than a damn tsunami. Wouldn't you be better off movin' on?"

"You saw she just thow'd me out again."

"But you'll be back in no time, right?"

The Skipper just grunted and sipped at his hot coffee.

Alex leaned in and spoke softly, not wanting those at nearby tables and the counter to hear. "What's this about you missing the channel comin' in Bulls Bay the other day?"

He watched an angry scowl come across his father's face. "That damn Robbie snitchin' on me again? I need to fire his ass!"

"Pop, I'm just worried about you out on the salt. Doesn't take much to get into trouble out there."

"What else am I gonna do? I got to run the business and pay the bills."

Alex said, "I know you got plenty of money saved and you can sell the *Maggie Mae* and settle back. You've earned it. Maybe spend some time down in the Keys and take the skiff to do some fishing. I'd go with you."

"Ain't never sellin' the *Maggie Mae*. Be like cuttin' off my right arm."

"Pop, you're movin' in on seventy. No shame in retirement and I think you need a change of scenery after all these years. Might meet a nice lady down there who isn't as damn crazy as you are."

The Skipper shook his head and looked out the window at cars passing on Main.

"Pop, you hearing me?"

His father looked back. "I know you mean well, Alex, but this is all I know, and I got no intention of startin' over somewhere else."

Chapter Four

Hanna was half-way back to Charleston, driving south on Highway 17, listening to country music on the radio and enjoying the beautiful morning and countryside passing by. Images of her recent weekend at the beach house with Alex kept coming back to her and she smiled as she thought about their recent time together. Alex Frank had become a treasured part of her life and she felt fortunate they had navigated the dark waters of the past year to come together again and continue on as a couple. There had even been some talk recently about living together full-time, but neither could agree on where, other than the beach house on Pawleys Island which had become their almost constant weekend refuge.

The lyrics from the song on the radio broke her thoughts. It was another classic country music story about *"a man's wife leaving town with his best friend ... and he missed him."* She laughed and turned the volume down when her cell phone rang on the console beside her. The caller-ID indicated it was her stepmother, Martha Wellman Moss. Hanna's delight in the coming day quickly soured as she considered letting the call go to voice mail. Her father's second wife was a constant irritant in her life, and she was in no mood to let the woman spoil such a marvelous morning.

The call ring ended and a short time later a chime indicated Martha had left a message. Hanna decided to listen to it when she got to the office.

Her free legal clinic in Charleston was continuing to attract more clients than she and her small staff could possibly assist, and she found she was referring more people than she would have liked to other free legal services. She was also balancing much of her week working with paying clients with the small firm she had joined on Pawleys Island. She still had bills to pay and college tuition for her son, Jonathan, up in Chapel Hill. After her husband's death and the near total financial collapse he brought down on their family, she had been able to at least hold on to the family's long-held house on the beach going back to the mid-1800's and her ancestors, the Paltierres.

She was not so fortunate in saving her home in Charleston along the Battery and now lived in a modest apartment above her legal clinic in an old historic house in a neighborhood just a few blocks from the city's center.

As hard as she tried, her latest episode with Martha crept back into her thoughts. The woman lived with her father in Atlanta in the quite-spacious Moss family home on West Paces Ferry Road north of town. The house dated back to family ancestors, the Coulters from the early 1900's. The Coulters ran the liquor trade in the South in the years before and after Prohibition. Tales of their nefarious exploits were still not so quiet gossip in Atlanta social circles. One of their sons, Mathew Coulter, had become a well- known novelist beginning in the 1930's. The house had passed along to Allen Moss's mother's side of the family in the 50's. Hanna had grown up in the house and was always embarrassed by the opulence of the place, though many of her friends lived in similar homes in the area.

Martha had called Hanna two weeks ago to complain that her father was thinking of selling the big house and getting a penthouse condo downtown that would be more convenient to his work office at the law firm where he had served as senior partner for many years. Martha was clearly more concerned she would lose the big house in the inheritance when Alan Moss finally passed. It was all Hanna could do to keep from hanging up on the woman. Two people living alone in a seven-bedroom, 10,000 square foot home was surely nonsensical, but Martha was twenty years younger than her husband and certainly had her sights on being matron of the *"Moss Manor"* in Buckhead society for many years to come.

Hanna had ended the call with a firm rebuke, stressing *that it was her father's house and he could damn well do what he pleased with it,* yet she knew this was far from the end of the drama. She hadn't bothered to call her father about it. He was certainly capable of handling the situation as he saw best.

Allen Moss had been back at work full-time for over six months since a near fatal heart procedure had slowed him considerably. Hanna had tried to convince him to step back his workload, but he would have nothing of it. The firm was his life and he would probably breathe his last breath in the big leather chair in his office looking out over the skyline of Atlanta.

Fortunately, in Hanna's mind at least, he had stopped trying to bring her back to the firm to begin moving her into a position to keep a Moss family member in a senior role. She had worked there in the first years of her career after law school and frankly, hated every minute of it, working with Atlanta's "upper-crust" with their divorces and other legal entanglements. She found far more satisfaction helping the community's under-served in Charleston.

The chaos in the front lobby area of her legal clinic was not surprising. Phones were ringing, loud conversations among different groups of lawyers and their clients were trying to be heard above the din. The old two-story home she had renovated to open the clinic had a daily flow of people needing help with housing, jobs, bankruptcies, various crimes and numerous other legal issues. Hanna had two other lawyers currently working part-time with her and two legal assistants. It was all they could do to keep up with the heavy volume of cases, but to Hanna, it was a labor of love.

Her long-time assistant, Molly, looked up and smiled as Hanna came in the front door from the street. Molly had a phone to her ear and both hands on the keyboard to the computer screen in front of her. Her expression echoed the fact it was a typical crazy Monday morning. She handed Hanna a tall pile of pink phone messages as she walked past to go back to her office.

She closed the door behind her and sat at the old oak desk against the far wall. One window on the side looked out through tall shrubs to the house very close next door. Taking a deep breath, she began sorting through her messages as she powered-up her computer and waited for her email in-box to load. On her cell phone calendar, she saw she had her first appointment in five minutes, a new case with a man's name she didn't recognize.

Her cell phone buzzed on her desk. It was Alex and she pushed the receive button. "Hey!"

"Just wanted to make sure you made it back okay," she heard him say.

"No trouble. Missed most of the early traffic." Then she remembered the phone message from her stepmother. It always galled her to consider the woman her stepmother She was barely a few years older and certainly played no motherly role in Hanna's life. "Martha called. More drama in Atlanta. Alan wants to sell the house." She always called her father by his first name. He thought it was more professional, certainly in public than, "Daddy". "I let it go to voice mail."

"You need to lighten up some on the woman," Alex teased. "She takes good care of your father."

"Other than the fact she's a gold-digging selfish boor, she's just great!"

Alex laughed and then said, "Look, I'm almost downtown. Stopped to see my father on the way down. He and Ella were going at it again."

"They're quite the couple."

"She was pissed he wouldn't have sex with her again before breakfast," he said, laughing again.

"What will we do with those two?"

"He also won't listen to reason about cutting back on the shrimp boat and won't discuss the memory issues."

"We just need to keep after him before something serious happens," she said.

There was a pause and then he said, "Okay, I'm parking. Got to catch-up with Lonnie. I've got some food in the fridge. I'll cook unless you have plans."

"I'll look forward to it... as long as I get to help in the kitchen." She was always hesitant about his ability to prepare an edible meal.

"Just bring a bottle of wine. I think we're out."

"See you tonight," she replied. "Hope your Monday isn't as crazy as mine is starting out."

He clicked off and she decided to listen to Martha's voice mail before her first appointment arrived.

The familiar "sugar sweet" southern voice came over the phone's speaker, "Good morning, Hanna. Hope y'all had a fine weekend. Hate to bother you but wanted to catch you before you hear from your father. We're having a little thing and I wanted you to hear my side of the story first. Please call me as soon as you can this morning." The message ended.

Hanna sighed and was tempted to disregard the request but decided better of it. Martha answered on the second ring. "Oh, Hanna. Thanks for calling back so quickly. I know how busy you are."

She tried to control her impatience and keep her tone calm. "What's going on with you and Allen?"

"We had a terrible argument last night... it just got really ugly."

"About the house?" Hanna asked.

"No, we're still discussing that, but your father is completely insane about something he has totally misunderstood."

"And what is that?" Hanna asked, her impatience difficult to hide.

"Your father thinks I'm having an affair..."

"What!"

"He's completely wrong about the whole situation, but he won't listen to reason."

"Give me the short version," Hanna said, "I have an appointment in two minutes."

"You know Robert Aylesworth, the investment banker your father and I have been friends with for years?"

"Yes, I know Robert."

"Well, your father has it in his head that Robert and I have been seeing each other and..."

"And are you?" Hanna said curtly.

"Not like that, Hanna. I swear."

"Why would Alan think otherwise, Martha?"

She hesitated before answering, then said, "Well, Robert and I do run in the same circles and end-up spending a lot of time together. We're in the same mixed-doubles tennis league at the club and he's been taking yoga in one of my classes lately, which your father doesn't feel up to doing either anymore."

Hanna was quickly losing her patience. "The man almost died from heart disease last year, Martha!"

"Of course, honey. I don't mean anything by that, but Robert and I were having a drink at the club after yoga last night and your father walked into the room and totally misread the situation."

"Martha, listen, I need to run. Someone's waiting to see me." She was trying her best to believe the woman's innocence but was doubtful at best. Finally, she said, "I know you love my father, but please don't do anything to hurt him or I swear..."

"Hanna, honestly, nothing's happening. I just wanted you to hear what's really going on before you speak with your father next."

Hanna doubted that Allen would even bring it up. His damn pride wouldn't let him admit to his daughter his wife might be shacking-up with another man. "Martha, I need to go."

"Bye, dear!"

Chapter Five

Alex wasn't even out of his car in the lot next to the police precinct in downtown Charleston when his phone buzzed. It was his partner and he touched the screen to take the call.

"Lonnie, sorry I'm late. I'm downstairs. I'll be up in a minute."

He could hear the concern in the man's voice. "Make it quick! We have a thing coming down fast on the "hitter" we've been tracking."

Alex ended the call and gathered a few items on the seat next to him including his service weapon, a 9mm Ruger semi-automatic that he carried in a shoulder holster. It was the same model he had carried during his tour of duty with the Marines in Afghanistan.

The "hitter" Lonnie Smith was referring to was a reputed hit man for the Dellahousaye crime family that operated across the South, with unfortunately, too much activity in the Charleston area lately in illegal drugs, gambling and prostitution. Connor and Beau Richards, who Alex had finally arrested a year earlier up in Dugganville, were wired into the organization although both were now serving long sentences in the state penitentiary.

Asa Dellahousaye ran the family and all the many branches and tentacles. At 72 years of age, he had remarkably managed to avoid arrest and jail-time over his long career in crime. He had a powerful stable of lawyers, judges, politicians and influential social and business leaders watching his back... and sharing in the hefty and illicit profits. His legitimate business enterprises included real estate and construction, and his generous philanthropic endeavors helped to mask the true nature of his empire.

The hitman was a deranged lowlife, reportedly operating out of the

Caribbean lately, named simply Caine. Alex never knew if it was his first or last name. He did know the man had a long sheet of attributed kills around the world including two recent murders in Charleston that appeared to be tied to the Dellahousaye family.

Alex and Lonnie had been following up on several leads indicating the man was in town with more work to be done for Asa D, as he was best known by "friends" and "associates".

Alex found Lonnie at his desk upstairs. The big man was breathless, and his face and shaved head were covered in drips of sweat from the early heat and humidity of the coming day. They had been partners for over five years and had grown to become close friends away from work. Alex was Godfather to Lonnie and Ginny Smith's five kids. Hanna had also grown close to the family over the past year. Lonnie was the first African American to earn his detective shield in the department and was highly regarded for his work. Many thought he was on track to be Chief someday.

"Just got a call from our friend Jeb down at his bar on King street," Lonnie said. "Says a man that looks like the picture we dropped off is on his second bourbon."

"We got back-up?"

Lonnie nodded as they both headed to the door. Two uniforms and Beatty and Mills from upstairs will meet us down the block from Jeb's in five minutes."

"We got the green light on this guy from the Captain?" Alex asked. "You know he's gonna be comin' out hot."

"Whatever it takes, Franky," Lonnie said, using his friend's popular nickname in the department.

Lonnie took the wheel of the unmarked car down in the lot and Alex took a fresh magazine loaded with fifteen 9mm rounds from his bag and slid it into his piece. He took another and put it in the pocket of one of the bullet-proof vests he pulled from the backseat. A 12-gauge Remington shotgun was secured in the rack between them, pointing up at the roof of the car. Ammunition was already loaded in the vest.

Lonnie drove with purpose, but with no lights or sirens. The bar was less than a mile from the precinct and they pulled up to the designated staging spot a block away. The two young street cops were already there. Alex saw the other homicide detectives, Nathan Beatty and Willy Mills, walking quickly up to join them. All gathered around Lonnie who would lead the take-down.

"Okay, listen up," Lonnie said, looking down the street in both directions. The bar was around the corner to the south. "The owner told me the shooter is at the bar in the back next to the door to the kitchen. Two other customers at the bar. No one at tables. I've been in there and it's gonna be dark. The kitchen leads to a back door into the alley that empties out in both directions." He showed a picture of the man to the group then motioned to the two uniformed officers. "I want you on both sides of the back door, far enough back to have good cover, but in position to make sure our man has no way out. If he comes your way, take no chances with this asshole. He will not hesitate to take your head off."

Beatty said, "How we runnin' this, boss?"

"Alex and I will go in the front door, looking like customers."

"No vests, then?" Alex said.

Lonnie nodded, then looked to Beatty. "You two cover the front entrance in case he manages to get past us. Do not come in unless you hear my signal on the radio or if shots are fired. Clear?"

The two detectives nodded their heads in agreement.

Within minutes, they were all in position. Lonnie whispered into his radio to confirm the two uniforms had the alley covered. Beatty and Mills had vests on and shotguns pointed at the ground. Alex and Lonnie had their handguns secured in their waistbands under the back of their untucked shirts. Lonnie put his radio receiver in his back pants pocket, again hidden by his shirt.

"Franky, we move quick here. No hesitation on this piece of shit," Lonnie said, his voice steady and assured.

Alex could feel a hum building in his ears and his pulse quicken. Images of similar moments during raids in Afghanistan came back to him. His hands felt cold in spite of the heat. He tried to put the memory of a similar attempted arrest here in Charleston a few years back that left him on the ground with a hole leaking blood from his gut. He heard his partner whisper, "Let's go."

He followed Lonnie through the front door and immediately struggled to get his eyes to adjust to the dark interior of the bar room. A long bar with bottles arrayed along the wall was to their right. Neon signs of beer brands seemed the only light. He came alongside Lonnie and quickly tried to assess what he was seeing. There were only two men at the bar, sitting together and hunched over half-empty beer glasses. There was no sign of Jeb the bartender or a third customer where Caine should have been sitting. *What the hell?*

Lonnie crouched low and moved quickly to the left through several tables toward the back of the bar. He motioned for Alex to proceed to the bar. The two men drinking looked up as Alex pulled his gun. They both pushed their stools back and stood with panicked looks on their faces. Alex signaled with his left hand for them to get on the ground. He was sure neither man met the description and picture he had seen of the shooter known as Caine.

Alex looked quickly over the edge of the bar, his weapon extended. "Clear," he said, loud enough for his partner to hear. He made his way cautiously around the two men on the floor, his gun extended and aimed at the metal door with a greasy window to the back-kitchen area. His heart was now pounding in his chest and the buzz in his ears sounded like a train rushing by. He could see that Lonnie had made it to the back wall of the bar and was positioned to the left of the door, crouched behind a table with three chairs. Lonnie signaled for him to take cover behind a table to his right.

Lonnie's voice echoed out across the dark room, "Charleston Police! We have multiple units at all exits!"

Alex heard one of the men on the floor beside him say, "Oh shit!"

Lonnie yelled out again, "Place any weapons on the floor and come through the door with both hands high above your head!"

No response.

Alex saw Lonnie look back to him, assessing the situation. He turned back to the kitchen door. "Caine, this is Detective Smith. We'd rather walk you out of here in one piece, not on a slab. I want you coming out that door, now!"

Alex heard a muffled sound from the kitchen like someone trying to speak out.

Lonnie got on his radio and alerted the teams outside to the current situation and ordered them to remain in place. He heard Beatty acknowledge from the front but there was no response from the two officers in the alley.

Shit! Alex thought and turned to the man nearest him on the floor and whispered, "Where's Jeb and the other guy?"

The man looked back through rheumy eyes, confused.

"Where'd they go!" Alex hissed.

No response.

The chaos and devastation that erupted in the next sixty seconds would haunt Alex for the rest of his life.

Lonnie motioned Alex forward to take position on the right side of the door into the kitchen, then radioed quickly for more backup.

Alex heard a low moan and garbled voice from beyond the door. He looked over at his partner.

Lonnie was breathing heavily, sweat staining his shirt. Quietly, he said, "I think our man is gone, he's probably taken out the boys in the alley."

The moaning from the kitchen intensified.

Alex tried to calm himself and keep his right hand holding his gun from shaking.

Lonnie whispered, "We need to see if there's anything we can do for Jeb."

Alex nodded back.

"I'll go in low left," Lonnie said. "You take the other side. Who's out back?" he said into the radio. Mills responded saying both plainclothes were down, no sign of Caine.

Alex felt a chill rush through him.

To Alex, he said, "Ready?"

Alex held his Ruger in both hands to steady himself. He tipped his head once that he was ready to go. He watched his big partner come up fast and push through the door, ducking left quickly and out of sight. He followed immediately and came into the kitchen low, his weapon extended. He first saw the bartender named Jeb laying face up on the floor near a door to the back alley, clutching his chest with bloody hands, moaning and struggling to rise. Alex saw Lonnie continuing to move slowly along the left wall past cabinets and shelves with food and cooking pots. The air smelled of grease and stale beer. Alex wiped sweat from his eyes. He felt like his pounding heart would burst through his chest. He saw two doors along the right wall in front of him. He moved quickly to the first and pulled it back, his gun extending into the room as he peaked around the door. It was a small dank bathroom and empty.

As he would reflect back later, over and over in tortured dreams and recollections, he recalled everything from that point moving in slow motion, sounds muted and distorted.

After a glance over at Lonnie who was kneeling low along the far wall, moving slowly toward the downed bartender, Alex started toward the second door. In his memory of the next few moments, the door flew open in his face, knocking him backward, his gun falling away and sliding across the floor. As he fell, he watched as a hand extended from behind the door with a silenced gun pointing out. He remembered trying to yell out as he fell, but never remembered what he was trying to say. When he hit the floor, he watched helplessly as the trigger was pulled in four quick shots, only a hissing spit sounding from the long silencer.

Alex turned on his side, reaching desperately for his gun as he watched the four rounds explode into Lonnie Smith's chest and face. The big man went down instantly in a heap and didn't move. Alex yelled out into the room, now smelling of cordite and fear, "Noooo!"

The man known as Caine came out through the door and turned toward Alex. A smile spread across his face as he turned his weapon toward Alex, lying on the floor, his gun still out of reach, now resigned to his ultimate fate.

Later, he would recall only a sudden calmness coming over him as he looked up at the sneering face of the hit man and the round barrel of the gun pointing at his own forehead.

Caine spoke, but Alex would never remember his words. As he watched the man's trigger finger start to pull back, the door to the alley burst open and Mills rushed in. The assassin's gun spit again and Alex felt the bullet tear through the side of his neck, a burning hot slice of pain, likely diverted from a kill shot by Mills arrival.

As Alex fell back, he saw Mills fire twice and then go down as Caine caught him in the face with deadly aim. Mills fell in the open doorway and Caine turned back toward Alex just as Beatty came crashing through the door from the bar behind him. Alex watched as Caine bent low and rushed toward the back door. He heard Beatty yell out, "Jesus!", as he fell beside him on the floor. Then the explosion of Beatty's weapon firing twice as Caine disappeared out the back door, wood splintering on the door jamb from the shots.

Alex heard Beatty yell out again, "Oh Jesus!" as he lost consciousness.

Chapter Six

Hanna was finishing up a call when her assistant, Molly, leaned into the room. "There's someone I think you need to see. She doesn't' have an appointment. Her name is Calley."

"Send her back, thanks," Hanna said, clearing a few files and stray papers on her desk. She looked up when a young girl, maybe sixteen, came through the door. She was dressed in faded jeans, bright blue running shoes and wore a tight sleeveless t-shirt with a yellow smiley face on the chest. Her blond hair was pulled back in a short ponytail. She wore no make-up and her face was deeply tanned.

"Hello, I'm Hanna, she said, walking up to shake the girl's hand and then leading her over to two worn leather chairs in the corner of the small office. "Sit down, please."

"I'm Calley Barbour. Thank you for seeing me."

Hanna said, "Can I get you some coffee or water?"

"No... no, I'm fine.

What can I help you with this morning?"

The girl hesitated, looking around the office, settling on the two diplomas on the wall. Finally, she said, "I think I need a lawyer."

"And why is that?"

Calley squirmed in her chair, then the girl's cell phone buzzed in her jean's pocket. She struggled to get it out of her pocket. As she looked at the screen, she said, "It's my parents. They must have gotten the call from school I didn't come in this morning." She declined the call.

"Why are you missing school?"

"I told you, I think I need a lawyer."

Hanna said, "Calley, tell me what's going on."

The girl took a deep breath and then stared directly into Hanna's eyes. "I'm pregnant."

Hanna thought for a moment before answering, pushing back memories of a similar situation she found herself in as a young girl in college. "Tell me what happened."

The girl pushed a stray bit of hair from her eyes and said, "I barely know this guy. We met at a party out at the beach at a friend's house."

"So, how far along are you?"

"I've missed two periods."

Hanna hesitated, then asked, "And why do you think you need an attorney?"

"I don't want the baby. My parents will freak. They're super-religious and will probably throw me out of the house."

Hanna felt a familiar sadness come over her, remembering a similar time. "So, you think you want an abortion?"

"I know I want an abortion," the girl said firmly. "This guy raped me… or that's what I remember. We were really drunk and ended up out on the beach making out. I wanted him to stop and I couldn't make him."

"Calley, I'm so sorry. You didn't report this to the police then?"

"No, like I said, my parents would go ape-shit. I'd been drinking and doing some weed, let alone having sex with this guy. I don't even know his name or where to find him."

"How old are you?" Hanna asked.

"I just turned sixteen."

"You know in South Carolina your parents will have to sign an authorization for an abortion until you're over seventeen?"

Hanna saw tears forming in the girl's eyes. She wiped at them with both hands and looked down. "I know that and that's why I need your help."

"Calley, the law is very clear on this. You need parental consent."

"But I was raped!" she cried out as she tried to hold back her sobs.

Hanna shook her head, trying to think through all the implications, legal and moral. She had faced these same doubts and fears when she found herself pregnant from a man who had left her in college and never knew about the child. Calley Barbour's crying brought her back to the moment. She looked at the sorrow and despair on the young girl's face. *I wish I'd had someone to help,* she thought. Despite her past experiences, Hanna remained a Pro-choice advocate and was sympathetic to the girl's situation.

Calley said, "I read on the website for the local abortion clinic that a judge could give a waiver. My parents wouldn't need to know."

"It's called a *Judicial Bypass*," Hanna answered, begrudgingly, not knowing the full extent of the legal ramifications.

"Right, a bypass," Calley said. "That's why I need your help."

Hanna thought for a moment, then said, "First of all, I'm not advising you to do anything yet, certainly not keeping your parents out of this decision."

"But I thought you could help me!"

"Please, Calley, let's take some time to really think this through. I know there are many constraints to a judge giving this release from parental consent."

"You won't go to my parents!" the girl said in panic. "You're a lawyer. You can't talk about my case unless I agree."

"Calley, I'm not your lawyer yet, but I do want to help you."

"Please don't go to my parents!"

"I won't speak to anyone about this until we understand all our options and agree together on how best to proceed."

Calley Barbour had just left her office when Hanna's cell phone buzzed. It was a local number she didn't recognize, but she decided to take the call. "This is Hanna."

There was a brief pause before an unfamiliar voice said, "Hanna Walsh?"

"Yes, who is this?"

"My name is Jim Guinness, I'm the Captain down at Alex Frank's precinct."

Hanna felt a numbing dread come over her. "What's happened...?"

"Alex is okay at the moment..."

"At the moment!" she cried out into the phone. "What's going on?"

Captain Guinness continued with hesitation in his voice. "There was a shooting this morning during an attempted arrest."

"Oh God!" Thoughts of a similar call from the police when her husband had been found shot and killed on a sidewalk in downtown Charleston flashed through her mind.

Guinness said, "Alex is at the hospital. He's stable, but not out of danger yet. I'm sorry, Hanna."

"How bad is it?" she pleaded.

"He has a gunshot wound in his neck. Again, they've stabilized the situation, but he's lost a lot of blood."

Hanna felt faint and leaned back in her chair. "What hospital?"

The police captain informed her where Alex was being treated, then said, "I'm afraid I have more."

"Oh, please..." Hanna said, her heart sinking.

"I know you were close to Alex's partner, Lonnie Smith."

Hanna managed to answer, "Yes?"

"He's gone, Hanna. Lonnie was dead at the scene from his gunshot wounds."

She couldn't respond but thought immediately about Lonnie's wife and family. She heard Captain Guinness continue, "I'm down at the hospital with Alex. I'm so sorry."

"I'm coming down," Hanna managed. "I'll be there as soon as I can. Who is with Lonnie's wife, Ginny?"

"I have a team of people over there with her."

Hanna didn't know if she could stand, let alone drive to the hospital. She said, "Thank you, Captain. I'll be down as soon as I can."

She ended the call and looked up to see Molly standing in the doorway. "Is everything okay?" she asked.

Hanna just shook her head. "I have to go down to the hospital. Alex has been hurt."

"Oh my God!"

"His captain says he'll be okay, but he's been shot, and it sounds bad."

"Oh, Hanna. I'm really sorry."

"His partner has been killed."

Molly didn't answer, tears starting to drip down her face.

"I'll be going to see his wife Ginny sometime later. I'm sorry to leave you with all this, but I need to go."

"Of course," Molly answered quickly. "Just let me know what I can do to help."

Chapter Seven

His first conscious thought was the image of Lonnie Smith falling to the floor with blood spreading out across his face and white shirt. Alex tried to sit up and felt a searing pain in his neck and lay back down. A bright light above was blinding and he put an arm over his eyes.

"Alex?"

He heard the voice and looked to the side of the bed. It was his captain, sitting in the chair beside him.

"How you feelin', partner?" Captain Guinness asked."

"What the hell happened?"

Guinness didn't answer, just stared back. Random fragments of memories were coming back to him and a sinking feeling in his gut made him think he might throw-up. He tried to gather himself and asked, "Where's Lonnie?"

The police captain took a deep breath. "He didn't make it, Alex."

He pressed back down into the pillow, staring up at the bright light on the ceiling. His first thought out loud was, "Oh my God, Ginny."

"I have people with her."

"I need to be with her," Alex insisted.

"You need to stay right where you are and tell me what happened. I got everyone in the damn department out looking for this Caine fellow."

Alex reached for the heavy bandages on his neck and winced again at the pain.

"You took a round through the side of your throat," Guinness said. "Nicked a damn artery. You nearly bled-out."

Alex closed his eyes and tried to calm his breathing. He remembered the last moments when the man named Caine turned his gun back on him and the puff of smoke as the gun silently bucked and tore off a slice of his neck. He looked over at the tubes running from his arm up to bags of red and clear liquids on a rack beside the bed.

"It was a shit show, Captain," Alex finally said. He closed his eyes and tried to remember more of those last horrifying moments. "What about the others?" he asked.

The two uniforms, Knapp and Armeda are dead, killed in the alley. Willy's gone, too."

Alex was shaking his head slowly, his eyes pressed closed.

"Beatty got two shots off on Caine, but thinks he missed. We're checking all the blood trails."

"Captain... I'm not sure..."

"Beatty stayed with you and Lonnie to try to stop the bleeding," Guinness said. "He didn't pursue."

Alex remembered the door crashing into his arm and face, his gun falling away and then the shooter coming out... Lonnie going down. He knew in his heart he had screwed-up. *Lonnie is gone!* He felt a terrible weight pushing him down into the bed. He didn't think he could move. He felt his hands trembling and his feet were cold.

Alex heard his captain say, "When you feel strong enough, we need to get this all down. For now, tell me anything that will help us find this guy."

Random images and flashes of memory came and went. "I just don't know, sir," Alex finally said. "Lonnie got a call from the bar owner. We know the guy. He had Caine at his bar. We'd shown the picture around."

"I know," Guinness said, "Lonnie checked-in with me before you left."

"What did Beatty tell you," Alex asked.

"I want to know what you remember."

Alex sighed deeply. He wanted to get it all out, but something inside was holding him back. He just wasn't clear on all that had gone down... *except he was sure he had cost Lonnie Smith his life.* He squeezed his eyes tighter and tried to hold back tears. He felt Guinness's hand on his arm.

"You rest a bit more. I need to check back on the search. I called Hanna.

She should be here soon."

Hanna. What was he going to tell her? That he hadn't been able to protect his partner? That he had gotten him killed. Hanna knew Lonnie and Ginny now, almost like family. *Goddammit!*

A deep sorrow pressed over him, as bad as when his father had told him and his brother that their mother had just died in a car accident, back when they were in high school.

He woke with a start and opened his eyes. The pain in his neck flared red and hot and he winced before turning to the door to see Hanna standing there. She rushed to the side of the bed and leaned down to hug him. He could feel her tears soak through the hospital gown on his chest.

"Alex, I'm so sorry about Lonnie," she whispered.

He didn't answer but pulled her tighter around him.

"The department has people with Ginny."

"I know," he said, the sadness in his voice like a dark fog hanging over the room.

Hanna pulled back to see his face. "Are you okay? Your neck?"

"I don't know. I haven't talked to a doctor yet."

She looked up at the IV's. "The captain said you lost a lot of blood."

He just nodded back at her.

"Alex?" she started, then paused as he looked away.

"Alex, what is it?"

He was shaking his head slowly, his eyes closed.

"Alex!"

He turned back to her, a frantic fury in his face. "It's my damn fault, Hanna!"

"What?"

"I screwed up!"

She reached out and held his cheek, then stroked it gently. "Alex, you can't blame..."

"I got him killed, Hanna!"

Their eyes met and he couldn't help the tears flooding out. She wiped at them with her fingers and then hugged him again. She whispered through her own tears, "Honey, I'm so sorry. I'm so sorry."

Chapter Eight

Hanna drove up the street to the Smith's house. She saw two police cruisers parked in the front and another unmarked car in the drive. She looked at her watch. It was just past noon. She found an empty space across the street under a big oak tree and pulled in. Walking up to the house, she couldn't put thoughts of Alex's tearful confession from her mind. He wouldn't tell her what had actually happened but insisted Lonnie's death was his fault. She couldn't imagine the grief and pain he was feeling. Her own emotions were nearly overwhelming.

Her heart beat faster as she walked up the lawn to the porch. *The kids are probably still at school*, she thought to herself. *God, how will they ever get through this? And Ginny?"*

The front door opened as she got to the steps. A woman dressed in a blue skirt and white plain blouse stepped out on the porch. She had deep red hair pulled back tight in a bun at the back of her head and heavy framed black glasses covering much of her face. A police shield hung from a lanyard around her neck. She held out a hand to stop Hanna. "I'm sorry, Mrs. Smith isn't seeing anyone right now."

"She's my friend," Hanna replied, then continued, "Alex Frank is my boyfriend."

"Are you Hanna?" the woman asked.

"Yes, yes I am. I know about Lonnie. Can I please come in?"

The policewoman hesitated then said, "Let me check a moment," before she disappeared beyond the door.

Hanna looked up and down the street. It looked like a normal day in this

Charleston neighborhood. The tall trees were shading the quiet street. She saw Ginny's flowerbed was filled with many colors and beautifully tended. She sighed deeply and looked down in despair. She looked up and Ginny Smith was standing in the door. Through the screen, Hanna could see her face was drawn and streaked with tears. She pushed open the door.

"Hanna, thank you for coming." Her voice was barely above a whisper.

The two women embraced in the doorway Their cheeks were wet together. Hanna said, "I'm so sorry, dear. I don't know what to say other than I'm so very sorry."

She felt Ginny's head nodding and then she pulled away and motioned for Hanna to come in. The woman who had first met her on the porch was standing to the side, her arms crossed. Hanna could see two other uniformed officers in the kitchen, both on their phones. Another plainclothes officer was sitting on the couch in the living room, watching them. His tie was undone and his shirtsleeves rolled up in the heat.

Ginny turned to the policewoman. "Can you give us a few minutes, please?"

The woman nodded, "Of course."

There was a small den at the back of the house. Ginny motioned for Hanna to take a seat on a plaid couch and then sat next to her on a stuffed armchair, pushing the ottoman aside.

"How is Alex?" Ginny asked. "I know he's been wounded."

"I just came from the hospital. He's apparently out of danger, but very weak. He lost a lot of blood." She saw her friend blanch and look away. "Ginny, I shouldn't have..."

"No, it's okay."

"What can I do?" Hanna asked quietly.

Ginny looked back at her and said, "I don't know how I'm going to tell the kids. They'll be home from school soon. The officers wanted to bring them home earlier, but I need more time and I didn't want them picked up by the police at school."

"Of course."

"Our minister will be here any time," Ginny continued.

"I'll stay here with you to help with the kids."

"No, you need to be with Alex. Thank you for coming, but..."

"He needs to rest," Hanna said. "There's really not much I can do down there." She thought again about Alex's deep sorrow and guilt at the loss of his friend and partner. She knew she couldn't say anything to Ginny about it... yet.

Ginny wiped at her nose with a tissue.

"Is there anyone I can call for you?" Hanna asked.

"Lonnie's department is helping with most of that. I've already called Lonnie's parents. They live in Nashville and will be coming in tonight. My parents live across town and are on their way over." She paused and wiped at her nose again. "You're sure Alex will be okay?"

Hanna felt guilty for some strange reason that Alex would likely survive, and Ginny's husband was gone forever. "Yes, the doctor said he should be fine after the wound heals."

Ginny said, "Did he tell you anything about..." She couldn't finish.

Hanna jumped in and knew she was lying, but said, "No, he's still trying to piece it all together."

The officers out there won't tell me much," Ginny said, "an ongoing investigation and all, for Pete's sake."

"I'm sure there's a process and protocol," Hanna replied and then regretted saying anything.

"As soon as I saw that woman through the door this morning, I knew something had gone terribly wrong."

Hanna reached over and took her friend's hand.

"Lonnie and I were going to take a weekend away this Friday and go to the beach down in Hilton Head. We haven't been able to get away in so long."

Hanna sighed and went over and sat on the arm of the chair, putting her arm around her friend. Finally, she said, "Alex and I will always be here for you and the kids."

Ginny looked up and said, "I know dear. I know."

Chapter Nine

Alex leaned back against the pillows in his hospital bed and listened to the phone ringing at the other end of the call to his father's cell. It was mid-afternoon and he hoped he would catch him still out on the water within a cell signal or onshore before he was off to another night at Gilly's and who knew what calamity with Ella Moore. He was about to end the call when the ringing stopped.

"Alex! That you, boy?"

"Hey Pop, yeah. You out on the water?"

"Just comin' in. Good run this morning. Damn near full hold of shrimp."

"Good, good," said Alex slowly. "Look, I needed to reach you so you wouldn't worry if you heard something on the news."

"What's up?" Alex could hear the roar of the big diesel below the deck of the *Maggie Mae*.

"There was an incident during an arrest this morning, Pop."

"An incident? You okay?"

"I'll be fine, Pop, but..." He paused a moment to gather himself. "We lost Lonnie, Pop."

"What!" the old man roared into the phone. "What in hell happened?"

"We tried to take down this shooter who's been leaving a trail of bodies around town."

"A shooter?"

"He's a hit man for the Dellahousaye organization."

"A bunch of bottom-feedin' sonsabitches!" the Skipper said. "Weren't the Richards boys tied up with that asshole?"

38

"That's right, Pop."

"And this guy got Lonnie? Oh shit, I'm sorry, son."

"Yeah, it's the worst, Pop. I haven't been out to see Ginny yet, but this is gonna be a terrible..." He couldn't finish.

His father broke in. "You sure you're okay?"

"Nothing to worry about," Alex said, not wanting his father to overreact. "I took a round on the side of my neck, but they've got me patched up. Didn't hit anything vital."

"Holy shit, son! That's too damn close!"

"I'm okay," Alex said. "I just didn't want you to hear something on the radio or TV. Three other police officers were killed."

"My God! They catch the guy?"

"No, not yet."

"They gonna give you some time off to heal up?" his father asked.

"Don't know yet. This just happened late this morning."

"You need to come up and spend a few days on the boat with me. Let the sunshine and salt air help with the healing."

Alex let out a deep breath of air as he thought about the next few days and the internal investigation into the shootings that was sure to ramp up and ring him dry in the process. Four police officers down... *there would be hell to pay.* He had to get his mind clear on all that went down, but his primary concern right now was to get back on the job and join the effort to find Caine before he killed again. While the thought chilled him, Alex knew he would never rest until he avenged the death of his partner. "I'll think about it, Pop. Let's see what the boss has in mind for me first. I'll keep you posted."

"You keep your damn head down, son," his father warned.

"Sure, Pop. I'll talk to you soon." He ended the call.

Hanna appeared in the hospital room door later that afternoon. Alex had been sleeping fitfully and turned when he saw her come in. He looked at the clock on the wall. It was just past 2:00. The nurses had been keeping him heavily sedated on something he couldn't pronounce. Hanna came over to the bed and sat beside him, leaning in to give him a kiss.

"Sorry to wake you," she said. "I don't even want to ask how you're feeling."

"Like crap, thank you," he said with frustration. "Sorry..."

"You don't have to apologize."

"Did you see Ginny?"

Hanna nodded her head *"yes"*, trying not to show the concern she was feeling.

"I need to go and be with them," Alex said.

"You need to stay right here until the doctor says otherwise."

"She must be taking this really hard. I can't imagine."

"She's a strong woman and mostly she's worried about the kids."

Alex knew Hanna wanted to reassure him, but it was a useless effort. He squeezed the bridge of his nose and pressed his eyes shut, trying to block the images of Lonnie's five fatherless kids.

Hanna said, "Her pastor is there with them, and both sets of parents will be staying and helping out as long as needed."

"What they need is their father, dammit!" Alex said, clenching his fists. He felt Hanna rubbing his shoulder in comfort and turned to see her looking down at him, a deep sadness on her face. He needed to step back and realize just how fortunate he was to even be alive, let alone have this woman to share these coming days with. He reached up and took her hand and pulled her close in a tight embrace. After a while, he said, "Thank you for being here for me."

"Of course."

"You've had to put up with a lot with this crazy cop life I lead," he said.

Hanna whispered back into his ear, "I've had my own share of drama."

Chapter Ten

Hanna stopped back at her office just before 5 o'clock to check in with Molly and try to gather some work she could get to through the evening. She had ordered takeout for Ginny and her family and would pick that up on the way back over to the Smith house around six.

There were still two groups of people waiting in her small lobby to speak with lawyers, an Hispanic man and woman with a small child and another young woman, also with a baby in her lap. Molly ended a phone call as Hanna came up to her desk.

"I hate to ask," Molly said, scrunching her face like she wasn't sure she wanted to know.

"Alex is okay. It's a pretty serious wound on his neck, but the doctor thinks he'll be up and around in a couple of days."

"Well, thank goodness."

"How we doing here?" Hanna asked, looking around the reception area.

"All set. Adam will be able to meet with both parties here before he leaves. She was referring to Adam Preston who had worked at the clinic with Hanna for several years. "I left a few things on the center of your desk you need to deal with. Sorry."

"No, that's okay. That's why I came back." Hanna looked over her shoulder and then turned to Molly. "Can you come back for a moment?"

Molly stood across the desk as Hanna pulled her notes from the meeting earlier that day with Calley Barbour. "If you get some time later or in the morning, will you see what you can find on case law regarding underage abortion?" Her assistant was studying to become a paralegal and often helped with research when she could take time away from running the front desk and administration of the office.

"Your meeting with Calley Barbour this morning?" Molly asked.

Hanna nodded and frowned, thinking back on the girl's difficult situation and decisions to be made. "She was raped and didn't report it. Now she's three months pregnant and doesn't want to keep the baby. She's convinced her parents will disown her."

"Does she want to pursue the rape charge?"

"No, she doesn't even know who the boy is or where to find him."

Molly nodded.

Hanna spent two hours at Ginny Smith's house, helping her feed and comfort her kids. The boys ranged from the oldest at fifteen, down to young Henry who was just six. Her parents and in-laws had arrived, and several close neighbors and church friends were also crowding the house. Hanna could tell it was all too much for Ginny to deal with, but she had no idea how to graciously ask everyone to give the woman some space with her children. Maybe it was best to have all the distraction, she thought.

The police department representatives had all left over an hour ago. Ginny had been assigned a counselor who would continue to help her through the coming days. Her pastor had also seemed to be a great comfort. Hanna was helping some of the visitors get food when she saw Ginny at the sink, working on rinsing dishes and silverware. She walked over and placed her hand on her friend's shoulder. "Can you please take a moment. I'll do this."

Ginny turned. "I'd rather keep busy, thanks."

Hanna moved in to help her at the sink, loading the dishwasher. "Did you learn anything more from the police people who were here?"

"I finally got them to share what they could," she said. "Lonnie and Alex were leading a team to arrest a suspect on some local murders. The man still hasn't been apprehended."

Hanna said, "Captain Guinness told me they have the whole department out looking for this guy."

"They think he's part of the Dellahousaye crime family," Ginny said, looking over at Hanna. "A professional assassin who's killed a couple of people locally in the past weeks. Lonnie got a tip where he'd be. Somehow, this guy must have known they were coming to get him in this bar downtown."

Hanna was shocked to hear Alex and Lonnie's assailant may have ties to a mobster. She knew Dellahousaye was a dangerous man, but had no idea it could be this bad, right here in Charleston. Alex had almost been killed by a professional hit man, and he was still on the loose. She remembered there had been a uniformed police officer stationed outside Alex's room at the hospital the whole time she had been down there.

Ginny interrupted her thoughts, "They'll have autopsy reports tomorrow sometime, but they were able to tell me from the Medical Examiner's early assessment that Lonnie died very... very quickly." She struggled to finish and used the dish rag to wipe at her tears.

Hanna put her arm around her shoulders and pulled her close. Ginny turned into her and wrapped her arms around her. Hanna said, "I'm sure they were just trying to give you some peace about all this."

Ginny didn't reply.

Hanna returned to the hospital and was walking down the corridor to Alex's room when she saw the clock behind the nurse's station. It was just after 9pm. In her mind, she was thinking about how such a fine day had turned so wrong.

The sun was beginning to set outside through the windows she was passing. The long hallway was dark and quiet. She saw a policeman sitting in a chair outside Alex's room, scrolling through something on his cell phone. He stood as she approached. They had spoken during her earlier visit and he greeted her with a tip of his cap.

"I think he's sleeping again," the man said, quietly.

"I'll just sit with him a while, thanks." She went into the room and Alex was lying awake, staring out the single window on the wall. The setting sun was shining its last rays through the blinds and it washed the room in a soft orange glow. He turned when she walked in and she was glad to see a thin smile come across his face.

"Hey, I told you not to come back today," he said. She leaned over to kiss him on the cheek. "You have plenty to do, I'm sure," he continued.

"I want to be here with you. The rest can wait." She sat beside him and held his hand.

"How are Ginny and the boys?" he asked.

"There are so many friends and family there, I guess it's a blessing to help keep her mind off things."

"Okay, good. The doctor's not gonna like it, but I'm going over there tomorrow, one way or another."

Hanna squeezed his hand. "I know you want to help, but let's just see how you're feeling."

"They take me off these tubes, I'll be fine. The neck's gonna be sore for a while, but they've got some amazing painkillers."

"Be careful with that stuff," she scolded. "Don't want you getting hooked on anything. I can't believe the stories I'm hearing about the opioid and painkiller epidemic."

"I'll be fine," he said, though Hanna sensed some hesitation.

She had been thinking about the Asa Dellahousaye connection to Alex's shooting. The thought of such a dangerous man and his people turning their wrath on Alex and the others was frightening. She wondered whether Dellahousaye had been involved in the trouble Alex and his father faced in Dugganville this past year, leading to the arrest of the Richards men. She was quite certain the Dellahousaye mob family had been involved with her deceased husband's failed land deal and ultimately, his murder. On the way back to the hospital, she decided it was best to let Alex know. "I need to ask you about something."

"Okay."

"Ginny tells me the guy from this morning works for the Dellahousaye crime family."

"The department shared that with her?"

"Yes, they told her they believe he's a paid assassin for this mob group."

"That's right," Alex answered. "Lonnie and I had been after this guy for

several weeks. Two local murders linked to people Dellahousaye would prefer
dead kept coming back to this hitman. His name is Caine. We got a tip this
morning from an informant. Somehow, he knew we were coming in after
him."

Hanna took a deep breath, considering whether she should complicate the
situation for Alex, bringing up her own fears about the gangster.

Alex continued, "Dellahousaye is known to have tentacles everywhere,
including the police department and the courts."

"Was he involved in the mess up in Dugganville with your father last
year?" she asked. "And what about Ben and Osprey Pointe?" she continued,
referring to her deceased husband.

"We don't know for sure. Nothing ever sticks to this guy," he said.
He grimaced before saying, "Dellahousaye has no moral compass, Hanna.
People who cross him end up dead or wishing they were."

An hour later, Hanna decided she needed to get home to catch up on some of
the work she'd left and to try to get some sleep. She gave Alex a long kiss and
then held him tight. "I'm so thankful you're going to be okay."

He didn't respond.

"I'll stop by in the morning," she said, standing beside the bed.

"You need to take care of business tomorrow and be with Ginny as much as
you can. I'll be fine and if my doctor isn't a total asshole, I'll be out of here."

"I don't think so."

"We'll see. Good night." She reached for his hand. "I love you, Alex Frank."

"I love you, too. Thank you for being here and helping with Ginny and the
kids."

She smiled and turned to leave. She looked back one more time as she was
going through the door and Alex was looking out the window, a small lamp
by his beside illuminating his face. She was struck by his sad expression but
knew he was dealing with the loss of his best friend and partner, let alone his
own near-death experience.

The cop was still there outside the room and he wished Hanna a *"good
night"*.

The hall ahead was dark and deserted. A few lights were bright up ahead at the nurse's station. A doctor in a full set of surgical scrubs was coming toward her, looking down at a chart. His face was obscured by the charts and he didn't even acknowledge her as he passed. She got to the elevator and the doors opened right away. As she started to get on, she looked back down the corridor and at the doctor who was approaching the officer outside Alex's room. The doors closed and she pressed the button for the first floor.

Chapter Eleven

Alex rubbed at the stubble of beard on his face as he looked out the hospital window at the last light of day. The pain in his neck was a dull throbbing pressure, deadened by the painkillers they were pumping into his arm. He knew he should have told the doctors of his past problems with these kind of drugs after his wounds in Afghanistan and an earlier gunshot wound years ago. It was a battle he knew he would fight for the rest of his life but had managed to keep at bay in recent years. At one point after his return from his last tour of duty, it had gotten so bad he was getting multiple doctors to write prescriptions. He had even bought drugs on the street when his prescriptions couldn't be filled anymore. After a night when he almost considered heroin to take the edge off, he knew he had to do something drastic. His father helped him check-in to a rehab clinic. He came close to falling down the same worm hole again after the last time he'd been shot on duty. He knew the danger. He knew the slippery slope and yet the pain in his neck this time was nearly unbearable.

He thought about Hanna who had just left. This was the second time she had helped him recover from a gunshot wound in their short time together. The last had been the previous year in Dugganville when a shooter hired by Beau and Connor Richards had tried to take him off the board after he got too close to their involvement in the murder of the shrimper, Horton Bayes, the man his father had been falsely accused of killing. He had always suspected Asa Dellahousaye was behind the drug ring the Richards were caught up in but could never make the connection. During that recovery, he had been able to lay off the hard meds.

He was grateful Hanna was still with him after all of that and the episode with his ex-wife, Adrienne, trying to lure him back. He wasn't sure how he was going to get through these coming days. His doubts about the take-down and his partner's death were eating at his gut and it was all he could do to stay tied down to this hospital bed. He needed to get back out there and find this guy. Hanna was the voice of reason he probably needed, he thought again. *How long is she going to keep putting up with all this?*

He heard some discussion in the hall outside as the officer assigned to guard his room was talking to someone, probably another nurse or doctor. In the next moment, his senses went on full alert when he heard the cop say, "Wait, wait just a min...", and then he heard the distinctive spit of a silenced weapon firing twice in close succession. There was the sound of a man crashing back against the wall, crying out and then hitting the floor.

Alex acted on pure instinct and reached for his own gun he had insisted he keep close during his stay. It was under the two pillows he was propped-up against. With the butt of the pistol secure in his right hand, he rolled to the far side of the bed away from the door and felt the pain in his neck searing through every nerve-ending in his body, at the same time the tubes connecting his arm to the IV bags pulled the rack crashing down across the bed.

He saw the gun and the man's arm come around the door first. He managed to get on his knees, release the safety and slide a round into the chamber as he aimed at the door with both hands. Before he could even yell out, Caine came through the door firing three rounds into the pillows at the head of the bed. Alex ducked instinctively and then came back up ready to fire. Caine had obviously realized he had lost the element of surprise and was already falling back behind the door jam.

Alex squeezed off two rounds that thundered into the stillness of the room and long hospital corridor. His pulse was racing, and he gulped for air to calm himself as he waited for Caine to come at him again. Instead, he heard the man running down the hall, then two nurses yelling before Caine hollered for them to "get down!"

Alex tried painfully to stand. He ripped the two IV needles out of the back of his hand and screamed out loud at the pain. He staggered to the doorway, feeling light-headed and afraid he might pass out. He got to the doorway and glanced around the frame. The officer he knew as Stricker was down and not moving. He hadn't even had time to pull his gun. There was an ugly hole in his forehead with blood flowing in a steady stream onto the gray carpet.

He looked quickly down the long empty hall. Caine was just reaching the end of the corridor and pushed open a door with a red "Exit" sign over it. The assassin looked back at Alex for just a moment and even in the dim light, Alex could see he was smiling, mocking him. Rage filled him as he watched the man lift the gun with the long silencer again and point it directly at him. Across the long distance, he heard Caine yell out, "Bang!" and then he disappeared through the door.

Alex knelt beside the fallen cop and checked his pulse. He couldn't find any sign of life. He reached for the man's radio and called in the *"officer down"* report.

Within minutes, Alex's room was full of uniformed and plainclothes cops. An *"All-Points Bulletin"* had been issued again for Caine, but in these early minutes, the man had apparently slipped away again. Alex wasn't sure if he had hit him with either of his two shots. There was no blood trail down the hall according to one of the officers first on the scene.

He was back sitting on his bed, breathing heavily as a doctor and nurse tried to reconnect his fluids and assess his situation. He looked up when he saw Captain Guinness coming through the door with his detective colleague, Nathan Beatty, the other survivor of the morning's failed arrest. Beatty had been by earlier in the day to check on him.

A forensics team was already trying to dig bullets out of the bed and wall and outside in the hallway where Alex had tried to take down Caine. He'd had a sudden fearful thought earlier that one of his rounds may have penetrated walls and possibly hit someone, but one of the first responding cops soon assured him no one had been injured. He was sitting at the end of the bed as the hospital staff worked to stabilize him.

Guinness said, "Damn, Alex!"

Beatty came up beside him, "Good thing you had your piece, man."

Alex just nodded back, then asked, knowing full-well what the answer would be, "What about Stricker?"

Guinness looked back, then turned and said, "They're working on him, but I think he's gone. The man rubbed his chin and grimaced, clearly upset he had lost another man to this killer.

Beatty asked, "You sure it was Caine?"

"No question. He stood right there in that doorway expecting me to be lying in the bed, probably sedated and asleep. Fortunately, Hanna had just been here, and I was awake and heard the attack outside the door." He thought about Hanna and said a silent prayer of thanks she had left the room moments before.

Guinness said, "We've been piecing this together most of the day. We still need more time with you, Alex, but it seems clear this guy got word or sensed you were coming in this morning. He had time to secure the bartender in the back of the place and was laying in ambush for our two men headed into the alley."

Alex was listening while the nurse continued to work on his IV rig.

Beatty said, "We can't figure why Caine didn't bug out after he took down our men in the alley. He came back in and was waiting for you."

Alex was thinking through the chaos of those few brief minutes again. He winced, not from the pain the nurse was inflicting on the top of his hand, but in the images of his partner going down and Caine turning his weapon back on him.

He put his head down, trying to gather himself as his captain said, "It's almost like he was on a mission to take everyone out who was coming after him. If Beatty hadn't knocked through into the kitchen when he did, Alex, I'm afraid you might be down at the morgue, too."

Alex looked over at the other detective. "Good timing, Nate."

Captain Guinness continued, "Caine must have been monitoring the news channels this afternoon. There's a media frenzy on this damn mess, even the nationals are in town. It went public that one of the surviving officers was being treated here at the hospital.

"Thanks for inviting the bastard," Alex said, not in jest.

"Yeah, I raised hell with our PR guy and the commissioner," Guinness said, "but they wanted to let the city know that two of you had survived. Helluva stupid way for the department to try to save face."

Alex said, "Can you get me out of here? I feel like a sitting duck now."

"Obviously this guy wants no witnesses left alive," Beatty said.

"Still can't figure why he didn't take out the bartender, Guinness said. "One theory is Caine tied him up in the back with a gag so he'd make enough noise to lure the cops through the door into the kitchen, then planned to shoot him too before he left."

"Makes sense," Alex said. "Have you got Jeb under wraps?"

"Yes, he was treated for the beating Caine gave him in the back before he tied him up. We've got him in a secure location."

Beatty said, "Alex, have you had time to sort through how this guy got the jump on you?"

Alex had thought of little else and he still hadn't given an official report of all that went down. On instinct, he decided to delay revealing his account as long as he could. He paused, then said, "I'm still trying to piece it all together. It came down so fast and then I'm out cold 'til the paramedics revive me in the ambulance on the way down here."

Guinness patted Alex on the knee and said, "If you're feeling better in the morning, we'll bring down the investigating team on this and get your statement, as much as you can remember, anyway."

"What about getting out of here?" Alex asked.

Guinness turned to the doctor who was shaking his head, *no.*

The captain said, "Let's give it until morning. We'll have every access point covered here tonight. You'll be safe."

Alex was trying to control his temper, but spit out, "Captain, I can damn well take care of myself. I want to get back out on the street and get this guy."

Again, the doctor was shaking his head.

"We'll see how you're doing in the morning," Captain Guinness said.

Chapter Twelve

Hanna was only three blocks from the hospital when she started to hear sirens, then two police cars raced by her heading in the opposite direction. She had the car radio tuned to a country music station with the volume low, as she continued to sort through the events of the day in her mind. She looked in the rear-view mirror as the lights from the two squad cars disappeared around a far turn. She turned the radio off so she could hear if any other emergency vehicles might be approaching. *"What's happening in this crazy city now?"*

She couldn't get thoughts of Alex out of her head and how close he had come to joining his fellow officers as a victim of this ruthless killer named Caine. She could also tell the guilt he was feeling in surviving the attack when his best friend and three others from his department had lost their lives. She couldn't imagine how difficult it would be for him to work through this and come to grips with the situation.

And then there was Ginny Smith who had lost her husband, her children's father, the person closest to her in life. Hanna had been through this when her husband was found shot and killed on the streets of Charleston. Later, she would learn more of Ben Walsh's transgressions and the cause of his death, but the early days of shock and grief in learning of her husband's violent death still kept her awake at night.

A few minutes later, Hanna pulled into the designated parking spot behind her office and apartment. She gathered her purse and leather bag that held her work papers on the seat beside her. The humid night air clung to her skin. Letting herself in the back door, she turned the bolt lock behind her and walked down the darkened hallway to her office. Molly had left a lamp on next to her desk and she sat down to sort through messages and files her assistant had left for her.

Outside, she heard sirens again and on impulse reached for the remote for the small television that hung on the far wall. She pushed for a local news channel and turned up the volume to hear a woman reporter standing in front of several police cars in the background with lights flashing.

"...we're waiting to hear from the official department spokesperson, but from what we've learned from informed sources outside the hospital..."

Hanna felt a chill race through her. She stood quickly and walked over to the television.

"... there has been a shooting and perhaps a fatality inside this facility."

Hanna turned quickly looking for her phone, trying to control the panic that was rushing through her. She grabbed her cell on her desk and pushed in the contact for Alex's phone. It rang four times before she heard his familiar voice answer, "Hanna?"

"Oh, thank God!" she cried out and then, "Are you all right? What's going on down there?"

Alex seemed confused when he responded. "Where are you?"

"I'm back at my office and watching a television reporter at the hospital. What's going on?"

"They're here already?" he said, again sounding hesitant and confused.

"Alex?"

"Hanna, there's been another shooting."

"That's what I'm seeing here on the news broadcast. What's happened?"

"Everything is under control here," he said, "but..." He hesitated again.

"Alex, what in the world?"

"The shooter came back..." he started. "He came back for me."

Hanna was stunned and couldn't believe what she was hearing. She tried to answer but stunned and distracted by the reporter on the television.

Alex continued, "I'm okay, but this asshole shot and killed the officer who was assigned..."

"The man outside your door?" she jumped in.

"Yes, Stricker. He's dead, Hanna."

"Oh, Alex..."

"He was obviously coming back for me."

"How did you...?"

Alex interrupted, "Hanna, I'm okay. Just a little rattled. I had my gun and I was able to protect myself."

She thought for a moment, thankful that Alex had survived this second attack. "Where is the killer?" she finally said."

"He got away. Half the department's out on the streets trying to track him down."

Hanna turned the television off and hurried back to her desk, reaching for her purse and car keys. "I'm coming back down."

"No!" Alex said quickly. "It's a madhouse down here and there's nothing you can do."

"Alex..."

"Please, Hanna, I'm fine. Just try to get some rest tonight. I hope to be out of here in the morning and..."

She couldn't control her fear and frustration any longer and burst out, "Alex, dammit! You're not going anywhere tomorrow, and I want to be there with you."

She waited for him to reply and could hear a lot of conversation in the background. "Hanna, I really need to go. The Captain is here and we're trying to sort through all this. Please, get some rest and I'll see you in the morning."

She was shaking her head and trying to regain her composure. "Are you going to be safe down there?"

"They have people on every door and access point," he replied. "Hopefully, they'll have him in custody soon."

Before the body count gets any higher, she thought to herself.

"Hanna?" she heard him ask.

"Yes..."

"I've asked for the department to place someone outside your apartment tonight."

"What!"

"I don't want you to get upset," Alex went on, "but I just don't know what this guy is capable of and who else he might be targeting to get at me."

Hanna turned and looked out the window at the dimly lit parking area behind her office and apartment. A chilling sense of dread and fear washed over her. She started walking towards her office door and then down to the front of the building. "Do you really think he'd come after me?" She got to the front of the office and looked out at the street. A Charleston Police cruiser was already parked in front.

"It's just a precaution, Hanna."

"Why is he doing this?"

"Apparently, he doesn't want any witnesses from the bust this morning who can ID him," he said and then paused for a moment. "He's also a crazy bastard..."

She sat on one of the chairs in the reception area, trying to calm herself. "They need to find this maniac, Alex," she said hesitantly.

"They're trying, Hanna. They're trying."

Chapter Thirteen

Caine sat in a back booth of an all-night diner five blocks from the hospital, his fishing cap pulled low over his face as he sipped at a cup of coffee. His senses were alert to any signs of approaching danger. He knew the cops would be crawling the streets looking for him. His gun was secured in a shoulder holster under his shirt.

The waitress came up and refilled his cup. "Get you anything else, hon?"

He smiled up at her and said, "You got any pie left?"

"One slice of blueberry."

They both turned to look outside when a police cruiser raced past with lights on and siren screaming.

"Wonder what's happening now?" she said, shaking her head in disgust.

"Get a little vanilla ice cream on that pie?" Caine asked.

"Sure thing," she said. "Be right back."

He watched her walk away and kept looking out the window for the appearance of any cops. He already had an escape route out the back scoped out. He planned to wait a few more minutes before starting to make his way back to his boat at the docks along the river.

As he waited, he kept thinking about the mess this morning at the bar. He was not one to tolerate loose ends, nor was his employer, Asa D. He cursed himself silently. He'd been working for the mob boss for over ten years off and on. This latest engagement was beginning to spiral out of control. The old man had too many people in his way who needed to be eliminated. Things were getting too hot and he was anxious to get all this behind him and return to his mountain home overlooking the bay on St. Croix. He smiled when he thought about sitting out on the deck next to the pool with his latest tanned young girlfriend.

He had developed his taste for killing when he'd connected with a group of mercenaries operating out of Paris. He found that he was not only good at it as his skills developed, but he also got a strange pleasure in watching people in the final seconds before their deaths. His body count had become his own perverse badge of honor. Eventually, individual jobs began to come his way and he'd been working on his own for years now taking contracts around the world.

When he got the call a bust was coming down this morning, he knew he could just slip out the back and avoid any confrontation, but the thought of taking out a few more of the bastards was just too good to pass up. He was upset that he wasn't able to take them all, but sometimes you need to cut your losses and clean up later. That's why he had tracked the one surviving cop to the hospital. He'd have to regroup on that one and he already had a plan for the other.

His contact on the Dark Web had provided detailed dossiers on both of them.

The waitress set the pie and ice cream down in front of him. "Enjoy".

"Thanks... Mary," he said, looking up at the name card on her peach-colored uniform.

He'd wait a few more minutes before taking back roads and alleys to the waterfront and his boat at the marina.

Chapter Fourteen

Alex woke with a start. He was sweating and he must have yelled out because a nurse and the new cop assigned outside his door came quickly into his hospital room.

"You okay, Lieutenant?" the cop asked.

Alex took a moment to clear his head. Fading images from a dream were still flashing in his brain. He saw the cold metal hole on the end of the silencer held by the assassin named Caine aimed straight at his face. He saw the body of his partner, Lonnie, falling in a heap across the kitchen, blood already pooling on the floor from the gunshot wounds he had just taken.

In the dream, Alex could still remember the helpless feeling of being knocked over by the door as Caine came out to confront them and then falling to the floor and watching his gun slide away out of reach. He had felt helpless, weighted down as if unable to move. His screams as Caine aimed the weapon back at him were silent in the dream. He couldn't seem to cry out to help Lonnie.

He tried to push that all away and looked up at the cop standing by the bed. "What...I'm sorry."

"Just checking," the cop said. "You cried out."

The nurse was checking the monitor next to his bed and then the IV bags on the rack.

The cop's nameplate read *Mcquire.*

Alex finally said, "I'm fine, thanks. Just dreaming, I guess."

"Helluva thing with Stricker last night," Officer McGuire said.

Alex looked at the young man for a moment and fought off the wave of guilt that was sweeping over him. "Yeah, helluva thing."

An hour later, his cell phone vibrated on the stand next to the bed. The caller ID read, *Hanna*. "Hey, good morning," he said, trying to sound more cheerful than he really felt. He looked out through the blinds on the window and saw a soft red glow in the clouds from the rising sun.

"You feeling any better?" he heard her ask.

"Got a little sleep."

"Good," Hanna replied. "There's still a cop car out front here at my apartment. Is that really still necessary?"

"I'm not sure what happened overnight, other than the new cop they've got outside my room here hadn't heard any updates about catching this guy."

"I'm going to take some coffee out, if that's okay," she said.

"I'm sure they'll appreciate it."

"The Captain will be back in a few minutes with the investigation team and an Internal Affairs person, I'm sure."

"Internal Affairs?"

"There will be an investigation into the whole incident. I haven't provided my official statement yet."

Hanna said, "I can tell you've got some serious doubt and guilt about this whole thing. I'm sure you did everything you could..."

"Hanna," he cut in quickly, a hint of irritation clear in his voice, "I wish I could say I had a clear conscious on how this all came down, but it was not good. I should have..."

"Alex, I'm sorry. I don't know what happened, but I know you're one of the best at what you do and..."

"We need to talk about this later," he said abruptly.

There was no response on the other end of the call, and he waited a moment, too, mad at himself for losing his cool with her.

"Hanna, I'm sorry. I'm just trying to sort this all out in my mind. It's going to take a little time."

"Of course," she said.

"Look, the IA team is here. I need to go."

"I'll be down to see you later this morning."

"Please go be with Ginny," he protested. "I'm going to get over there this afternoon, one way or the other."

When Hanna reluctantly signed off on their call, Alex pressed the call button for a nurse. When she came in, he said, "Can you crank up the dial on those meds? My neck is killing me. We need to take the edge off a little."

"Let me check with the doctor."

Alex hesitated, then said, "No really, that's okay." He didn't want to give the doctor any further excuse for not letting him out of here.

The Internal Affairs team included two men and a woman who Alex knew from the Department but had no real relationship with. They were all business and had taken two hours to walk him through his account of yesterday's events and then the attack the previous night from the killer named Caine. He had decided to share everything he could remember, including the loss of his weapon and inability to protect the flank of his fallen partner. He told them everything about the return attack the previous night and the shots fired in trying to protect himself from the assassin.

After they left, he had an uneasy feeling about the whole situation. He was sure there would be more interrogations and questions before they were through. They didn't seem to react one way or the other about his accounts of both episodes but did continue to press him on how the killer may have been tipped off to their attempted arrest. He could provide no logical explanation.

His police captain, Guinness, had come in toward the end of the interview and had finally pressed the team to finish up so that Alex could get some rest.

It was early afternoon when he touched the call button for the nurse again. His neck was on fire and the meds weren't making a dent in the pain. He wasn't going to ask for more, but rather to have her disconnect the IV tubes to let him get out of the hospital.

"You need to speak to the doctor," the nurse had scolded, then left the room.

Hanna had come by earlier before leaving to spend more time with Ginny

Smith and the children. He apologized for being short with her earlier on the phone.

A few minutes later, one of the young doctors who had been treating him came into the room. He didn't wait for Alex to speak. "I strongly discourage you from getting out of this bed for at least another day or two. You need to let that wound heal. You've got internal stitches holding your neck together that are very susceptible to pulling apart."

"Doc, I'm getting out of here, with your permission or not, so you might as well get the nurse to unhook me before I pull these damn needles out myself."

The Uber car pulled up to the street in front of the Smith house. Alex sat in back, trying to push aside the pain in his neck and the uncertainty and guilt he was feeling in having to see the widow of his friend and partner. He didn't see Hanna's car and concluded she must have gone back to her office.

He walked up the steps onto the porch and rang the doorbell, his heart pounding in his chest. He felt light-headed and occasional bouts of nausea kept washing over him. He reached out for the brick wall of the porch to support himself. He stepped back when the door opened. Lonnie and Ginny's youngest son, Charlie, stood at the door.

"Uncle Alex?" the little boy said quietly.

"Hey, Charlie. Can I come in?" He pulled open the door and then knelt in front of one of his five godsons. "How you doing, big man?" Alex asked.

The boy shook his head and looked down. Alex pulled him close and hugged him. "I'm sorry about your dad, Charlie. I wish..." he said and then couldn't continue. He looked up as Ginny came into the room. He squeezed the boy tight then stood and took Ginny Smith in his arms. They both started crying and neither spoke, holding each other.

Finally, Alex pushed back and said, "Whatever you need..."

"Alex, please..." They watched as her son ran into the other room to join the others.

Alex wanted to tell her that none of this should have happened, that if he'd done his job, her husband would still be alive. Ashamed, he couldn't bring himself to make the confession.

Ginny broke his thoughts and quietly said, "I know you loved Lonnie as much as we did."

He nodded, wiping at his tears. "I promise you, I will get this guy."

"I know you will," she answered. "I heard he came after you again last night."

He nodded.

"Another officer killed?"

"Right," he answered, tentatively.

"Who is this monster, Alex?"

He was feeling faint again. "Can we sit for a minute?"

She led him over to a couch and sat beside him. "I can't believe they let you out of the hospital already."

"They didn't."

"I should have known," she said and then managed a slight smile.

Alex took one of her hands in his. "We think this Caine fellow is working for Asa Dellahousaye, the mob boss. There's a gambling bill pending in the state legislature that the man will likely profit from handsomely. People opposed to the bill have started dying and disappearing."

Ginny was shaking her head, trying to understand why her husband had died.

"We'll get these guys, Ginny."

"You first need to rest and get well. I don't want to be losing you, too."

"You saw Hanna this morning?"

"She's been a blessing, Alex."

He thought about the chaos he kept bringing into people's lives. Hanna had dealt with so much in her own life and since they'd been together, he'd only brought on another layer of turmoil and danger.

"Alex?"

Ginny startled him back to the present. "What can I do to help... with the boys, anything?"

"We're managing," she said, tears welling up in her eyes again.

Alex pulled her close and she rested her head on his shoulder.

He wanted to tell her this was all a terrible mistake, that her husband should still be with her and the kids, that their lives shouldn't have been upended by his failure to do his job. He wanted to come clean with her but then he knew he was only trying to manage his own guilt and his admissions would do nothing to help with Ginny Smith's grief.

She pulled back and wiped the tears from her face. "None of this seems real yet. It's like I'm in this fog that won't clear, and I know he's really gone, but I can't bring myself to accept it yet."

Alex took a deep breath, trying with all his will to be strong for this woman, to help her through the loss. He had never felt more helpless.

Chapter Fifteen

Hanna was sitting behind her desk and disconnected the call she'd been on with Alex's police captain. He was looking for Alex who had abruptly left the hospital even though the doctors had advised him to stay at least another day. She was certain he would be going first to the Smith house to be with Ginny and she had told the captain that.

She knew Alex would leave, but she was more than worried about his wound and overall condition to be back out on the street. On impulse, she called his number. It rang several times before going to a mailbox that was full and wouldn't allow her to leave a message. They had planned to meet for dinner if he was able to leave the hospital. Apparently, he was feeling strong enough.

Molly came in and put a file on her desk. "Here's what I could find in South Carolina law on underage abortion laws."

"Did you find any more detail on this *Judicial Bypass* exception?"

"Very specific requirements and conditions… you'll see."

"Okay, thank you," Hanna said, starting to look through the documents Molly had printed out.

"Hanna, I know it's not my business, but are you really thinking about helping this girl do this without her parents knowing?"

Hanna bristled at the challenge for a moment, then said, "You're right, it's not your business…"

Molly stepped back, clearly regretting bringing it up.

"Molly, I'm sorry," Hanna said, quickly. "I didn't mean…"

"It's okay," her assistant said. "Let me know if you need anything else." She walked out of the office quickly before Hanna could respond.

Hanna stood when Molly showed Calley Barbour into her office. She walked over and took the girl's hand. "Hello, dear. Come in."

Molly closed the door as she left.

They sat across from each other at the small conference table. Calley was dressed less casually this time, like she was prepared for a day in court. She had pressed white slacks and a blue buttoned top on with nice leather sandals. Her hair was let down and curled slightly. Just a trace of make-up on her eyes and face gave her the appearance of a young woman, certainly older than sixteen. Her expression was bright and full of expectation.

"So, what have you learned, Hanna?"

Hanna looked down at the file in front of her and thought again about what she had read and confirmed about a *Judicial Bypass* to avoid specific written approval from her parents to proceed with an abortion. She had given all of this a lot of thought and was now convinced this young girl should have the right not to carry a child to term who was the result of rape and could perhaps alienate her from her parents forever. But, she still had some issues she felt Calley needed to think through very carefully.

"Calley, the laws of South Carolina state that a woman under the age of seventeen needs the consent of at least one parent or grandparent to have an abortion."

The girl was clearly growing impatient and upset with her methodical approach. "But, what about..."

"Calley, please. Let me continue."

"I'm not going to tell my parents!" she insisted. "All they would think about is what their church would say. Those people all have their head in the sand about what's really happening in the world today. They would disown me, I swear."

"Before we go into the other options that may be available," Hanna began, trying to remain calm and supportive, "there are counselors available we can work with to help you think through terminating this pregnancy. I know your parents will not be supportive of any solution, but adoption is certainly an option I think you should seriously consider before we move forward with any waivers or releases to receive an abortion."

"Hanna, I've told you, they'll throw me out on the streets! They'll be so ashamed they'll never let me back in their house."

"Calley, I understand all of that." She paused for a moment to gather her thoughts. "I want to share something with you. I'm not trying to convince you of anything, but I want you to consider everything here."

Calley put her face in her hands in desperation. "I thought you would help me!"

"Please, just listen to me for a moment and then we can walk through all the possible scenarios."

The girl didn't look up and just kept shaking her head.

Hanna proceeded anyway. "When I was away at college, I became pregnant with a boy who I had been dating. I was on birth control, but somehow it didn't work. By the time I knew I was pregnant the boy had left school for a job in Europe. I knew he would never come back, and I was right."

"He didn't know about the baby?" Calley asked, looking up.

"I never had a chance to tell him. He had already gone." Hanna walked over to her desk and brought back her cup of coffee before sitting again. "I was so upset about his leaving and the prospect of being a single mother. It was all too much, and I elected to have an abortion."

"So, he never knew."

"I've seen him since, but I couldn't bring myself to tell him," Hanna said. "Obviously, I've lived with this decision for a long time now and I have deep emotions on both sides of my decision. Honestly, I try to convince myself I didn't do it in anger over his leaving me. I thought we were in love."

Calley sighed and then said, "I'm sorry, Hanna, but..."

Hanna interrupted, "I continue to support Pro-choice to allow women to deal with these situations as best they can, but there are very few days when I don't think back about having that baby and where it would be in my life today."

"Hanna, he raped me!"

"I know, dear," she said and then took a deep breath. I know this is a very different situation. I want to work through this with you and help you make the best decision."

"I've made up my mind and I can't have this baby! I couldn't live with it knowing the circumstances and I can't go through with the pregnancy for an adoption if I want any chance to stay with my family, at least until I'm old enough to go out on my own."

"There is counseling available for both you and your parents to work through this."

Calley stood and was shaking in anger. "You're not listening to me! I thought you would help me!"

Hanna tried to speak calmly. "Please, Calley. Sit down. Let me explain all of this to you." She opened the file folder in front of her and looked through her notes. Calley sat back in her chair. "As I said, the age of consent for abortion in our state is seventeen. There are waivers for special circumstances including a medical emergency or a pregnancy resulting from incest. Neither is the case here."

"But what about a judge's *bypass* or whatever it's called?"

"Yes, I've confirmed there is a process for a minor to seek a *Judicial Bypass* to proceed with an abortion without parental consent. The judge has to consider several factors including the maturity of the minor, any threat of violence in the home, or a pregnancy that is the result of rape or incest."

Calley's eyes grew wide in expectation. "Hanna, I didn't go to the police about this rape because I was afraid of what my parents would do, but that is exactly what happened on the beach that night."

"Yes, I understand," Hanna said. "We can file a request with the local courts to schedule a confidential hearing with a judge."

Calley jumped up and came over and leaned down to wrap her arms around Hanna. "Thank you! I knew you would help me."

Hanna returned the girl's embrace and closed her eyes, trying to convince herself she was doing the right thing.

Hanna had left the office downstairs and was looking through her refrigerator for something to eat. Alex still wasn't answering his phone and she was mad enough at him, she vowed she wouldn't try again. She knew he was dealing with an impossible situation, but... *answer your damn phone!*

She was just sitting down at her small kitchen table when her phone rang. Thinking it was Alex, she didn't even look at the call screen. "Where in hell are you?"

There was no response for a moment, then, "Hanna? It's Allen, your father."

"Allen! Oh, I'm sorry, I thought you were Alex."

"How are you, daughter?"

"Fine," she said, lying. She took a bite of her frozen whatever meal just out of the microwave. She burned her mouth and spit it back on the plate. "Damn!"

"What?" she heard her father say in surprise.

"Sorry, I just burned my mouth. I swear this microwave cooks to 5000 degrees sometimes."

"Eating fancy again, I see."

She didn't take his ribbing. "What's up, *father*?"

"I'm seeing all this about the Charleston Police Department on the television. Please tell me Alex isn't in the middle of all that."

"He's smack in the middle of it," she said. "He was one of the officers shot yesterday, Daddy."

"I was afraid of that. How is he?"

"He was lucky, but his partner, Lonnie Smith... we've talked about him."

"Yes, I know who you mean."

"He was one of the officers killed. It's just horrible. Alex and I are very close to the family and Alex feels responsible." She went through Alex's story and lingering guilt.

"So, he's in the hospital. Is he the one who was almost killed last night?"

"Yes, this crazy man came back after him again."

"How is he doing?"

"Well, he's out of the hospital already, but I can't seem to get in touch with him. We were supposed to have dinner tonight."

"I'm sure he'll call. Give him my best." He paused, then, "Do you have a minute, Hanna?"

"Of course." She blew on another spoon-full of nuked pasta and tested it before taking another bite.

Her father said, "I wanted to let you know I've decided to sell the house."

"Okay..."

"Martha is furious, but it's my damn house and I'm tired of rattling around in that big old place and the traffic and drive downtown will kill me if my heart doesn't give out first."

"Daddy!"

There was silence on the line for a moment and Hanna took another bite and sipped at the wine she had poured.

"I also wanted you to know Martha and I have been having some issues and she's moved out, just for a while, anyway."

Hanna put her spoon down. "Allen, Martha called me about your concerns about an affair. Are you sure?"

"She called you?"

"You know Martha, always playing both sides of the aisle. Where did she go?"

"Staying with a friend."

"Not the other man?"

"No... no, one of her many girlfriends... lives nearby here in Buckhead."

"I'm sorry, Daddy," Hanna said, trying to be sympathetic. "I know how much she means to you."

"We'll work this out," he said. "I just wanted you to know. I'm really sorry to hear about Alex and your friend. Terrible! Give Alex my best."

"I will," she replied, then without really thinking it through, said, "You and Martha should get away. You need a break. The firm will be just fine."

"I may just do that, thank you," she heard her father say. "I love you, dear."

"I love you too, Allen."

Chapter Sixteen

Asa Dellahousaye was a surprisingly quiet and private man. His reputation for flamboyance and opulence was well deserved, but he preferred privacy and seclusion. His extravagant parties were attended by notable names from industry, politics and particularly celebrities from film and television and music. His appearance at these gatherings was typically brief and usually at the end of the evening when most were quite inebriated or stoned and might later recall never having seen their host. An invitation to a Dellahousaye event was a badge of honor for those who wanted to run in the vaunted circles of the rich, powerful and famous. The fact that much of the man's wealth was earned from questionable and corrupt businesses seemed little deterrence.

Asa D, as he was most often referred to by friends, family and business associates, preferred to watch these lushly catered events from afar, often from the privacy of his study in whatever home he was residing in at the time, viewing the comings and goings and often coupling of his guests from the many security monitors on the wall. He was usually accompanied in these private sessions by his young fourth wife. She was a former South American beauty pageant beauty who had captured his heart with her striking looks, sense of humor and other exceptional skills that kept him energized even in his later years.

Having just reached his 72nd birthday, Asa D still cut a fine and handsome figure when he did make public appearances. He traveled with a personal trainer and chef who both kept him fit and healthy with the best food and workout regimen. He had inherited his father's imposing stature, standing near 6 foot, four inches, with a barrel chest and thin waist. His deeply tanned face showed few wrinkles and was offset by striking silver hair kept long and combed straight back. His clothes were hand-tailored and always quite elegant.

His security detail was considerable and led for many years by a man named Etienne, an equally large and imposing man of Cajun heritage similar to his boss who never spoke to guests or meeting attendees, but was clearly present behind Asa D at all of these types of public affairs and other meetings. Several more men and women were discreetly staged throughout whatever venue was being used. All guests were welcomed through metal detectors as they arrived, but few seemed to care in this age of terrorists and deranged killers. No one appeared overly concerned their host had a reputation for extreme violence in his personal and business dealings, though no formal charges or indictments had ever been brought against him.

On this particular evening, the party was being held at Asa D's sprawling beach front home on Isle of Palms, on the Atlantic coast just north of Charleston. It was one of numerous estates he kept in places like Miami, Malibu, Vail, Long Island and New Orleans. The invitation list was close to one hundred and clusters of finely dressed men and women could be seen, and were being watched, throughout the lower level of the house and out onto the lawn and terraces that featured a massive pool and entertainment area overlooking the dunes and ocean beyond. A jazz band played discreetly to the side of the pool and a few guests were dancing with drinks in hand. There was no official occasion being celebrated, just the latest opportunity to be seen at an Asa D party. The guests had flown and driven in from around the country and many nearby homes had been rented for the days leading up to and following the event for people to stay.

It was nearing midnight and Asa D knew he had to make at least a brief stroll through the gathering. His wife had fallen asleep on the couch next to his desk and he decided not to wake her. She had earned a good night sleep, he thought with a smile. He took one last look at the high definition monitors on the wall of his study. A United States Senator and one of the many lawyers he had at his disposal were talking in the kitchen, away from the noise and gaiety beyond. He needed to have a word with the honorable Senator from

South Carolina.

When he opened the door, Etienne was waiting for him and followed him down the dark and beautifully decorated hallway from the southern wing of the house toward the kitchen. He was dressed in a finely tailored white suit with a light blue silk shirt and kerchief stuck in the breast pocket. His shoes were freshly polished black Italian loafers that shined even in the low light.

Yes, he needed to have a word with the senator.

Phillip Holloway stood talking with Senator Jordan Hayes. They both held glasses of white wine, but neither had much to drink throughout the evening. This was about business and about keeping on the right side of their host, Asa D. Holloway was a partner in a prominent law firm based in Charleston. He and his firm were closely aligned with the political and business interests of both the senator and Mr. Dellahousaye, mostly with his legitimate businesses, but on occasion, those interests that were not particularly ethical.

Both the lawyer and the senator had attended the affair alone. Holloway's wife, Grace, was in a state penitentiary after being caught-up in land fraud and murder charges of his former partner, Ben Walsh, his dear Hanna's deceased spouse. He continued to lust after Hanna Walsh, but she had repeatedly rejected his flirtations; not surprising considering Mrs. Holloway had been having an affair with Ben Walsh and was held at least partially responsible for his murder. It was all such an ill-fated sequence of events as the land deal Ben had gotten involved with Asa D on had gone south and several of those involved became unfortunate and dead victims of the whole affair. Phillip had managed to stay above the fray on that particular transaction but knew Asa D held him partially responsible. He had numerous sleepless nights thinking about the fragile and dangerous, yet highly profitable relationship he had with the charming gangster.

The senator's wife rarely left Washington. In fact, she rarely left their brownstone in Georgetown. Her debilitating depression and heavy drinking were not conducive to a public life, certainly not in the nation's capital. Senator Hayes had long ago given up on helping his wife battle her demons. He was too busy with his political career and outside business interests. He also had another woman in DC to help with other more personal needs.

Holloway was listening to the senator rattle on about the fundraiser being organized for next fall's campaign. He would be up for re-election for his fourth term in the U.S. Senate and was expected to win in a landslide. Regardless, money needed to be raised and the right people and forces aligned to ensure victory. Phillip had been instrumental in each of the senator's previous campaigns. Asa Dellahousaye was a large contributor to the senator's re-election efforts over the years and both men hoped to have a few words with their host tonight to deliver the necessary show of appreciation.

The senator turned the conversation to the recent rash of violence in the nearby city of Charleston and Phillip's attention perked up. Four police officers had been killed and Hanna Walsh's detective boyfriend had nearly been taken out. How convenient it would have been, Holloway thought, to have his rival for Hanna Walsh's favors to be suddenly out of the picture.

Two other high-profile community leaders had also been found dead under mysterious circumstances in the past month. Holloway cringed every time he started connecting the dots. They all seemed to come back to the man who was hosting tonight's affair and his efforts to bring legalized gambling to the state. Just two days ago, a South Carolina state representative leading the efforts to bring the bill forward in the State House had gone missing. Authorities were investigating. Family members and friends were hoping the woman had just left on an unscheduled vacation, but most including the police, felt she had fallen to some sort of foul play. The investigation continued.

Senator Hayes and Phillip Holloway turned when they noticed a commotion and scurrying of guests behind them. Asa Dellahousaye came out through one of the large sliding glass doors along the front of the big beach house. He was, of course, followed closely by the towering body guard, Etienne. Asa D stopped briefly along the way to greet some of his guests. Others pushed in to voice their appreciation for the invitation. He tried to remain patient with the distractions as he scanned the crowd for the senator. He saw him by the pool with the idiot lawyer, Holloway, and began making his way in that direction.

After a final exchange with another guest, he walked up to the two men. "Good evening, gentleman."

Hayes offered his hand, "Asa, nice to see you again. Thank you for the invitation on this beautiful evening."

Holloway stood to the side and said, "Hello Asa."

Ignoring the greeting from the lawyer, Asa D said, "Senator, could we have a moment?"

"Of course."

Holloway took the obvious slight without protest and excused himself.

Asa D looked around to make sure they could speak confidentially. "Senator, I'm sure you're aware we have complications in Columbia with the proposed bill. Our friend in the State House decided she had other interests in conflict with our plans... not a wise decision I have to say."

"Yes, Asa, I'm well aware. Please tell me her sudden disappearance has nothing to do with this."

Dellahousaye's face remained impassive. "That's none of your affair, but where the honorable representative is at this point is beyond me."

Hayes scowled, trying to remain calm in the intimidating glare of the gangster.

"I need your help, Senator. We need to reassert our control in the State House to make sure this bill gets to the floor and gets passed. I don't need to tell you the financial gains at stake here... for all of us."

Hayes hesitated, thinking through how best to navigate these dangerous waters. "Asa, give me a day or so to make some discreet contacts. I think we can get this back under control."

"I want you to call me tomorrow with an update," Asa D demanded.

Chapter Seventeen

Alex had spent time with all the Smith boys. It was one of the most difficult experiences of his life. As he looked into each of their eyes, he couldn't help but think it was his responsibility to protect their father and he had failed. He'd left the house with a final hug for Ginny and assurances he would be available to help her with anything, though he knew he was going to have more than he could handle trying to get his head straight and at the same time, get back on the street and find this killer.

As he drove back across town, he knew he was supposed to meet Hannah for dinner at her apartment. He had hesitated to call but couldn't put his finger on why. The pain in his neck was growing unbearable. He remembered some painkillers from a past prescription back at his house. He turned at the next corner and headed home.

Rifling through a cluttered cabinet next to his bathroom sink, Alex finally found the prescription for Vicodin. He had been prescribed the drug by his doctor for the bullet wound in his arm during the episode with the Richards back in Dugganville. The bottle still had a dozen pills. He went to the kitchen for a glass of water. He noticed his hand shaking when he lifted the glass to wash down the pill.

His cell buzzed and he looked at the screen, expecting to see that Hanna was calling again. It was his captain down at the department. "Hello, Jim."

"Alex, where in hell are you?"

Alex cringed and sat in one of the kitchen chairs, his legs a bit unsteady. "I'm home."

"You should be in the hospital! You trying to kill yourself?" the captain admonished.

"I'll be okay," Alex responded. "I just couldn't lie there anymore. I need to get back to work."

There was a pause on the other end of the call before Captain Guinness said, "Alex, I'm going to ask you to step back. I'm putting you on a medical leave of absence. You need to take time to get well."

"Captain...!"

Guinness continued, "You know as well as I do in a case like this, we need to put you on the sidelines until we get everything sorted out."

"Captain, you need every person available to track down this Caine killer."

"I'm well aware of that, Alex, but as of now, you are on paid leave until further notice."

Alex felt his heart sink and a deep fury begin to build as he thought about the assassin and the havoc he was causing in people's lives.

Guinness said, "And you need to get some rest and let that wound heal. Do you hear me?"

Alex didn't answer. The painkiller he had taken was already beginning to dull his thinking. He placed the phone on "speaker" and set it on the table in front of him. Holding his head in his hands, he said, "Jim, I can't sit by on this."

"You will damn well stay out of it until I tell you otherwise! Are we clear?" Alex didn't answer. "Alex!"

Finally, "Yes sir, I hear you."

"The IA team may have some more questions for you tomorrow. Keep your phone handy."

"Yessir."

Alex ended the call and sat looking out the window of the kitchen. This wasn't the first time he'd been placed on leave from the department but this time, he knew he couldn't sit back and let someone else do his job. He would find Lonnie's killer or at least do all he could to stop this guy from killing again.

When he stood, he stumbled and had to reach for the chair to keep from falling. The drug was really kicking in now and he felt some relief from the pain and the old familiar buzz of contentment these damn pills gave him. He pushed thoughts of past dependencies aside.

He held the walls as he made it back to his bedroom and laid down on the bed. He thought of Hanna and pulled his phone out of his pocket. Rather than call, he decided to send a quick text... *Sorry, really need to get some rest back here at the apartment. See you tomorrow. Love, A.*

He was in a deep drug-induced sleep within minutes.

Chapter Eighteen

Hanna was starting to pour her second glass of wine when her phone chimed indicating a text. As she read the message from Alex, she was relieved that he was home safe and getting some rest. *But why couldn't he call?*

A stack of files stared back at her on the small kitchen table. At least she would be able to get caught up on some of the backlog at the office, she thought, deciding that she'd had enough to drink and needed to get some work done.

The top file was for Calley Barbour and she thought again of the young pregnant girl facing one of life's most difficult decisions. She had Molly send a formal request to the Office of the Court for a judicial hearing on Calley's case. They were told to expect a call back within the week as well as a request from the clerk to send over the relevant background information for the judge to review before the hearing. Hanna needed to prepare that brief this evening.

She began by looking through her notes again from the first two meetings with Calley. Then, she re-read the legal summary that Molly had prepared. As she went over the legal ramifications and requirements for the judge to consider in granting this waiver of parental consent, Hanna was concerned about the rape allegation that had not been reported by Calley. Would the judge require formal charges to be filed before he would consider that stipulation? Calley claimed to not even know the boy or where to find him. She decided to call a friend in the Public Defender's office in the morning who dealt with a lot of sexual assault cases.

In her mind, Hanna had come to terms with the fact she would be helping a sixteen-year-old girl obtain a legal abortion without her parent's knowledge or consent. The law provided for this type of situation, although she still had some concerns about Calley's claims about the rape and her parent's reaction if they were to discover she had been drinking, doing drugs and got pregnant by someone she didn't know and couldn't identify. She tried to think about how to get more background on the parents without violating client privilege. It seemed a gray area, but as Hanna thought about it more, she decided she needed to know more about the Barbour family. She would talk to Molly about it in the morning.

For a moment, memories of her time in college came back to her; long sleepless nights with Sam gone off to Europe, probably never to return, his baby growing inside her. She was legal age for an abortion at the time and worked through the haunting decision alone, uncertain who to bring into her confidence for guidance and advice. She often found herself rationalizing her ultimate choice as the best decision at the time. The abortion had been in the sixth week of her pregnancy. The recovery was physically difficult, but emotionally, a virtual roller coaster of depression and doubt. Ultimately, she had turned to her closest friend at school and together they worked through Hanna's recovery in the coming weeks until a time when the emotions began to dull and the rationalizations seemed more justified, and her life simply moved on. The demands of school were very difficult. She lost herself in her studies and tried not to dwell on her decision.

There had been an opportunity some years later when Sam did come back to the U.S. for a short visit. He contacted her in Durham, and they met for coffee. Throughout that brief reunion, she could barely hear him tell of his travels and work. She had been too preoccupied with how or whether to tell him about the baby. In the end, he left without knowing and still didn't know.

She started in on the next file on the stack and soon found herself nodding off, partly from the wine and partly from lack of sleep over the weekend out at Pawleys Island. When she and Alex were out there most weekends, they tended to stay up too late, drink too much wine and wake far too early each morning.

She went to the counter and put on a pot of coffee to try to rally for another hour or so on the work files. Then she thought about Alex, hopefully in a restful and recuperative sleep. What he had endured in the past two days was unimaginable. She scolded herself with being impatient and upset with him earlier. *I'll call him in the morning and offer to help with whatever he needs... Ginny Smith and her kids, whatever.*

Caine watched as the police cruiser finally pulled away in front of the legal clinic in downtown Charleston. He had driven by several times through the day to check. It was now just past 9:00 pm. He wasn't sure why they would decide now to leave their post watching the cop's girlfriend. Maybe they were off for a quick cup of coffee, or maybe they'd been called off permanently. He kept driving past, watching the cop car in his rear-view mirror. When they were out of sight, he turned around and pulled up to the curb two houses down from the law offices of Hanna Walsh.

He had all the latest background on Hanna Moss Walsh... schools, degrees, work history, her free clinic here now in Charleston, her other home out on Pawleys Island and legal work with a firm up there. His background investigators were exceptionally thorough, but he paid them well to be. His business and survival depended on it.

There was a light on over the front porch of the old converted house, but the office windows were dark. Upstairs, light showed through two windows with closed blinds.

Caine sat and thought about how best to close out this particular chapter with the police detective who had luckily survived yesterday's gunfight. He had received an encrypted message from his employer to clean up the mess quickly and leave no loose ends. He was a man who followed orders from his clients diligently, particularly from Asa Dellahousaye.

He certainly knew where Alex Frank lived and also knew he had left the hospital later in the day. It was quite likely, however, that he was here with the lovely girlfriend, Hanna, having her help nurse his wounds. He quickly formulated a plan, thinking that even if the cop wasn't here, he could take the woman as bait for their ultimate reunion.

Just when he reached to open the car door, headlights in his mirrors caught his attention. He slumped down as the police cruiser pulled past and parked in front of the house. There were two cars now between them. Caine waited five minutes, then put his car in gear, pulled out and drove slowly away past the cruiser and down the block. *Another time, Ms. Hanna and Detective Frank.*

Chapter Nineteen

Despite the Vicodin, Alex woke with a splitting headache and when he tried to sit up in bed, his neck flared with a fresh assault of deep tissue pain. He fell back into the pillow and cursed, closing his eyes and trying to focus on anything but the pain coursing through his neck and head.

He managed to get up and to the bathroom and shook another pill from the prescription bottle. He washed it down, drinking from the faucet and then slowly made it out to the kitchen, his right hand up on the wall along the way to steady himself.

With coffee brewing, he looked through the messages on his phone. His father had called again, but his voice mail was full and not accepting any more messages. He started clearing and deleting some of the calls and making mental notes to return some of them. The phone buzzed in his hand and his father's number flared up on the screen.

"Morning, Pop."

"Hey Alex," Skipper Frank said, the sounds of *Maggie Mae's* diesel pounding in the background. "You get your ass up here today, you hear me."

"Pop, I told you, I got work to do."

"I know you're on leave, son. Had Pepper check with your office." He was referring to County Sheriff Pepper Stokes, their friend who ran the Dugganville Sheriff's Office.

"All you had to do is call me," Alex said in frustration, then remembered his father had tried to call.

"You're gonna need some rest, son. Get on up here. I'll be back in port by noon. I'll meet you up at the house. You can get some rest and we'll fry up some fish tonight, maybe get a nightcap down at *Gillys*."

Alex's doorbell rang from the box downstairs. "Let me call you back, Pop. Somebody's at the door."

"Just get your ass up here. See you this afternoon."

Alex passed the front windows of his condo and saw the patrol car parked down in the lot. He looked through the security hole in the front door and saw Hanna standing there, talking on her phone. He opened the door and she quickly ended the conversation and came gently into his arms, not wanting to aggravate his wound.

He felt the warm comfort of her holding him close. She pulled back and said, "You get any rest last night?"

He stepped aside to let her come in. "Enough."

Hanna stopped and looked at his face. "I'm sorry, but you look like hell!"

He remembered what had stared back at him from the bathroom mirror earlier... pale skin, dark circles and bags under the eyes, hair going in all directions and a bandage the size of a softball on his neck. "Thank you... I feel like hell, too. These pain meds aren't making a dent and my head's splitting apart."

"What are you taking?"

"An old prescription of Vicodin."

"What did your doctor say?"

"I didn't ask before I left," Alex said, walking back toward the kitchen. "He wasn't exactly in favor of my departure."

Hanna shook her head and followed. Alex poured coffee for both of them and they sat at the dining table.

"You should know," Alex began, "I'm officially on paid leave until they've completed their investigation of the shootings and the doctor thinks I'm healthy enough to go back to work."

"Well, I'm pleased to hear they want you to rest," Hanna said.

Alex squeezed his eyes tight, trying to ward off another surge of pain in his forehead. "I thought I could get back out there and help find this guy, but I can barely walk from one room to the next."

"I noticed," Hanna said. "Why don't I drive you up to the island. You can stay as long as you want until you feel strong enough to get back on the job."

Alex thought about her invitation for a moment, then said, "Skipper asked me to come home for a few days. I think I should take him up on it. If I'm laid up, I really should spend some time with the old coot and see just how bad he's getting along."

"That sounds like a good idea. I don't think you should drive with those meds in your system, though," she offered. "I can drive you up there later this morning. Shouldn't take more than an hour round trip if we let the morning traffic clear. I do need to get back to the office. It's a little crazy down there."

She stood and kissed him on the cheek. "What if I come by around ten?"

He nodded. "You sure you have time?"

"Just be ready at ten."

Caine watched from a parking lot across the street next to another building as Hanna Walsh came down from Frank's condo. She waved to the two officers in the police cruiser and then got in her own car and drove off.

He thought for a moment about going after her but thought better of raising suspicion with her police escort. *There will be the right time and place.*

Hanna picked up Alex as scheduled at ten and they were soon out of town and headed up Highway 17 to his hometown of Dugganville. Their police escort followed with two officers assigned to continue to watch their back.

Alex looked over at her from the passenger seat. She noticed his stare.

"What are you looking at?" she said, smiling back at him.

"Why do you put up with me?" he said, seriously wondering again why this woman had the patience and fortitude to deal with his work, his ex-wife and all the other craziness in his life.

Hanna drove for a while without answering, then turned again and asked, "Are you serious?"

Actually, he was, he thought to himself. Other women in his life had endured far less and decided he was not worth the effort. "I feel so badly about putting you in danger like this."

She smiled and tried to make light of the situation by saying, "I'm not particularly wild about an insane assassin on the loose, but for some reason, I still think you're worth it."

Alex started to respond when she changed the subject. "I wanted to share something with you, something from work that's been bothering me."

He was somewhat relieved she had squelched his invitation to dump him, but his doubts about the danger he had placed her in still was eating at him. "What's going on?"

Alex listened as she told him about a client who needed her help with an abortion. As he listened to her explain the situation without revealing who the girl was, he found himself shocked that Hanna would agree to help this underage girl go behind her parent's back for something so serious.

"There is certainly legal precedent for a case like this," he heard her continue. "We're waiting on scheduling for a hearing before a judge to rule on this girl's request."

Alex looked over at her as she drove and tried to understand her position, but he was struggling with her decision to proceed with this. Finally, he said, "I have to tell you, I'm really surprised you're agreeing to help with this."

"I thought you might say that," Hanna said, her hands squeezing tighter on the steering wheel. "I'm a little uneasy about it myself."

"We've never spoken about the abortion issue," Alex said and then paused, looking out the front window. "I've always leaned to the side of the unborn child's life needing to be protected. I'm no advocate or active pro-life supporter, but it's just how I've grown up feeling about all this. Fortunately, I've never had to deal with it personally."

Hanna drove on for a while without responding, then said, "Well, I did have to deal with it back in college."

"And what happened?"

She told him the whole story.

When she finished, he could tell she was shaken about what she had dealt with those many years ago and what she was dealing with now. "Hanna, I'm so sorry," he said. "I wish there was something I could say."

"What do you think about her not filing a police report in the sexual assault?" Hanna said, getting back to her client's situation.

Alex thought about it for a moment. "It would certainly make the case easier to argue in front of the judge. Not sure if the girl won't be asked to file charges, even if she can't identify the attacker."

"I have an inquiry out to a friend," Hanna said. "She works in the Prosecutor's office and handles a lot of these types of assault cases."

"Okay," Alex said in a measured voice, "but let me ask you this, and I know it's not a fair question."

"Then why ask?"

"You asked for my advice and opinion on this case," he said sharply.

"What then?"

"If this girl was *your* sixteen-year-old daughter, how would you feel about an attorney and the courts helping her abort a pregnancy in the hope you would never find out? And what if you did?"

Hanna drove for some time in silence, then turned and said, "And what if all of this is really best for the girl?"

Chapter Twenty

Senator Jordan Hayes was normally a patient man, but he was trying his best to not lose his composure as he sat across from the maddening fool of an attorney, Phillip Holloway. The two men were sitting in the dark and elegant lobby of the Dilworth Hotel in downtown Charleston. Two cups of coffee and a silver carafe lay in front of them on a low table. Their chairs and all the furniture in the lobby were deeply stuffed and richly upholstered. Ceiling fans spun quietly above them, and the early morning light streamed through the wooden plantation shutters on the windows across the front of the hotel.

There was no one within listening range and Holloway continued on about his stellar connections in the South Carolina state capital in Columbia. "Really Jordan. Let me make a few calls for you. We can have a meeting set up by this evening. We'll have this gambling bill back on track in no time."

Hayes had finally had enough. "Holloway, you're wasting my time."

The lawyer sat back, apparently stunned by the rebuke. "But Jordan..."

"Listen to me!" the senator said sharply, leaning in and trying to control the level of his voice. "I invited you here for a single purpose. Do you or do you not have any leverage on Dellahousaye we can use if this all goes south?"

"I'm his attorney. I can't reveal..." Phillip began.

"Bullshit! You're one of fifty lawyers at the man's disposal and he could give two shits if you continue to work for him."

Holloway looked like he'd been slapped in the face.

Hayes continued. "This is a very dangerous game, but I need some assurance there is a card to be played to keep Asa off our backs if this all blows up."

"Jordan, anything I could divulge would get me disbarred and send me into witness protection, for God's sake! You know as well as I do, Asa would not hesitate to put a bullet in our heads if we betray him."

"That's exactly why we need this insurance policy that you damn well better come up with."

Holloway sat back and sipped at his coffee, then placed it back. "There's something I'm a little worried about?"

"What's that," the Senator said impatiently.

"You've heard that Sarah Talbot has been missing for several days?"

"The state representative you've been working with in Columbia?"

"Yes, she hasn't shown up for work and her family has issued a "missing persons" with the police."

Hayes looked around the lobby before speaking. "She was chairing the committee on the gambling bill?"

"Right, and for some reason, she started making noise about her opposition to the bill."

"I thought you had her wrapped up."

"I was supposed to meet with her two days ago to sort this all out, but she never showed up."

"This has Dellahousaye written all over it," the Senator said, his nervous voice betraying his efforts to remain calm.

The hotel manager on duty walked up. "Can we bring you anything else, Senator."

"No, thank you, Richard. We're fine right now."

"It's our pleasure to have you staying with us again Senator Hayes. Please don't hesitate to ask for me if I can help with anything during your stay in Charleston."

Hayes nodded and said, "Of course, Richard. Thank you."

The man walked away, and Hayes reached for his coffee cup, draining the last few sips. "Holloway, this meeting is over. I have to get upstairs for a call with Washington. You need to get to the bottom of this Talbot disappearance and make sure we have enough votes on the committee to get this bill to the vote."

"Already on it."

"Even more reason we need a trump card for Dellahousaye. If you have anything we can use, call my personal line. Otherwise, I don't expect to hear from you until the fundraiser up in Myrtle Beach in September."

Holloway stood with the senator. "I know what you're trying to do, Jordan. Let me give this some thought. I'm sure we can come up with something."

Chapter Twenty-one

Hanna pulled her car to a stop in front of the Frank house in Dugganville. The small one-story sat up on a grassy rise from the street in the shade of several towering live oak trees. Across the street, the river stretched out in both directions lined with small piers and boats tied up or on hoists. She saw Skipper Frank's shrimp boat, the *Maggie Mae*, coming up slowly from the east. The Skipper's mate, Robbie, was along the starboard rail, ready to help bring the old boat into the pier.

"Good timing," Alex said, slowly getting out of the car and holding his neck while he watched his father bring the *Maggie Mae* in. Their police escort pulled up behind them and parked along the road in the shade.

Hanna got out and walked around to the front of the car and sat on the hood with Alex. "What does he do with all the shrimp?"

"He's already unloaded them down at the commercial pier," Alex said. "I'm sure he's kept a few dozen to steam up. We'll put some on ice for you to take back to Charleston."

She saw Alex's father lean out the window of the pilot house and wave. They both waved back.

"Should we go help them?" Hanna asked.

"I'm not too steady yet. Don't want to fall off the dock. They'll be fine. Skipper's docked his boat ten thousand times."

She looked down the river to her left and saw the small-town waterfront of Dugganville in the distance. The morning sky was still free of clouds and a deep blue against the trees and foliage that lined the river. The summer heat and humidity were building, and her sleeveless blouse felt sticky against her skin. She thought back again about the conversation in the car with Alex about her case with Calley Barbour. They had not found any common ground on the issue and she almost regretted bringing it up with him. A text had come in from Molly on the drive up that a hearing had been scheduled for the following day. The judge who would preside had a case delayed which opened up a slot on her calendar.

Hanna knew Judge Louise Kraft, both personally and professionally, though they were by no means close friends. The judge had presided over several other cases for Hanna's clients over the years. She had always been a fair and compassionate judge in Hanna's opinion, and she was encouraged when Molly told her who would be hearing the case.

She watched as Alex stood and walked slowly back to the police cruiser. He leaned in the window and spoke with the officer driving. She couldn't hear what they were discussing and turned back to watch Robbie jump down to the pier and grab a heavy line to secure the boat. She looked back in surprise as Alex stepped away and the police car made a wide turn in the road and drove away.

As Alex came back over to her, he said, "Enough with the armed escort."

"You told them to leave?"

"I can take care of myself up here," he said. "They're going to get some food in town and then follow you back to Charleston when you're ready."

"So, your department has no leads on this guy yet?"

"Not that I've heard."

Alex's father jumped over the rail onto the pier, surprisingly agile for his age, Hanna thought, and walked up to them. He was dressed in stained Levi shorts and a light blue fishing shirt with the sleeves rolled up above his elbows. His feet were bare in old flip flops and a well-worn Atlanta Braves cap covered his wispy gray hair. He walked with an angle in his posture like one leg was slightly shorter than the other.

"What a nice surprise," Skipper said. "Beautiful lady on a beautiful morning."

Hanna gave him a hug and kiss on the cheek.

"How you been, Hanna?"

"I'm okay, just a little worried about your son."

The old man said, "How you feelin', boy?"

"Been better."

"Looks like that guy took a helluva chunk outta your neck."

Alex didn't respond, watching his father's mate finishing up securing the *Maggie Mae*.

"How'd you do out there?" Hanna asked.

"A bit slow last night. Been gettin' tougher to find the little bastards the last few years."

Alex finally said, "Pop, Hanna needs to get back. Thought I'd stay a couple days and let this neck heal some."

"Okay, great. Sure you can't stay for lunch, Hanna?"

"No, I really need to get back to the city, but I'll come back for Alex whenever he's ready." She gave Alex a hug and whispered, "Please get some rest." She could feel him nodding against her shoulder. She kissed Skipper Frank goodbye and he gave her the bag of iced shrimp he was carrying. She got back in her car. As she drove away, she looked in the rear mirror and saw Alex's father put his arm around his son and help him up the lawn to their house.

Back in Charleston, Hanna came in the back door of her offices and locked it behind her. She went into the small kitchen and drained the water and ice from the bag of shrimp before putting it in the refrigerator, then went to her desk. Her police escort had pulled around to park in the front. She called Molly up in the lobby to let her know she was back.

"I've got something for you if you have a minute," Molly said.

When she came in, Hanna said, "Close the door," then sat with her assistant at the conference table.

Molly slid a file across the table. "You really need to read about Calley's parents, Warren and Jenna. I took some time to find what I could on the usual sites. They're quite a pair. He's the pastor of a small church on the south side, very strict, all fire and brimstone type. Serious teetotalers. You won't believe the church website."

"What about the mother?"

"Found a little on *Facebook*. Some serious rants with her friends about the evils of Pop Culture and Hollywood. I'm surprised I even found her on social media. She works in a daycare center for homeless kids."

Hanna was looking through the copied documents in the file. "Anything else?"

"There was some news coverage two years ago about the church. Another family was pressing charges against the father and the congregation for being a cult and indoctrinating their daughter. Pretty messy."

Hanna looked at the copies of the press clippings.

Molly continued. "Calley has an older sister, Carolyn. Looks like she's mid-twenties. Lives in Florida. Lots of tats and piercings. I suspect she left the family a long time ago but can't really tell. *Instagram* portrait says she's working as a bartender. No college mentioned. Couldn't find any connection with her parents now, so it's likely they're estranged."

Hanna closed the file and looked up at her assistant. "This should give Judge Kraft some serious doubts about the merits of bringing the parents into this. They'll obviously go out of their minds and who knows how they'll react. One daughter is already gone.

Chapter Twenty-two

Alex peeled the last shrimp on his plate and dipped it in the homemade sauce his father made. He watched Skipper finish his lunch and stand to go to the sink to wash his hands of shrimp shells and slime.

"Not bad, hey boy?" Skipper said.

"Nothing like a fresh catch right off the boat."

Skipper came back to the table. "So, how you and Hanna doing?"

Alex looked up, surprise on his face. "Fine, why?"

"That woman must be a damn saint to put up with you."

"I tried to tell her that just this morning."

"You're a lucky man."

Alex shook his head and winced at the pain in his neck. "Yeah, lucky." He took the bottle of Vicodin from his pocket and shook out another pill. "Need to take the edge off."

"Damn sorry about Lonnie," his father said. "He was fine man. I know how close you two were."

"Yeah..." Alex looked away, trying to control the sadness and guilt washing over him again. "Pop, this killer isn't through yet. You know he came back for me and I doubt he's giving up. We need to keep our heads up."

"Hope that sumbitch comes callin'. We'll park a 12 gauge in his brisket."

Alex's phone buzzed and he pulled it out to see it was his boss back in Charleston, "Hey Captain."

"Alex, you up with your old man?"

"Hanna drove me up this morning."

"They tell me you sent the boys back with her. No one staying there with

94

you."

"I'll be fine up here."

"You and your father better be ready for the worst."

"We can take care of ourselves," Alex said, a shiver racing through him as he thought of the assassin, Caine, in the doorway of his hospital room.

Captain Guinness said, "You seen the news?"

"What news?"

"Turn on CNN or Fox or any damn channel."

"Why?" Alex asked as he got up and went over to the small television in the corner of the kitchen and turned it on.

"Seems one of the men from your unit in Afghanistan saw the coverage about the shootings, the fact you were one of the survivors."

"Who is that?"

"Caption on the screen says *Adam Grove, U.S. Marines.*"

Alex felt his heart sink as he saw the face of his former squad member. He turned up the volume, but the segment was ending. "What's he saying, Captain?"

"Seems you two had a difference of opinion about an operation over there that got out of hand."

Alex's memory was suddenly flooded with images of a small village, battered from the war, gunfire coming from everywhere.

"Alex?" he heard his boss say.

"A difference of opinion?" Alex asked.

"Says your unit got shot up pretty bad... and he claims it was your fault."

Alex felt like he might be sick. "There was an inquiry."

"The man says it was bogus, that you led them into an ambush and panicked."

"Captain..."

"I just wanted you to know this was out there," Guinness said. "Don't be surprised if the media sniffs you out up there."

"Thank you, sir."

"I think Internal Affairs will want to spend some more time with you. They have a few more questions. We can do it on the phone. I'll let you know."

Alex ended the call and changed the station to find more coverage of Sergeant Adam Grove.

"What the hell's going on?" he heard his father say.

On the screen, CNN had Grove being interviewed saying, "he got six of us killed that day and when it all went bad quickly, he panicked and nearly got us all killed."

Alex knew Grove's account was flawed. He knew he hadn't panicked, but he did make mistakes that cost men their lives. He had lived with those mistakes every day since.

Skipper came up and stood beside his son. "I thought all that was cleared up a long time ago."

Alex didn't answer.

Later in the afternoon, Alex was sitting with his father at *Gilly's Bar*. It was his father's favorite haunt and Alex had spent too many late nights there as well.

Gilly, the proprietor, came up. "Another round, gentlemen?" the old bartender asked, gesturing to the two near empty bottles of beer in front of them.

Skipper Frank swallowed the rest of his beer and pushed the bottle across the bar. "Two more."

Alex was feeling the effects of the painkiller and the beer and was a little unsteady on the barstool. "I'm okay, Pop." He knew he shouldn't be drinking while he was taking the meds, but the news report of his former team member in the war had sent him over the edge. He couldn't stop thinking about the terror of that day in Afghanistan and all that came down in the aftermath. He had been cleared ultimately in the inquiry that followed, but in his heart, he still held himself responsible for the death of those men. He also knew what had really happened that day and the memories still kept him up a night.

"Oh shit!" he heard his father say. Sergeant Grove was on the television above the bar, this time on Fox News. "Hey Gilly! Turn that crap off!" Skipper yelled, pointing to the television.

The bartender came over and switched the television to ESPN. He turned and gave Alex a concerned look. "Sorry about all this, kid."

"Thanks Gilly."

"Sure I can't get you another beer?"

"Yeah, why not."

Alex felt a hand on his shoulder and turned to see his former mother-in-law, Ella Moore.

"Hey handsome," Ella said, leaning in to kiss him on the cheek.

As Alex turned, he cringed at the pain, still not dulled from the drugs and alcohol. "How you doing, Ella?"

Skipper pushed away from the bar, a look of disgust on his face at the woman's arrival. "Need to take a piss!"

Ella said, "Oh sit down you old fool."

Skipper walked away and Ella sat down beside Alex. Gilly placed a bottle of Bud Light on the bar in front of her and gave Alex a wry smile, shaking his head before walking away.

"Nearly scared us half to death, boy," Ella said. "How you feeling?"

"I'll be okay."

"You don't look okay." She took a long pull on the beer. "What's all this nonsense on the TV?"

"Old news."

"Yeah, I remember when that all came down. About broke Adrienne's heart when we all heard about the investigation."

Alex tried to remain calm, thinking about his ex. "Ella, nice to see you," he finally said. "Look, I gotta go." When he stood, he lost his balance, nearly passing out. He fell into the bar and Ella helped him to steady himself.

"A little early to be this tanked, ain't it?" she said.

"Taking some strong stuff for this neck," he said slowly, trying to clear his head.

Ella took a drink from her beer, then said, "I'm gettin' a little worried about your old man."

"How's that?"

"I swear some days, he don't even remember his own name."

Alex nodded, not wanting to comment on his father's condition.

Skipper came up behind him. "Why don't I get you home. Get some rest."

Ella said, "I need a word with you, Skipper Frank!"

The man just grunted and reached in to take Alex around his shoulders. "Come on, let's get you home."

"Really, Skipper. You get your ass back down here," Ella said with her hands on her hips. "You know we need to talk."

Alex's father just grunted again and led Alex toward the door. His legs felt wobbly and again, he thought he might pass out. From behind, he heard, "You take care of yourself, Alex."

Chapter Twenty-three

Reverend Jerome Townsend waited inside the wide wooden doors of his Baptist church on the west side of downtown Charleston. The fifty-eight-year-old senior pastor of the church was dressed in his full Sunday robes, though most of his congregation were not present on this week-day afternoon. He was a towering man, standing six and a half feet tall, with a massive girth pushing his maroon robe out to its full capacity. His head was shaved, and his dark brown skin glistened with drops of perspiration. Three other pastors of nearby churches stood nearby huddled and talking among themselves.

Townsend held his Bible in his right hand as he looked through a small gap in the doors at the large crowd assembling outside below the steps up to the church. A podium was placed on the top landing and several media microphones had been set-up there. Television trucks from all three local stations were parked out on the street. All would have feeds to the networks back in New York.

Let them wait, he thought, smiling at the continued attention he was getting, hopefully soon across the country.

Caine stood in the center of the growing crowd of reporters and onlookers in front of the church. He looked up at the towering spire reaching into the afternoon sun. *Praise the Lord*, he thought to himself. He looked at his watch and then scanned the crowd for cops and other potential threats. He had dressed in casual business attire to blend in with the assemblage of reporters, congregation members, community leaders and others who had come out from nearby office buildings.

The doors to the church finally pushed open and he watched as the Reverend Townsend led his small entourage of preachers up to the podium above, about ten steps up from the sidewalk. The other men stood beside the taller Townsend and all looked out solemnly at the crowd. Townsend adjusted the microphones up closer to his mouth and then took a white handkerchief from his pocket to mop the sweat from his forehead.

Caine could sense the anticipation in the people around him. To his left, he saw two Charleston cops walk up and stand at the edge of the crowd. He pushed back behind a taller man to hide his face, but he could still see the Honorable Rev above, preparing to speak.

"Good afternoon, ladies and gentlemen!" Townsend's voice boomed out through the loudspeakers placed on each side of the church landing. Reporters stood next to their camera people, preparing to take notes.

Caine had his hands in his pockets and felt the reassuring press of a small 9mm semi-automatic he was carrying under his shirt at the small of his back.

"Thank you being here today," Townsend continued. "Our community and our state face a grave crisis."

Caine watched the heads of the other church leaders nodding beside the big man.

"As many of you know, forces are at work to bring the evils and depravity of gambling to our cities and towns. It's bad enough that our honest citizens are already tempted by the offshore casino boats to throw away their hard-earned money. This is a scourge and disgrace the people of South Carolina can ill-afford and we should all be outraged that our politicians are even considering this legislation."

Caine pressed closer as Townsend paused for effect, looking out across the crowd of faces, nodding to several that he recognized in the front. He thought to himself, *This guy is good.* A few "*amens*" could be heard through the crowd.

"We as honest, God-fearing people need to stand up against this evil!"

More "*amens*" and nodding heads all around Caine.

"I have a list of names, brothers and sisters... names of our elected and so-called community leaders who are signing on to this abomination,"

Townsend said, his voice echoing off nearby buildings. "I want you to take a copy of this list." He held a sheet of white paper high over his head. "I want you to go to these people in their offices, their churches and their homes and tell them this is unacceptable! We will not stand by and let this invasion of our moral principles take over. We need to be heard and vote with our voices and our wallets to tell these people we will not support their businesses, we will not vote for them in the next election, we will shun them from the doorsteps of decent people!"

"Amen!" the man next to Caine yelled out. He had heard enough and started slowly making his way to the back of the crowd, keeping his head down. *Asa D was right*, he thought, *this guy is a problem. He better hope his place in heaven is assured.*

Chapter Twenty-four

It was late afternoon and Hanna was reading through some additional case law Molly had assembled for the court hearing tomorrow in Calley Barbour's abortion ruling. There was a light knock on her open office door, and she looked up. Staring back at her was a face she hadn't seen in over twenty years, other than in pictures in the press and a documentary film the man had produced. She felt her chest go empty as if the air had been sucked out. She stood slowly, her hands pressed down on her desk.

"Hello, Hanna." The voice was warm and familiar. For many years, she had imagined reuniting with Sam Collins. Memories of their time together in college in North Carolina were occasional guilty pleasures; the fun times, the quiet times, the lovemaking. He had been her first and then he had left her for work in Europe. She had seen him once a couple of years later, but then he had never come back... until now. All of this was racing through her mind as she looked at his face, clearly older as he was now in his forties, but still youthful, strong, deeply tanned with a couple of day's growth of beard, his light brown hair long over his ears and down to his shoulders, swept back in an unkempt yet natural way that seemed washed with the sun and salt of his many travels.

"Oh my God!" was all she could manage to say and then quickly regretted sounding so foolish. She watched as Sam came into her office and across the space between them. She remembered the slow easy pace of his movements.

"You look incredible, Hanna," he said, smiling and coming around the corner of the desk holding out his arms.

She turned to him and let his arms encircle her waist and pull her in.

Tentatively, she reached her arms up around his back and lifted her face for him to kiss her on the cheek. "Sam, what are..." she started.

"Just in town for a few days. Had to look you up."

Hanna pulled back to look up at him, his eyes a few inches above hers, still a deep piercing green with flecks of brown. "Why are you in Charleston?"

"Got an assignment to do a photo essay on homes along the Battery for one of those coffee table magazines."

She was still trying to gather herself, to calm a heart that was racing. She tried to tell herself it was the shock in seeing him after so many years, not some long-held infatuation she couldn't shake.

He pulled her close again and softly said, "I'm sorry it's been so long."

She heard the words but didn't respond, resting the side of her face on his shoulder, feeling the smooth cotton of his t-shirt, a plain navy blue. His shorts were rumpled white linen and his tanned bare feet were barely covered with brown leather flip-flops.

"Hanna?"

She pushed back again, struggling to collect herself and stop acting like a schoolgirl. "You just caught me by surprise," she said.

"I'm sorry I didn't call. I don't have your cell, so I left a message with your front desk. I heard you were running a legal clinic here in town. I guess you didn't get the message yet."

Hanna looked down at the pile of message slips Molly had left for her earlier, still unread. She felt his hands reach for hers and he stood back to look at her. As she looked down at their hands together between them, she heard him say, "Where has the time gone? I swear I was just in Chapel Hill a few days ago with you."

She looked up into his face and saw a warm smile that she had remembered so vividly all these years. She felt her emotions ebbing from surprise to confusion and now a sudden sadness as she thought of their last times together and how it had all unraveled.

Sam broke the silence between them. "I was wondering if you were free for dinner tonight. We need to catch up, obviously," he said, almost apologetically.

Pulling her hands away and stepping back, she stumbled into her desk chair and turned to catch herself on the desk. She heard him laugh quietly and say, "Still as graceful as ever."

"Sam, I'm sorry. This is just such a surprise... it's been so long."

"We can catch up on all that tonight. Please join me for dinner. I want to hear so much about what you've been doing, about your son..."

"You know about Jonathan?" she asked, both surprised and happy that he had been keeping up with her life.

"Social media," he replied. "I'm a terrible stalker."

She looked back at him, nodding and thinking that she too had kept close tabs on his many travels and women, including his wife. She looked down at his left hand and didn't see a wedding ring. *What's happened to the French woman? What was her name? Angela?*

"I'm sorry for barging in like this," he said. "I know you must be terribly busy. Your front lobby looks like Grand Central Station. Please, let's get some dinner tonight. You pick the place and I'll meet you there. How about seven?"

Her next thought was Alex and what he would think about her reunion with the first love of her life and having dinner with the man... and what he would think if he knew how much she still had feelings for this man who was still a boy when they had last seen each other.

"Seven o'clock?" she managed to say.

"Does that give you enough time to get through all those piles?" he asked, looking down at the clutter of her desk.

In an instant she decided that of course she had to see him tonight, to learn more, to fill in some of those many years apart. *To talk about their last time together?* "Seven will be fine. How about the *Peninsula Grill*? It's not far."

"I'll find it." He leaned in and kissed her again on the cheek.

She felt the wet trace of the kiss on her skin as she watched him turn to leave.

Sam stopped and looked back at her. "It really is wonderful to see you, Hanna."

She smiled back but didn't respond, her mind and emotions still swirling from the surprise of his visit.

CHAPTER TWENTY-FOUR

"Seven o'clock then." he said.

"See you there." She watched him walk out the door and away down the hall. She sat back in the comfort of her chair and let her head fall back, looking up at the cracked white plaster on the ceiling above her. *And what will Alex think about all this?*

Chapter Twenty-five

Alex was dozing on the front screen porch of his father's house, nestled down into the cushion on an old wicker chair. His feet were stretched out on a small ottoman. It was nearing dark and the night air was alive with the relentless chorus of birds and tree frogs in the big live oaks surrounding the house.

The sound of a car door slamming woke him from a dream where he was running toward his fallen partner, Lonnie Smith, yelling out something unintelligible, ignoring gunfire from some unseen assailant, wanting only to reach the man and protect him. As he was shaking off the last fragments of the dream in his mind, he heard, "Alex, is that you?"

It was a woman's voice and he opened his eyes to see a shadowed figured standing outside below the steps. He started to sit up but the pain in his neck flared like a white-hot iron laid across his skin. He fell back, cursing to himself.

"Alex, it's Amelia... Amelia Richards."

Alex managed to stand, wincing at the pain. He started toward the front door to the screen porch thinking *why in the world would Beau Richards' wife be here to see him?* He had helped to send the man away to prison this past year after it was found that Richards and his son, Connor, were behind a significant drug smuggling business as well as several other illegal operations. This woman's husband had also hired a local lowlife to kill him when he started getting too close to the Richards' crime enterprise. He hadn't seen Amelia Richards since the final day of the trial when her husband was convicted and sent away to the state penitentiary.

Alex switched on the front porch light and he could see her waiting for him at the bottom of the steps. He pushed open the screen door. "Amelia, what are you doing here?"

"Do you have a minute?" she asked, her voice resonating in the faint Italian accent of her birthplace. She was a tall and stunning woman with a dark complexion and soft hazel eyes. Alex had always been surprised at her marriage to the much older Beau Richards. He guessed she must be in her thirties at most. Her long brown hair was pulled back and tied in a thin blue ribbon at her neck. Her bare shoulders and arms were exposed by a flowered sun dress that hung to just above her knees.

Alex gestured for her to come up on the porch. He held the door as she went by him and he could smell the perfume and scent of her shampoo as she passed. "Have a seat," he said, leading her over to the grouping of wicker furniture. They both sat down. "How have you been, Amelia?"

"Some days better than others," she replied, her accent a surprising sound in the Low Country of South Carolina.

"Are you still staying out at the ranch?" Beau Richards owned a large ranch out east of town with a beautiful home that Alex had visited on a couple of occasions.

"For most of the year," she said softly. "In the hot months here in the summer, I go home to Italy to see my family."

Alex thought again about the night this woman's husband had tried to kill him personally when the hit man had failed. Alex had overcome Beau Richards, leading to his arrest and eventual incarceration. "What can I do for you, Amelia?"

"I heard you were in town and thought you might be down at *Gilly's* with your father, but I didn't see you there."

"I came home a while ago." He placed his hand on the bandage on his neck. "Need to get some rest."

Amelia said, "I heard about your injury on the local news. Such a terrible tragedy losing all those men."

Alex didn't answer.

After an awkward silence, Amelia said, "I need your help with something."

"I'm not much good for anybody at the moment," he said, touching his neck again.

"It's been very difficult since my husband went away."

"Look Amelia, I'm sorry, but your husband was involved in some very bad business and deserves to be where he is today."

"Oh, I know," she said quickly, pushing back in her chair and crossing her legs. "When I first met Beau, I had no idea what he was involved with. At the end, I was surprised at all he was doing."

Alex was finding this difficult to believe but at this point, it didn't matter. There had been no evidence Amelia Richards was involved personally in any of the illegal activities of her husband and stepson, and she was not arrested or charged when her husband was sent away. "What do you need help with?"

"My husband was working with some very dangerous men, I'm coming to find," she answered. "The drug business, you know?"

"Yes, we traced it back to a gang that operates across the South and a cartel in Mexico. 'Dangerous' is an understatement."

"I've been visited on several occasions by a man who says he represents the business interests my husband was involved with," she said. "He is a very frightening man."

"Is he one of the Mexicans?" Alex asked.

"No, he's an American," she said, pulling up the fabric of her dress and kneading it with her hands. "Do you know of a man named Asa Dellahousaye?"

Alex leaned back in surprise. "Dellahousaye came to see you?"

"No, one of his men."

Alex had long suspected the man known as Asa "D" was behind the drug business along the Atlantic coast if not beyond, but they hadn't been able to firmly make the connection in the Beau Richards case. The mention of the man's name caused his temper to flare as he thought of the killer this man had unleashed on his fallen friend and colleagues, let alone his own near-death experience. "And how do you know this man works for Dellahousaye?"

"They've been to our house before... back before Beau was arrested."

"And what do they want?" Alex asked.

"Soon after my husband went away ..." She paused to collect herself as her voice broke and then became very soft, as if someone might be listening. "When he went away to prison, just a few days later this man came to see me. He thinks Beau has records and money. I told them the police had taken everything, but they insisted he must have a hidden safe or cache of papers and money."

"And does he?" Alex asked.

"No, not that I'm aware. The small safe in his den was emptied during the investigation after his arrest. There was some money and guns and any paperwork was seized by the police."

"Yes, I remember."

"They've been back several times and I've let them look around the house and the hunting camp we have up in the mountains. They even wanted to search the house out in Colorado which I arranged before it was sold, but I don't believe they've found what they're looking for because the man was back again yesterday."

"Why haven't you come to the police sooner?" Alex asked, leaning forward and pushing back the pain searing into his neck.

"These are very scary men, Alex. I worry even coming to see you. If they knew, I don't know what might happen."

Alex thought about the relentless efforts Hanna had endured when her husband had been caught up with this crime syndicate and ultimately killed. They had kidnapped her son and the boy may likely have been killed if the FBI and Charleston Police Department hadn't intervened in time. *God knows what would have happened to Hanna,* he thought. "What do you think I can help with?"

"During the investigation, was there anything seized, any papers these men may think are of value?" she asked, leaning forward, expectantly.

Alex thought for a moment about the thick file of evidence gathered in the arrest and conviction of Beau Richards and his son, Connor. None of it had any reference to or direct ties to Asa Dellahousaye. The old gangster had covered his tracks very well in this particular case, but obviously he was worried about something Richards must have hidden away. He shook his head as he looked at the face of Amelia Richards. "I wouldn't be able to share any of the specifics with you anyway," he said, "but I don't recall anything that had to do with Dellahousaye, or we would have pursued it."

He watched her expression sag and she sat back in the chair.

"I'm sorry to bother you, Alex. I shouldn't have come." She stood to leave, and Alex pushed up from his chair trying to minimize the pain shooting through his neck.

"Let me think about it some more," he said.

"Thank you." She walked over to the screen door and then turned. "Again, I'm sorry about your friends in the department."

He nodded as she turned to walk down the steps. He decided it was best not to tell her that Asa Dellahousaye was behind the police shootings in Charleston. He watched her walk down the path to her car in the dim glow of the porch light and then drive away.

And what does Asa D think Beau Richards had on him?

Chapter Twenty-six

Sam Collins stood as Hanna walked up to his table at the restaurant. She noticed he had changed into a pressed white shirt open at the neck and rolled up at the sleeves. His hair was combed back wet and he had shaved the few days of beard she had seen earlier that day. His bright smile stood out on his tanned face and she suddenly felt a swirl of conflicting emotions... pleasure in seeing him again after so many years, uncertainty about her feelings for the man after all the years apart, guilt in meeting Sam without telling Alex yet. She scolded herself for even acknowledging there was anything to feel guilty about, dinner with a long-lost friend... *and former lover?*

He opened his arms to give her a hug and she turned her face so they could kiss each other's cheeks. She had showered and dressed quickly, running behind as usual at the office. *And why did you take so much time in front of the mirror doing your face?* she thought, angry at herself for worrying about how she would look at dinner with him.

"I'm sorry I'm running a little behind..." she started.

"Not a problem. I should have given you more notice," Sam said. "Thank you again for making time. I really am looking forward to catching up."

He held her chair and then sat across from her. The restaurant was near full as always and Hanna quickly looked around the room for familiar faces, not because she was concerned with being seen with another man, she thought. *Right? Why am I so worried about this?*

She heard Sam say, "You must be awfully proud of the work you're doing down there at the clinic."

Turning back to him, she smiled and said, "It's wonderful and challenging and frightening at times.

"Oh, I'm sure."

"I also work for a small law firm up near our beach house on Pawleys Island. It helps pay the bills."

"I remember visiting the beach house when we were back in school," Sam said.

Her mind suddenly brought back images of their times together on the beach, around a beach fire, making love in the dunes on dark nights.

"Hanna?"

She focused on his face across the table from her and pushed the past from her thoughts. "Yes, it's a marvelous place," she said.

"I'd love to see it again sometime," he said. "I wish I was going to be in town longer on this trip."

"Maybe the next time."

Sam turned the conversation to her son, Jonathan, and she brought him up to date on his time now in Chapel Hill at UNC. The conversation inevitably led to her husband and his tragic death. Hanna had long ago come to grips with the loss, and the discovery of his infidelities and illegal dealings had left her with only the nagging irritation in not seeing through the man's faults earlier before it all fell apart.

Wine and then dinner were served as they continued to talk about Hanna's path since they had last been together. As the waiter was clearing their plates, it occurred to her she hadn't mentioned Alex Frank. Without hesitating, she said, "You'll have to meet the man I'm seeing now. He's a detective with the Charleston Police Department. He helped me through all the mess with Ben and then Jonathan's abduction."

Sam quickly said, "I'd like to meet him. He's a lucky man."

Hanna smiled back at him trying to read his face. Deciding to change the subject she asked, "I read somewhere you had married?"

He nodded and waited for the waiter to take his plate and step away before saying, "Yes, we were married nearly ten years. She finally got tired of the travel and my time away. It's better for both of us really."

So, you're divorced now?"

"Yes, nearly a year. She lives back in Paris where she grew up. She is a wonderful woman and a saint really for putting up with my crazy schedule as long as she did. We left on very good terms and I've seen her a couple of times when I'm back in that part of Europe."

The waiter came and asked about dessert. They both declined but agreed to another glass of wine. When the man walked away, Sam said, "I wanted to talk to you about that last night back in Chapel Hill."

Hanna felt a rush of nervous apprehension.

He continued, "I've always felt there was something you wanted to tell me that night, but I couldn't get you to talk about it. I know you were upset, but..."

Hanna felt tears start to well-up in her eyes and she wiped at them with her napkin. She had often wondered if they would ever have this conversation and if she would have the courage to tell him what had happened.

She had missed her period for the second time just a week earlier and hadn't been to the doctor yet. When Sam had told her that night he was leaving school to take a photo assistant's job in Europe, it had broken her heart. She was so upset she couldn't bring herself to tell him she might be pregnant. He left a few days later and never came back. When she confirmed she was pregnant, she was in such a downward spiral from the emotions of Sam's leaving and the prospect of a child when she was only twenty at the time, it had all overwhelmed her. Two weeks later she had an abortion. There were so many times she could recall wanting to contact Sam and let him know what had happened, but she could never bring herself to do it. They had exchanged letters and an occasional phone call from some remote location he was working for a few months and then the contacts became less frequent. Eventually, she knew in her heart it was over and she began the process of moving ahead. The guilt in not telling him about their child though had never gone away.

She heard him say, "Hanna, what is it?"

She took a long drink from the glass of white wine and let the slow comfort of it ease down into her. She looked directly into Sam's eyes and wrestled with the thought that she had already had too much wine to have an intelligent conversation about the fact she had aborted the birth of their child twenty-some years ago.

"Hanna, please. Let's just get this all on the table."

She let all her emotions flow out. "If you hadn't left, it would have all been okay."

"What are you talking about?"

She hesitated again and took another sip from the wine. "I just didn't know what to do."

"About what?"

She put her napkin on the table and crossed her hands on it, trying to stop from crying anymore. "I was pregnant, Sam."

Her words hung in the air and she watched as he absorbed what she had just revealed. He leaned back in his chair. He just looked at her for a few moments, the expression on his face both confused and then angry. "When I left school?"

Hanna nodded.

"So, when... ?" Sam started.

"I had an abortion, Sam," she said softly, not really caring what the others at nearby tables might hear but finding it difficult to say the words out loud.

She watched as he stared back at her intently, blinking a couple of times as he tried to absorb what she had just told him. Finally, he asked, "And why didn't you come to me? Why didn't you tell me about this?"

"You were gone!" she said more forcefully. "You had left me!"

"Hanna..."

"Please," she interrupted. "It was a long time ago. I've given up debating whether I made the right decision. It's done."

Sam pulled his hand back and looked down at his plate for a few moments, then took a drink from his wine glass.

"I'm sorry I've never told you about this," Hanna said. "I should have come to you, but you were so far away, and I knew you weren't coming back."

She watched as he looked back at her and said, "Hanna, I'm so sorry you had to go through this alone. I wish you had told me, but I understand."

"It was a long time ago."

CHAPTER TWENTY-SIX

"Yes, it was. We were still kids, weren't we?"

Hanna nodded, searching his face for what he might really be feeling. She could tell his mind was swirling through the implications of it all.

"And if you had told me?" he finally said, clearly thinking outload. "Where would we be today? Where would our child...?"

"Sam, please don't!" she pleaded.

"I'm sorry," he said.

"I think we should go," Hanna said, pushing her chair back.

Sam walked Hanna back to her office and apartment through the dark streets of Charleston. It was near 10:00 when they reached the front steps to her building. They had walked in silence the whole way. At one point, Sam had reached to take her hand, as if in apology for raising the question of what might have become of them as a couple and of their child together. She had pulled her hand away and continued on without speaking.

She turned to him and could see his face in the dim light from a lamp across the street. This time when he reached for her hand she didn't pull away.

"Hanna, I didn't expect this evening to bring back so many difficult memories. I'm sorry."

She didn't reply.

"I've always felt badly about how it ended between us," Sam continued. "I was stupid for leaving the way I did, but one thing led to another with my work and then so much time had passed between us."

"You don't need to apologize for anything," Hanna said.

"I knew something was bothering you that night I told you I was leaving. It's always nagged at me even after all these years. Again, I'm so sorry."

He pulled her close and she didn't resist. She reached around to hold him near. They stood together in silence for a few moments. The tears came again, and she felt them on her cheeks, dripping onto his shoulder. She pulled back to go up the stairs.

Sam held her arms softly and leaned in to kiss her on the cheek. "I'm sorry it's been so long, Hanna. "I'm sorry..."

"Please, no more apologies."

"Okay." He stepped back to leave.

"It's been nice to see you," Hanna said. "I hope you have a good shoot here in Charleston."

"Thank you," he replied. "I wish I had more time while I'm here, but..."

"Sam, let's leave it at this, okay."

He nodded back and then turned to walk away. "Goodbye, Hanna."

Hanna closed the door to her apartment and locked the bolt on the door. She turned on the kitchen light and opened the refrigerator. A half empty bottle of white wine was in one of the door shelves and she pulled it out and poured herself a glass before sitting at the small table. Her evening with Sam Collins was sending a rush of mixed emotions through her brain and her hand trembled as she took a sip from the wine. She felt some relief in finally telling him about what she had done. Then there was the guilt again in having seen him and not telling Alex yet, and what had she felt when Sam Collins had walked away, leaving her again? *No, let's not go there*, she thought.

She reached for her phone in her bag and didn't see any messages. She pushed the link to Alex's phone and heard it ring four times before going to voice mail. *The meds*, she thought. *Hopefully, he's getting some sleep.* She didn't leave a message.

Chapter Twenty-seven

Alex woke the next morning when he heard his father crashing around in the kitchen of their small house. He tried to shake off the haze of the night's deep and drug-induced sleep. The pain in his neck was an instant reminder of where he was and why. He managed to sit up, still feeling groggy. The bottle of painkillers was on the nightstand beside him and he took another, washing it down with the half-empty glass of water sitting there. The smell of dark rich coffee drifted in from down the hall.

He reached for his phone and saw a call from Hanna the previous night. She hadn't left a message. He pressed the entry to return her call, but it went to her mailbox which he was then informed by the maddening robotic voice that it was full. He looked at the time on the phone... 8:30.

After breakfast and a few calls back to the department in Charleston, he tried Hanna again and couldn't connect or leave a message. He called her office and her assistant, Molly, told him Hanna had not come in yet. She had already missed her first appointment. Molly had gone up to the apartment and knocked, but Hanna wasn't there.

Alex's senses immediately went on full alert. His captain had told him yesterday that he was pulling the protection detail. The department was stretched too thin already and the threat to Hanna from Lonnie Smith's killer had thankfully not materialized.

He had expressed his concern but couldn't convince the man to keep the men on assignment to watch Hanna's back.

He felt a sick feeling in his stomach, seeing the twisted face of the killer,

Caine, in the kitchen where Lonnie was killed and then again in the doorway of his hospital room.

He called Hanna's cell again and was surprised and relieved when he heard her answer, "Good morning."

"Hanna, where are you?"

"I'm finishing up a run and heading back to the office."

"I've been trying to reach you. Molly didn't know where you were and... "

"I'm fine," she said, "just needed to clear my head. I have this hearing today on the abortion case and..."

Alex waited for her to continue but there was only silence on the call.

"Hanna, what is it?"

Again, she didn't answer right away.

"Hanna?"

"I need to talk to you about something, but it can wait."

"No, I don't think it can," Alex said. "What's going on?"

He could hear Hanna breathing heavily from her run and hesitating, then she said, "I had dinner last night with an old friend."

"An old friend?"

"I've told you about the boy back in school I was seeing, the boy who left."

Alex couldn't suppress the doubt and jealousy already creeping into his thoughts. "Yes, you've told me. I assume he's also the father of the baby..."

Hanna cut in, "Yes, he was."

Alex walked out the front door of the house and down toward the docks across the street. "And he didn't know?"

"No, I never told him... until last night."

"And how did that go?"

"I'm glad I finally had the chance to tell him about all that. He was surprised of course and had a lot of questions..."

"So, how did you leave it with him?"

"He walked me home and we said *goodbye*."

"He walked you home. That's it?" Alex asked, regretting immediately that he was sounding like the typical jealous boyfriend.

Hanna said, "He's only in town for a few days. He's doing a photo shoot and I won't see him again."

Alex's mind was racing. *Hanna sees this man she was madly in love with in college, the man who fathered her first child, the child she had aborted without telling him, and they were both going to just walk away for another twenty years?*

"Alex, please don't be upset. I'm sorry I didn't tell you yesterday I was meeting Sam for dinner. I should have called."

He swallowed and took a moment to calm down. "It's okay, really. I didn't mean to sound like a jerk."

"You're not a jerk."

Alex couldn't help thinking again about what a burden he was to Hanna, and even a danger. He knew his mind was clouded by the painkillers he was on and he tried to push the thought aside. He quickly decided to move on and change the subject. "I hope your hearing with this young girl goes okay today."

"Thank you. I'm really struggling with all of that, actually, but I think we're doing the right thing."

"Well again, good luck."

"What are you doing today"? he heard her ask.

"I spoke with one of our men back in Charleston this morning. Seems your old friend, Phillip Holloway, was seen with Asa Dellahousaye. Did you know he was working with the man or that they were acquaintances?"

"No, I didn't," Hanna replied. "Phillip hanging out with a gangster?"

"Apparently. I'm having my dad drive me down to Charleston later this morning to have a word with Holloway. I still don't want to drive with these pills I'm taking."

"You think he might be involved in any of this with Lonnie and the killer?" she asked, surprise clear in her voice.

"I don't know what's going on, but I'm going to find out."

They ended the call with promises to touch base at the end of the day. Alex was out at the end of his father's pier now, standing beside the shrimp boat, the *Maggie Mae*. He couldn't get the thought of Hanna with her old boyfriend out of his mind and yet he thought, *maybe it's best. I'm dragging her right down with me... if I don't get her killed in the meantime.*

Chapter Twenty-eight

The Reverend Jeremiah Townsend said *good morning* to the gathering of church workers at their desks on his way back to his office at the back of the massive church complex that he oversaw. He was dressed smartly in an expensive blue summer suit with gray pinstripes, all set-off by a bright red silk tie. He walked with a slow and confident gait, comfortable in his role as the senior pastor of one of the state's largest churches. He was also feeling particularly good about the publicity he'd been seeing the past few days since taking a very public stand against the proposed gambling bill currently being considered at the state capital. His parishioners were solidly behind him, other community leaders were joining the bandwagon and most importantly, contributions were flooding in to the call center to support the church's "courageous" efforts to stare down the expanding scourge of gambling in their state.

Townsend walked into his palatial office and closed and locked the door behind him. He had several confidential calls to make and didn't want any interruptions. He took off his suit coat and placed it on a hook on the coat stand behind his desk. He sat down and began logging into his computer, the lush leather chair moaning at the extreme weight of the man. He reached for the phone on his desk and began dialing his first call.

He didn't hear Caine coming up behind him from the small kitchen attached to the office and jumped when the man's hand reached from behind him to disconnect the call. The reverend turned quickly in alarm.

"Who are you?" he bellowed.

Caine placed his finger to his lips. "Not so loud, Reverend. Don't want to alarm your congregation." He walked around the desk and stood facing the church leader. He had a large backpack hanging from one shoulder.

"Again, who are you and what are doing here?"

Caine just smiled back at the man, then said, "I was at your press conference, Reverend. You really are getting people riled up about the gambling bill."

"Well I hope so!" Townsend said, the arrogance and self-righteousness dripping off him. "This state has enough vices. Our good people don't need more opportunities to make poor decisions."

"I think you've made a poor decision, Reverend," Caine said, his eyes narrowing and smile disappearing.

"And how is that, sir?"

Caine reached into his pack and pulled out a long hunting knife. He watched as Townsend's eyes grew large in surprise and then fear. The man tried to get up, but Caine came quickly around the desk and forced him back into his desk chair with the tip of his knife against the man's nose.

"I'm going to call security..."

"Just shut-up, or I'll slice that nose off your face," Caine hissed.

Townsend sat back in his chair, his hands visibly trembling.

With quick movements, Caine placed a long piece of silver Duct Tape over the man's nose and mouth and then secured him to the chair with a length of rope from his backpack. When Townsend would start to squirm or try to get up, he was quickly subdued with the point of the knife held just in front of his face. Caine pulled out another long length of thick rope from his pack. He stepped back and threw one end up and over a large exposed beam twelve feet above the desk and spanning the high peaked ceiling.

He came close to Townsend's ear and whispered. "You've made some friends of mine very unhappy. When they get unhappy, people usually have to pay a price. Are you ready to pay the price, Reverend?"

The man stared back with frantic eyes, moaning some garbled response beneath the tape over his mouth.

"Are you good with the Lord, Reverend?" Caine asked. "I would hope so, a man of the cloth such as yourself."

In an instant, Caine had the one end of the rope around the man's neck and quickly secured a tight slipknot. Townsend struggled and tried to rise again, but the knife point quickly forced him back into his chair. Caine loosened the restraints holding the man to the chair and pulled the other end of the rope tighter until the tension on his neck pulled the man to his feet behind his desk. His free hands quickly went to try to release the choking tightness of the knot around his neck. Caine pulled harder and watched as the man lifted off the ground, his feet kicking and his hands frantically trying to remove the tightening rope around his neck.

When Townsend was four feet off the ground behind his desk, Caine secured the rope to a doorknob on the nearest wall. He stood back and watched the man continue to kick and squirm as the rope cut into his neck and cut-off his last gasping breaths. Townsend's face was now bright red, his eyes bulging in terror. Urine leaked out from the bottom of one of his pant leg openings.

Caine came around and faced the dying Reverend Jeremiah Townsend. "Your suicide will be seen as an act of deep regret for your corrupt life running this church and stealing your congregation and television ministry blind," Caine said. "I hope you rot in hell, pastor."

The killer kicked the desk chair over to make it look like the Reverend had stood up to secure the rope around his neck before kicking it away to kill himself. Asa D had wanted him to make this look accidental or self-inflicted, after one more death of a vocal critic of the gambling bill might be one too many.

As Caine picked up any remaining evidence of his presence and prepared to leave out a back door, he looked up to see Townsend had stopped moving. He hung now with his hands at his side, his head tilted above the slipknot of the rope. He had a distant and vacant look now in his bulging eyes. Caine smiled, satisfied with his handiwork and left silently out the back.

Chapter Twenty-nine

Just before noon, Hanna had worked through a couple of client meetings and the files that needed attending to for the morning. She had also assembled all the work she needed to take to the courthouse after lunch where she was meeting Calley Barbour for her hearing. As the morning had progressed, she kept getting distracted with thoughts of her dinner with Sam and then her conversation with Alex about the whole thing this morning. She was also feeling apprehensive about Calley's hearing and how Judge Kraft would rule on their request for Calley to receive an abortion without her parent's knowledge. She was having to continue to convince herself she was doing the right thing for this girl. All the thoughts of her own abortion years earlier with Sam the previous night had not helped to build her confidence in the path they were taking.

Her office phone rang. It was Molly telling her a Mr. Collins was out front and needed to see her. Hanna's first reaction was surprise that Sam had come back to see her so quickly. She had thought it clear he would be busy with his work for several days, then leaving town. Her second reaction was a bit of panic when she started thinking about what he could possibly want. "Send him back," she finally said.

Hanna stood and tried to make herself presentable, pulling her hair back behind her ears and tucking her blouse back into her slacks, then realized how ridiculous she was being. *Really, Hanna!*

She saw Sam walk through her door. Immediately, she knew something was wrong. His face was tired and drawn, his clothes disheveled.

"I'm really sorry for just barging in," he said and then came over quickly and stood across the desk from her. "I've been up half the damn night. I couldn't keep focused on my work this morning. We need to talk, Hanna."

"I have to meet my client in court at 1:30, Sam. This isn't a good time."

"Are you going to eat? Let's go get some lunch. We need to talk," he insisted.

Ten minutes later they were ordering sandwiches at a deli down the street. When they had their food, they found a table in a shady courtyard outside.

Hanna took a deep breath, then asked, "So, what's so urgent?"

Neither touched their sandwiches as they sat across from each other. Sam said, "After last night, after dinner with you... I got back to my hotel and started thinking again about what an idiot I was, leaving you like I did, not being there for you when you had so much to deal with."

"Sam, we talked about that and agreed, no more apologies."

"Hanna, you need to know, there were so many times during those years after I left that I wanted to come back to be with you, not even knowing about the baby. Every time, either work would get in the way, then I heard you were seeing this guy in law school. Then you were married with a son. It just never seemed right for me to come back and get in the way of all that. You need to know it killed me I couldn't come back."

Hanna was stunned at what she was hearing. She never had any indication Sam had regretted his decision or had ever considered coming back to her. "It's a little late for second-guessing all that."

"Why is it too late?" he asked.

"Sam, we're not kids anymore. We've moved on."

"What if I told you I'm tired of moving on. I feel like I've been running from something my entire damn life."

"What are you talking about?"

"I want us to have another chance, Hanna."

"Another chance?"

"I know you're seeing someone and I'm sure he's a great person or you wouldn't be with him, but..."

"Sam, I can't just throw everything in my life out the window," Hanna said, her heart pounding in her chest and her mind blurred with all the implications. "Alex and I have something special and I can't just leave and follow you around the world while you work. I have a life and a career here, and my son is here."

"I'm not asking you to walk away, Hanna. I'm tired of the travel, the hotels, living a life mostly alone. I want to settle somewhere, get connected, have a real relationship."

Hanna was feeling an overwhelming sense of panic and couldn't respond.

"I can find work here in South Carolina when I need to. Fortunately, I've spent very little of the money I've made over the years."

"Sam, this is crazy!" Hanna said, pushing back her chair and standing. "I can't even begin to process all this."

He stood across from her. "Can we please just give this some time for both of us to think it through."

Hanna was feeling an anger start to build. "You and I were kids when we were together."

"Look, I'm sorry for springing this on you so suddenly."

"Sudden is right! You're back for twenty-four hours and you're ready to abandon your career and take back a woman you haven't seen or known for decades." She reached down for her bag. "I can't even begin to process this, Sam. I need to get down to the courthouse to meet my client."

Sam came around the table and stood between her and the exit. "Can we please just give this some time... spend some time together to sort this all out?"

Hanna thought about Alex. She had never felt closer to a man than she did Alex Frank at this very moment. They had been through so much together and their lives now were good... *weren't they?* Sam Collins isn't real. He's a distant memory. "Sam, I have to go."

He stepped aside, a sad and strained look on his face.

Chapter Thirty

Phillip Holloway had been passed through the security gate at Asa Della-housaye's beach house on Isle of Palms and had already been frisked at the door by Asa D's primary bodyguard, Etienne. He sat waiting in the man's office, windows looking out at the panorama of the beach and bright blue sky. The hulking Etienne stood nearby watching him warily. Holloway tried to keep his composure and remain calm as he waited for the gangster. This was a discussion he was not looking forward to.

A door to the side of a massive and ornate wood desk opened and Della-housaye walked in and sat down in the rich black leather desk chair, not acknowledging the presence of one of his lawyers. He began sorting through some papers and then pulled out a cell phone and made a call. He finally glanced at Holloway and nodded, whispering, "Just be a second."

Holloway listened to the brief call and could make little sense of who he was speaking to or what the conversation was about. Asa D hung up and looked over at Holloway. "What's up, counselor?"

"Asa, thank you for seeing me..."

"Did I have a choice?" Asa D cut in.

"I just need a few minutes."

"What is it?"

"Senator Hayes sends his best. He wants you to know that we are both doing everything in our power to keep the gambling bill on track in Columbia."

"I appreciate that, Phillip. I'm paying you both very well to do exactly that."

"Yes, of course," Holloway said, hesitant in having his complicity in this scheme spoken out loud.

"When can we expect this to come up for a vote?" Dellahousaye asked.

"Certainly by the end of this session in September."

"We need to get this through as quickly as possible, counselor."

"Trust me, Asa, we're leaving no stone unturned."

"Is that all?" the gangster asked, standing behind his desk as a signal for Holloway to leave.

"One other thing," Holloway said, his voice cracking noticeably. He swallowed hard. Finally, he summoned enough composure to say, "The senator and I need some assurances..."

"What kind of assurance?" the gangster said strongly, a look of deep anger clear in his face.

"We certainly trust you, Asa..." Holloway said, thinking at the same time what bullshit that was. "We trust you, but we need your assurance and support that our involvement will never be linked to this transaction."

"Transaction?"

"The gambling bill..."

"Holloway, tell me what in hell this is about, now!"

"You need to understand that what I'm about to tell you is only in the spirit of protecting our own interests if for some reason our efforts are discovered, made public, whatever."

"Whatever?" the gangster repeated.

"The senator and I have filed documents in a secure place that provide great detail of our relationship with you and ..."

Dellahousaye broke in, furious. "Are you threatening me?"

Holloway stood to face the man, trying as hard as he could to remain steady and not show the fear that was coursing through him. "Of course not..."

"What the hell is this, then?"

"These documents and records of meetings and discussions simply characterize all of this work we've been doing for you as routine legal work for some investments you plan to make in the state."

Asa D seemed to calm some and sat back down.

Holloway swallowed hard and continued. "You also need to know there is another set of files that provides great detail on the true nature of our work to ensure this bill gets passed in Columbia. If for any reason, we believe our interests and involvement will be compromised, we trust you will back up our story. However, Jordan and I want you to know..."

"Enough!" the old gangster shouted. "Get the hell out of here! If we didn't go back as far as we do, I'd have Etienne carve you up right here in my office and drop you offshore for fish food."

Holloway blanched, feeling like he might be sick right here on the man's lush carpet. "Asa, you have our full support..."

"Get the hell out of here now, Holloway!"

"I'm only telling you this to make sure we're on the same page if anything goes south."

"I'm tempted to send your puny ass south, about 100 feet below the Atlantic," Dellahousaye said slowly and emphatically.

Holloway started backing toward the door. He sensed the bodyguard moving behind him to block his path.

"Let him go," Dellahousaye said. Etienne moved to the side. "Counselor, I expect this bill to successfully pass before the end of the month. I will hold you personally responsible if there are any delays."

Holloway summoned what little courage he could and replied, "It's in all of our best interests for that to happen, and as I said, the senator and I have all our resources focused on making that happen."

"It damn well better."

When Holloway closed the door to leave, Dellahousaye turned to his big bodyguard, shaking his head. "We need to get some new lawyers and politicians."

Chapter Thirty-one

Alex watched the road sign indicating ten more miles to Charleston. He rode in the cab of his father's old Chevy truck, the seats worn and dirty, the dash and floor filled with trash and papers, a pungent smell of shrimp and sweat heavy in the air. Looking over, he watched as his father drove calmly along, listening to old country music on the radio and humming with each tune. The old man seemed clueless to the deep spiral of booze and hard living that was clearly taking its toll. The man's face was weathered and creased with deep lines from age and wind and weather. The paunch above his belt nearly touched the steering wheel and Alex noticed his hands trembled slightly as he drove along, occasionally cursing loudly when one of *"them damn city drivers"* cut him off.

He was also more concerned than ever that his old man was sinking into deeper signs of dementia. In his brief time at home he had seen numerous occasions when his father would repeat himself or forget where something was stored in the kitchen. Just this morning, he had told Alex over coffee to go get his brother up for school. His brother, Bobbie, had been dead for nearly ten years, lost to one of the many senseless battles in the Middle East.

"Where am I headed, son?" Skipper Frank growled over the music and wind rushing in his open window.

"Take the next right." Alex pulled out his phone and found the address for Phillip Holloway's law offices to confirm their destination. He suddenly felt light-headed and leaned back against the rear glass of the truck cab. Closing his eyes, he tried to press down the throbbing pain spreading out from the gunshot wound across his neck. He reached down for his bag on the floor and found the bottle of pain meds. *Only two left,* he thought, placing one on his tongue and then washing it down with a bottle of water on the console beside him. He made a mental note to remind himself to get the prescription refilled while they were in town. He closed his eyes and waited for the welcome numbness of the drug to start kicking in again. He knew he was on a dangerous path of dependence with these damn drugs. He'd been there before, more than once, he thought, memories of his time in Afghanistan after "the attack", and then later with two earlier gunshot wounds. *I need to keep my damn head down,* he thought, feeling groggy already.

His father pulled up in front of Holloway's office building. "I'll probably be thirty minutes or so," Alex said, gathering his bag and the water bottle. "There's a donut shop just around the corner, parking on the side. I'll meet you there."

"No hurry, kid. Brought along a copy of the morning paper. Need to keep my ass current with all the news of the day."

"Thanks for driving me in, Pop. I won't be long." Alex got out of the truck and walked up to the imposing ten-story granite and glass building that housed the offices of Holloway's law firm. A security guard sat behind a long counter in the lobby.

The guard looked up as Alex approached. "Can I help you, sir?"

"I need to see Phillip Holloway up on ten," Alex said.

"You got an appointment?"

"No, but let him know that Detective Alex Frank needs a few minutes." He showed the man his badge. "He'll see me."

After a lengthy phone conversation with the office upstairs, the guard finally hung up and said, "Sign the register and go on up."

Another long reception counter greeted him as he walked through the glass doors into the lobby of the law firm. Two women, each dressed in finely tailored dark business suits looked up to greet him. Both immediately seemed to be obviously concerned with his dress, old faded jeans and a t-shirt with a fishing reel logo on the front. He was unshaven and his hair was uncombed.

"Detective Frank?" the woman on the left asked, uncertain at both his appearance and reason for wanting to see one of the senior partners of the firm.

"Yes, ma'am."

"I've notified Mr. Holloway you wish to see him. He's with a client but finishing up soon. Please have a seat," she said standing. "Can I get you some coffee or water?"

He held up his water bottle. "No thanks." As he sat down, he noticed both women continued to eye him suspiciously, then finally looked away and got back to their work when he stared back at them unapologetically.

Five minutes later, Holloway came through another glass door on the right side of the lobby. He was dressed immaculately, as always, in a finely pressed pair of suit pants, a starched white shirt with heavy gold cuff links and a bright purple silk tie. "Good morning, Alex! It's been too long." His voice was deep and assured, his smile broad and gleaming white, not a hair out of place on his sweeping gray cut.

"Phillip," Alex said, standing and taking the man's hand. "Sorry to stop in unannounced, but I just need a few minutes."

"Of course. Let's grab a room down the hall." Holloway led them back through the door and a quick left into a well-appointed conference room with floor to ceiling windows looking out over the skyline of downtown Charleston.

"How're you feeling, Alex? Heard about the shooting and really sorry to hear about your partner and those other officers."

"I'll be fine," he answered, trying hard to control his emotions in front of this man who was not only a continuing nuisance with his ongoing romantic come-ons to Hanna, but also with his possible links to the mob family of Asa Dellahousaye who was quite likely responsible for his partner's death.

Both men sat across from each other at the elegant walnut conference table. "What can I help you with, Alex?"

"We're investigating the shooting you're referring to," Alex began. "Do you know a man named Asa Dellahousaye?" He watched Holloway's face and reaction to his question and was not surprised to see a calm and casual expression staring back at him.

"Everyone knows Asa Dellahousaye," Holloway said. "I was just out at his house a couple of nights ago with about a hundred other guests. One of his typical big gatherings at the beach house out on Isle of Palms."

"And why would you be on the invitation list for a party thrown by a known gangster?"

Again, Holloway easily kept his composure, the only sign of nervousness when his right hand swept back along the line of his hair. "That's a bit harsh Alex. Mr. Dellahousaye runs a considerable number of legitimate businesses across the country."

"Cut the bullshit, Phillip!"

"Excuse me?"

"Dellahousaye is a mob boss and a killer and don't give me this shit about legitimacy. What the hell were you doing out there?"

Now Holloway's calm demeanor was beginning to show some cracks. He stood and walked to the wall of windows and then turned. "My relationship with Asa Dellahousaye is, frankly, none of your damn business."

"Is your firm representing him?" Alex said, remaining seated.

"I'm not at liberty to discuss who is or isn't a client of this firm."

Alex stared back at the man, letting the words hang between them. Finally, he asked, "And what were you doing back out there yesterday? Our people didn't mention a party."

Holloway's eyes squinted in surprise. "You have people following me?"

"We have people watching Dellahousaye's house. We know you were out there to see him again yesterday. Why did you neglect to tell me about that visit."

"Like I said, I'm not a liberty to discuss my relationships..."

"So, he is a client?" Alex cut in.

"I think we're through here, Detective," Holloway said, moving to the big paneled door to the hallway.

"Phillip, Asa Dellahousaye is under investigation for hiring the man who killed four Charleston Police officers this week and several other murders we're looking into."

"I find it hard to believe..."

"Shut-up, Philip!" Alex said sharply.

Holloway turned as he pulled open the door. He stood there, unwilling or unable to respond.

Alex continued. "Tell me about Dellahousaye's interest in the proposed gambling bill coming up for a vote in the State House. Our sources tell us he's more than interested in expanding his current gambling enterprises."

"I don't know what you're talking about, Frank," Holloway said, his indignation clear as he struggled to regain his practiced composure.

Alex pulled a photo from his bag on the table and slid it across the table. "Have you seen this man before?"

Holloway walked back to the table and looked down at a photo taken across a busy plaza of the killer known as Caine. He picked it up to take a closer look. Shaking his head, he placed it back down.

"The man's name is Caine. He's a hired killer for the Dellahousaye family and God knows who else around the world," Alex said, taking the photo back."

"I really need to get back to my client, Detective."

"I don't have to tell you, Phillip, these are very serious men. More people are going to get hurt or killed if we don't put a stop to whatever Dellahousaye and this madman Caine are ginning up. I don't think you want to be a part of that."

Holloway seemed totally calm again and said, "Alex, I don't know where you're getting all this, but you are way off base and I can assure you, this firm would have nothing to do with any of what you're describing."

Alex stood, shaking his head slowly and staring back at the lawyer. "You better hope to hell not!"

As Alex walked down the sidewalk to meet his father at the donut shop, he was thinking about his quick discussion with the lawyer, Phillip Holloway. The man was clearly linked to the mobster, Asa Dellahousaye, though it was not clear in what capacity. The guest list the night of the party that Holloway attended was extensive and included celebrities, politicians... even a U. S. Senator. The man's circle of connections was extensive. Holloway was likely representing Dellahousaye on some sort of legal issue, but what? *Is there any connection to this gambling bill and the people who are ending up as worm food?*

His cell phone buzzed in his pocket and he looked at the screen. It was his captain down at the station. "Captain?"

"Alex, where are you?"

"Just back in Charleston…"

"I need you to come down to the station."

"What's up?"

"Just get your ass down here, now!" The connection went dead.

Skipper Frank dropped Alex at the precinct and told his son he was headed off to find some lunch. They agreed to meet up later.

As Alex walked into the large office room of the police station, he was getting some strange and cautious looks. He said "hello" to a couple of people who didn't respond and kept heading back to Captain Guinness's office. He could see the man at his desk on the phone through the glass partition. Guinness waved him in, still on the phone and motioned for him to take a seat across the desk. He hung up the phone and looked up at Alex, a strained look on his face. He stood and walked over to close his office door and then sat on the corner of the desk, reaching for a clear evidence bag that held a small flip cell phone.

"You care to tell me what the hell this is?" Guinness asked, holding the bag between them.

Alex hesitated, peering into the bag. It looked like a cheap "burner" phone you could pay cash for with pre-loaded minutes. "Looks like a burner, why?"

"Internal Affairs found this in your desk."

Alex felt a chill run down his spine. He tried to think back why he would have kept this evidence bag in his desk. "Okay?"

"It's yours then?"

"No, don't recall ever seeing it."

Guinness stood and walked around to sit behind his desk, placing the bag in front of him. "We got a serious problem here, Alex."

"And what's that?'

"Seems there's a call on this phone placed to a number about fifteen minutes before you and Lonnie went in on the bust to take down Caine."

"And why is that my problem?" Alex asked.

"There were several calls to that number on this phone, up until you got shot and haven't been back to the precinct."

Alex's thoughts were racing now, trying to sort through what Guinness was implying. "And who do you think was on the other end of those calls?"

"IA seems to think it was Caine."

"What!"

Chapter Thirty-two

Hanna and Calley Barbour sat in the reception area for the office of Judge Louise Kraft. They had met just a few minutes earlier down in the lobby of the courthouse. On the way up the elevator, Hanna had advised Calley on what to expect in the private meeting with the judge. The woman had their request for the abortion permission waiver and would certainly have some questions. Hanna insisted that Calley answer all questions directly and honestly, though she would not be under oath as this was not an official hearing.

Hanna watched as Calley sat silently across from her engrossed in something on her cell phone. As she studied the girl's face, she couldn't help thinking back to the days leading up to her own decision to have an abortion those many years ago. She recalled being terribly upset and hadn't slept for several nights when she finally went in for the scheduled procedure. Calley seemed understandably nervous and fidgety, she thought.

Hanna leaned in and whispered, "Calley, please put the phone away."

The girl did as instructed. "What?" she asked, perturbed.

"We've been through the complete series of events leading up to your pregnancy. Is there anything we haven't discussed? I don't want any surprises in there."

Calley shook her head no, seemingly distracted by another person coming into the judge's offices.

"Calley, please focus here. We've given the judge your full account of what happened. She will certainly want to have you walk back through all that again."

"I know," the girl said. "Will we get her permission today?"

"I don't know."

"I don't want to have this baby, Hanna!" Calley said, starting to tear up.

The assistant at the desk across the small reception area took a call and then stood. "The judge will see you now."

Hanna let Calley walk ahead into the office of Judge Louise Kraft. She was seated behind her desk, pulling some papers together in front of her. She did not have her judge's robe on and was dressed in a white short-sleeved blouse with a small gold brooch pinned on the collar. She was an imposing woman, sitting tall in the leather chair behind her broad maple desk. Her light gray hair was pulled back from her face and gathered at the back, her features sharp and angular. Hanna had worked with her before and knew her to be straightforward, stern, but fair.

"Good morning, ladies, please sit down."

Hanna and Calley took the two chairs across the desk from the judge.

"Hanna, how have you been?"

"Fine, thank you, Your Honor."

"Miss Barbour."

"Yes, Judge..." Calley said, her voice quiet and uncertain.

Judge Kraft continued. "Miss Barbour, I've read through your case and I must say this is a very difficult and delicate matter. The law is very clear on the requirements to justify a waiver of parental permission for minors in cases like this, but often, the circumstances of the pregnancy and person's personal home life can create numerous questions and issues."

Calley just nodded and Hanna reached for her hand to help calm her.

"Let's start with the pregnancy." The judge paused and stared at Calley for a moment before proceeding. "It seems you had intercourse with a man or a boy at a party and you claim not to know the identity of this person. Is that correct?"

"Yes, ma'am," Calley answered, almost in a whisper.

"Please speak up," the judge demanded.

"Yes, Your Honor!"

"You are not under oath here, young lady, but I want to remind you it is a severe problem to be untruthful in a proceeding like this."

"I'm sorry, Judge Kraft," Calley began. "I shouldn't have been drinking that night..."

"And I understand you were under the influence of marijuana as well."

"Yes ma'am."

Hanna stepped in. "Judge Kraft, there were of course, no toxicology tests taken that night. Our office, however, has interviewed two other friends of Calley who attended the party. They both confirmed the alcohol and drug consumption."

"Yes, I see that in your brief, Hanna. And neither of these girls could identify the boy in question, correct?"

"That's right."

The judge was looking down at some notes on the papers in front of her. She looked up and said, "Calley, you know that being drunk and stoned is no excuse for the waiver you're seeking today."

Hanna watched as the judge's stare burned into her client's eyes.

"Yes, Judge Kraft."

"Let's talk about your family for a moment," Kraft said. "I understand your father is senior pastor at a church here in town."

Calley nodded.

"You obviously don't feel your parents will be supportive of your decision to have this abortion."

Calley started shaking her head, looking down at her lap.

"Calley?" the judge asked.

Hanna squeezed the girl's hand tighter and they looked at each other. Hanna gave her a reassuring nod.

"My father would throw me out of the house, if not kill me first, Judge."

"Has he been physically abusive or hurt you in the past?"

Calley sat forward and quickly answered, "No, no never."

"Then tell me why you're so concerned about your parent's reaction to all this, beyond the obvious religious feelings I'm sure they hold strongly."

Calley sat up and spoke forcefully, surprising Hanna. "My father preaches about the evils of alcohol and drugs and pre-marital sex every Sunday. Many people in the church have been shunned or thrown out in the past."

CHAPTER THIRTY-TWO

"I see."

"Judge, this would be a terrible embarrassment for my mother and father."

"Yes, I realize that," Kraft said.

They were interrupted by a knock on the door and the judge's assistant peaked in. "Judge Kraft, there's a young woman here who insists she needs to join this discussion."

"And who is that?" Kraft asked.

"She won't say, ma'am."

"Tell her this is a closed meeting..."

The door pushed open and a woman rushed past the assistant at the door. Hanna immediately recognized Calley's sister from the pictures she had seen on-line. She was clearly older than Calley but of similar size and even through the short spiky hair dyed pure white and multiple piercings and tattoos, there was a remarkable resemblance.

"Carolyn!" Calley said in surprise. "I told you not to come."

Chapter Thirty-three

Captain Guinness led Alex down a long dark hallway and opened the door to a small interrogation room. He switched on the lights and pulled out a chair for Alex to take a seat. Standing across from him, Guinness slid a file folder across the table.

"Seems we have another vocal critic of the proposed gambling bill, not among the living any longer," Guinness said.

Alex opened the file. The top photo was of a large black man in a dark suit hanging from the rafters of an office. Alex leaned in to take a closer look but didn't recognize the man.

"His name is Reverend Jeremiah Townsend," Guinness said. "He's the pastor of the big church and telemarketing ministry over on the south side. His staff found him this morning in his office about an hour after he came in."

"A suicide?" Alex asked.

"Appears so, but the forensics team is taking a close look."

"I've seen him on television," Alex said.

"The man held a big press conference yesterday to publicly condemn the gambling bill," Guinness said, sitting across from Alex. "A day later and he's hanging from the rafters in his office. Doesn't add up."

Alex looked through a few more pictures in the file, thinking about the likelihood of Caine being involved with this.

"You've never met the man," Alex heard Guinness say and then he looked up.

"No! I've never met this guy and I had nothing to do with it. I'll put ten bucks down that Dellahousaye and Caine are behind this."

Guinness stared back for a few moments, then said, "I think you're right."

"Captain, about this phone," Alex began.

"Internal Affairs will be in here in a minute."

"I don't know anything about the damn phone and I sure as hell didn't tip off of this Caine maniac to kill my partner and best friend. Come on, Captain!"

"IA pulled the phone records on the burner number and ran a map program to locate the calls," Guinness said. "That call that went out on this burner just before you and Lonnie left for the take down was received in close proximity to the bar, if not right inside where you confronted Caine."

"Captain, I swear to you..."

"Save it, Alex."

Two hours later, Alex walked out of the police precinct, squinting at the bright afternoon sun. The two members of the Internal Affairs team and Captain Guinness had grilled him relentlessly about the phone and the calls to whom they believed to be Lonnie Smith's and the three other police officer's killer. In the end, they let him go, though reluctantly. There had been no identifiable fingerprints on the phone and definitely not Alex's.

Alex was still groggy from the pain meds and stunned at the discovery of this phone in his desk. It was clearly planted there by someone he thought, as he pulled his own phone out and called his father. He was around the corner at a diner and Alex headed in that direction.

Who is trying to set me up here? Alex thought, his anger burning a hole in his gut.

In great detail, he had gone through the few minutes he had returned to the precinct the morning Lonnie was killed and the short interval he was there before they headed out together to meet the back-up team on the Caine bust. He had tried to account for nearly every moment and action, but his memory was not totally clear on all that had gone down that day after the trauma of his partner's death and his own wounds. There was certainly some time that he could not account for that would have allowed him to make the call to Caine.

He had repeatedly asked the investigators how they could possibly think he would put his partner and the other men in danger. As usual, their responses were minimal, but it was clear they felt he had tried to tip the man off about the impending arrest to give him time to get away. For whatever reason, Caine had decided to stay and inflict considerable damage and loss of life.

Internal Affairs was also implying he was on the pad for Dellahousaye, though they had zero evidence. *Where is this coming from?*

He arrived at the diner and tried Hanna's number before he went inside to find his father. He knew she had an appointment down at the courthouse on the abortion case but didn't know when she expected to be done. The call went to a full voice mailbox again.

Inside, Skipper Frank was sitting in a back booth, half a tuna sandwich on a plate in front of him and half a beer in the bottle beside it. He looked up as Alex approached. "Where you been?" the old man asked.

"I'll tell you about it on the way back home. You okay to drive?" he asked, looking down at the beer.

"Just had a couple. Thought we'd be leaving sooner. You had lunch?"

"Not hungry, thanks," Alex said, sitting down across the booth. "Finish up and we'll get out of here." He took the bottle of pills from his pocket and shook out the last of the painkillers, washing it down with a sip from his father's beer. He looked up the number for his doctor and after a long wait and several discussions, was able to get the doc to renew his prescription for the drug.

Thirty minutes later after a stop at the drugstore to pick up his prescription, they were on Highway 17 on their way back up to Dugganville. Alex was in the passenger seat with the window down letting the wind whip his face and take some of the heat out of the truck cab. He couldn't stop worrying about the IA investigators thinking he was dirty with Dellahousaye. His boss, Captain Guinness, had remained quiet through most of the interview and did not come to his defense when the two IA clowns started pressing him about being on the take.

In a moment of sudden clarity, he started thinking about who else would have been in the department that morning with any opportunity to make the alleged call and plant the phone in his desk. Lonnie Smith was of course there, but he would trust Lonnie with his life and could not imagine the man being on the pad for Asa Dellahousaye or have any reason to frame him in this.

Captain Guinness was there that morning, but Alex hadn't seen him before they rushed out to arrest Caine at the bar. Then there was Nathan Beatty and his partner, Willy Mills, who was now, unfortunately, dead along with Lonnie and three uniforms who went down that day. There were probably a dozen other people on the floor that morning who could have done this, but he couldn't place anyone close enough to the case with any reason to do this.

His thoughts kept coming back to Nate Beatty. He'd known the man for over ten years and never had any issues with him or reason to believe he was dirty. He tried to piece together the events leading up to and after the shootings, then again later that day and night at the hospital. Beatty was obviously upset about the loss of their colleagues, but Alex couldn't recall any other warning signs or questionable behavior. During the arrest, Beatty had been the last to come into the kitchen from the bar area after the shootout with Caine began. *He had probably saved my life*, Alex thought, as Caine had fled when the man came through the door.

Skipper shouted out over the noise of the radio and rushing wind, "What the hell happened down there today?"

Alex filled his father in on the accusations and case the department was trying to build against him.

"Them sons of bitches!" Skipper yelled out. "After all you've done for them over the years and you take a damn bullet for your partner and they try to hang this on you?"

"It's a little more complicated than that, Pop."

Chapter Thirty-four

Asa Dellahousaye sat in a deeply cushioned white leather chair on the aft deck of his large yacht, *Adrenaline*, drifting offshore about five miles from Charleston. The afternoon clouds were building, but the sun was still hot. The blue surface of the ocean was blinding in the late day glare. Several gulls dipped and climbed behind the stern of the yacht, hoping for an easy meal to get tossed over.

One of the crew brought up a fresh gin and tonic on a tray and Asa D exchanged glasses with the young woman. He watched her walk back inside and as usual, admired the round curve of her ass and long tanned legs in the white shorts the crew wore. He picked up a pair of binoculars to check on a boat that was approaching from the west. It was a thirty-something fishing rig and he soon confirmed it was Caine, as scheduled. Within minutes, the crew had the two boats tied off on the calm surface of the ocean and Caine jumped over and joined his boss in another chair.

Asa ordered a drink for the man and when they were alone, said, "Nice work on the pastor this morning."

Caine just nodded back, looking vacantly out across the long stretch of water and distant land on the horizon behind the boat. A man of typically few words, he was not one to brag or boast about his work.

Asa D said, "You know we need to clean up the rest of this now, right?"

"You mean the cop I didn't finish off yet?" Caine asked, his voice low and menacing.

"Yes, we've got him on the hot seat with his department, but I don't think they're going to able to prove anything against the man. Besides, he's seen your face twice now and that's a loose end we don't need."

"I understand, boss. I won't miss again."

The woman came back on deck with drinks for both men and told them dinner would be ready in about twenty minutes. When she was gone, Asa D said, "We have one other problem."

"What's that?"

"One of my attorneys has lost his mind and decided to threaten me with some bullshit evidence if he gets implicated in this gambling scheme."

"The one who's handling the bribes with the politicians?" Caine asked.

"Right. His name is Phillip Holloway."

"I know who he is."

"The dumb bastard really thinks he can threaten me."

"I'll take care of it, boss," Caine said.

"This guy is too high profile to just take off the board," Dellahousaye said. "This has to look like an accident and before you take him out, I want to know what the hell he's holding against me and where it is. Do whatever you have to."

Caine squirmed in his seat, clearly delighted he would be able to inflict a little additional pain before taking out the lawyer.

"Holloway is also very close to the Senator," Asa D said. "I want to know if he's in on this, too."

"Absolutely!"

Chapter Thirty-five

The sisters, Carolyn and Calley Barbour sat across from Hanna at the small conference table in her office. The meeting with Judge Kraft had come to a swift halt when the older sister had barged in and insisted on talking to Hanna and Calley before the proceedings went any further. The judge had suggested they continue the next day. She had an hour open after lunch.

The two girls had remained quiet on the short walk back from the court-house.

Hanna started, "Carolyn, please tell me what's going on here."

The two Barbour sisters exchanged looks, then Carolyn turned to Hanna. "Calley called me a couple of days ago to tell me what was happening."

"And she told you about the waiver we're seeking for parental permission on the abortion."

Carolyn seemed confused and Calley started to interrupt.

Hanna said, "She did tell you why we're meeting with the Judge today?"

"I thought you were there to get a ruling on an underage abortion," Carolyn said. "I didn't know about the parent issue, but of course, they would have to be involved. Calley has told you about our parents, right?"

"Yes, it's the fundamental argument in the discussion with the judge."

"But she hasn't told you everything?" Carolyn asked.

"What do you mean?"

Calley jumped in. "Hanna..."

"She didn't tell you everything about our father?" Carolyn asked, obviously knowing the answer.

"Calley, what's going on here?" Hanna asked, standing to walk over behind her desk and grab the file for the case. She could see the girl was starting to cry.

Carolyn blurted out, "She didn't tell you our dear father has been having his way with both of us since we were twelve years old?"

Hanna was stunned and looked down at Calley who now had her face buried in her hands.

"I finally got out and left when I was eighteen," Carolyn said. "The bastard came into my room again on the night of my birthday for God's sake and started taking his clothes off. I'd taken a golf club from his bag in the garage, knowing he would be coming for me again. This time I had decided enough already, and I'd be able to take care of myself. I hit him across the back of the head as hard as I could with the golf club. I hoped I'd killed him with the first blow, but he was on the floor moaning and bleeding and I just couldn't bring myself to finish him off. I left and have never been back. I've been trying to get Calley out of there, but I swear they have her brainwashed or something."

Hanna couldn't believe what she was hearing and was trying to sort through the implications when Calley said, "There was no boy on the beach, Hanna."

"What are you talking about?"

"It was my father. It was always my father. I'm surprised I didn't get pregnant years ago, but he would give us pills, birth control."

Hanna was absolutely flabbergasted at what these girls had endured. "And you've never tried to report this to anyone? What about your mother?"

"She didn't want to know, or she was afraid of my father, too," Calley said. "I'm not sure."

Hanna sat back down across from the girls. "We have to report this to the police."

Carolyn said, "I've wanted to do it for years, but Calley always talk me down, tells me he was leaving her alone now, everything was okay."

"But it wasn't okay?" Hanna asked.

Calley nodded, wiping at her eyes.

There was a deep anger and disgust burning in Hanna and she tried to keep her composure she was so mad. Finally, she said, "I know someone at the police department. Let me talk to him tonight." She could see panic in Calley

Barbour's eyes. "I won't do anything until I talk to you tomorrow. We need to meet in the morning, before we have to go back over to see Judge Kraft.

Appointments and calls backed up through the afternoon and Hanna wasn't able to leave the office until after seven. She ran up to her apartment to change clothes. She had planned to get up to Dugganville earlier, but as usual, work continued to take precedent. She was still fuming about Calley and Carolyn Barbour's father. *What a monster! Hiding behind his self-righteous pulpit.*

She needed to talk to Alex about how this would all go down if the girls agreed to bring charges against their father. Certainly, it would help with Calley's case for an abortion. Incest was on the top of the list for reasons to grant the waiver of parental approval. The Reverend Warren Barbour would be taking a hard fall.

Thoughts of Sam crept back in. She'd managed to keep their discussion over lunch at bay through the afternoon as she had been consumed with the Barbours and then ten other issues at the office. *Sam wants to move to Charleston! He wants to "give it another chance."*

She couldn't think clearly with all that was racing through her mind. How many years had she been thinking about Sam Collins since he had left her in their junior year in college? How many times had she secretly thought about what it would be like if he were ever to come back to her? And now, here he was, and it was scaring the crap out of her. *And what about Alex? She didn't even know Sam after all these years!*

She was ten minutes out of Charleston when her phone buzzed. It was Judge Louise Kraft. "Hanna, what in hell's going on?"

Hanna tried not to panic and blurt out all she had just learned. "Judge, I'm sorry, but there are some new developments. I'm looking into it and I'll be able to fill you in tomorrow when we get back together."

"I sense there's more to this than our young Ms. Barbour is telling us," the judge said. It wasn't a question.

Hanna hesitated a moment, then replied, "That would be correct. Again,

I'll have an update for you by tomorrow afternoon.

They ended the call and Hanna threw the phone down on the seat beside her.

Chapter Thirty-six

Skipper Frank signaled for Gilly to bring two more beers. Alex hadn't finished the second sitting in front of him at the bar. He knew he shouldn't be drinking on top of another Vicodin for the day he'd just taken an hour ago, but his investigation by the Charleston Police Department had him totally flustered and upset, and frankly a little afraid if any other trumped-up evidence would suddenly surface tying him to Asa Dellahousaye and the killer, Caine.

He looked up when he heard his father yell out, "Gilly, turn that damn thing off!" The television screen above the bar was set to a network news station and his old Army comrade, Sergeant Adam Groves, was on the air again talking about the ill-fated mission in Afghanistan they had both survived. The local papers and broadcast stations had also picked up the story and it was all over the news.

The man was up close in the studio, dressed in a suit sitting next to the news anchor. Alex heard him say, *"Lieutenant Frank totally freaked out on us when the attack began. We shouldn't have been there to begin with. We were pinned down with rounds coming in from everywhere. Several of our guys had already gone down. The rest of us had to take control of the situation or we would have all been killed out there."*

The newsman asked, *"So what do you know about this latest police shooting incident in Charleston?"*

"Only that Alex Frank was in the middle of a shit storm again... sorry, can you bleep that? He got his team in the middle of a mass casualty event and four men died. Somehow, he managed to survive again. From what I'm hearing on the news, he didn't back-up his partner and the man died. I'm not at all surprised."

The newsman turned to the camera, *"We're talking about the fatal shooting in Charleston of ..."* Gilly finally came over and grabbed the remote to turn the sound down and change the station.

Alex felt his blood burning hot and his head felt dizzy. He reached for the second beer and finished it in one swallow. He sensed his father's hand on his arm.

"Don't pay no attention to that bastard."

Alex tried to block images racing through his brain of that day in Afghanistan and as soon as those went away, the chaos in the Charleston bar kitchen echoed in his brain. He could still smell the cordite in the air from the gunfire. He could still see his friend Lonnie's blood on his hands when he finally got to him and realized he was already gone.

Was Grove right? How many men have I gotten killed? How many times have I asked myself that question?

He was well into the third beer when he felt a hand on his shoulder. When he turned to see who it was, he almost fell off the barstool, the drugs and the beers quickly taking effect. He saw the face of Amelia Richards looking back at him.

She reached out to help him catch his balance and they fell into each other. She helped him back onto his stool and sat beside him. "You okay, Alex?"

Her Italian accent again seemed out of place. He forced his eyes to focus and saw her tanned face looking back at him with a concerned stare. Her hair was pulled up in random swirls on top of her head and she was wearing a thin-strapped yellow sun dress that showed off her well-toned shoulders and arms. Alex steadied himself on the high stool, one hand on the bar to make sure he didn't tip over again.

"Alex?"

"What are you doing here?"

"I've tried to call you. I found something I need to talk to you about," she said. Over the loud noise in the bar, they were almost shouting to be able to hear each other. "Can we go in the back for a moment?"

Alex turned to his father who had just noticed Beau Richard's wife talking to his son. "Back in a minute, Pop? Alex saw that Ella Moore had come up and was sitting on the other side of his father. The two had obviously made up and were in deep and for the moment, affectionate conversation.

Amelia helped him down and held his arm close as they made their way through the crowd to a back room that still had a few empty booths and was a bit quieter. She helped him into the booth and then sat across from him. A server came up and asked for their order. Amelia told her to bring two waters and black coffee.

Alex took a deep breath to gather himself, his head weaving and eyes trying to focus on the face of this woman.

"I told you about the men looking for something they think Beau left behind before he was sent to prison," she said.

Alex nodded, trying to recall the details of their earlier conversation.

"I was out on our boat today," she continued. "I had the crew take me out to get some fresh air and think about what I was going to do with Beau being gone for at least ten years."

"It's not my place, Amelia, but I'm not sure you should be waiting for a guy like that. You know he tried to kill me and how many others did he hurt or kill trying to run all that illegal business?" He knew his words were slurred but he could at least string a sentence together.

"I know, Alex. It's all I've been thinking about since he's been gone."

The girl brought over the water and coffee Amelia had ordered.

Alex lifted the coffee cup with both hands to keep from shaking, first sniffing the strong brew and then swallowing a long hot gulp.

"What did you want to tell me?" Alex asked.

"On the boat today, we have some kayaks and I wanted to get out of the water for a while. It was very calm and one of the boys pulled a kayak from the lower bay for me. When he was helping me in off the stern of the boat, I felt something with my feet down at the end of the kayak. When I was away from the boat and crew some, I reached down and pulled out a sealed bag."

"And what was in the bag?"

She took a sip from the water glass in front of her and looked back intently. "There were several thumb drives."

"Thumb drives?"

"Beau had a recorder on his office phone. I knew it was there because I came into his office one day and he was listening to some telephone conversations on his laptop."

Alex was trying to keep concentrating on what she was telling him. The coffee had given him a small shock of clarity, but he found her face coming in and out of focus. He placed a hand on the table to steady himself and took another sip from the coffee. "And have you listened to these recordings?"

She nodded. "I know why this Dellahousaye man is sending people to search our homes. There are several conversations Beau had with him about their business."

"About their business?"

"There are discussions about some very bad things... even murder."

"And how do you think Dellahousaye knows about these recordings?" Alex asked

"I don't know. Maybe Beau told him about them as some sort of insurance, maybe even to protect me."

Alex was trying to think through all she was telling him when he noticed someone walking up to the booth. He turned to see Hanna stop just a few feet away. Even in his diminished, drug-induced state, he knew the scene didn't look good, him sitting in a back booth at a dive bar with a beautiful woman. He didn't even try to stand because he knew he might fall over again. "Hanna!"

He watched as she stood for a moment, obviously taking in the situation. He was sure she was going to come to the wrong conclusions. "Hanna, come here. I want you to meet someone."

Hanna came the rest of the way up to the table and didn't wait for Alex to make introductions. She held out her hand to Amelia Richards. "Hello, I'm Hanna Walsh."

"Amelia," she answered, taking Hanna's hand in a quick shake.

Alex started to speak but his gesture knocked over the water glass in front of him and most of the water spilled across the table into Amelia's lap. She slipped out of the booth quickly, reaching for napkins to wipe at her dress. Alex tried to get up too and nearly fell into Hanna, who helped him back on his seat, then stepped back and said, "I'm sorry to interrupt. Bad timing." As she turned to walk away, Alex could see her face was either confused, angry, disappointed... he wasn't sure. Her last words before walking away were, "Call me tomorrow." And then she was gone through the crowd. He knew he could never navigate the way to go after her.

Alex tried to open his eyes. There was birdsong and then the roar of some motor... a leaf blower? He laid back on the pillow, his head feeling like it might explode. He saw blood on the pillow from his neck wound. As his eyes focused, he realized he had no idea where he was. He glanced around at an elegantly furnished large bedroom with two windows looking out over a long field down to a line of trees. He forced himself to sit up against the padded headboard. There was a glass of water on the nightstand and he gratefully took a long drink to quench the dryness in his mouth. He looked down and saw he was wearing only his plaid boxer shorts. The rest of his clothes were on a chair in the corner. *What the hell?*

He had no recollection of where he was or how he had gotten here.

The door opened and Amelia Richards walked in carrying a tray with a carafe of coffee and two cups. She was dressed in a short silk robe and was barefoot.

"Good morning, Alex,"

"Amelia...?

He tried to clear his head, to think about the previous night. He had been at Gilly's with his father. Amelia had come in, then... then Hanna had been there. *Hanna!*

Chapter Thirty-seven

Hanna had driven straight back to her apartment in Charleston the previous night after leaving Alex in the bar with the woman in Dugganville. In her heart, she knew she had over-reacted, and on the entire trip back she kept trying to rationalize what she had seen, how she had responded. A half bottle of wine in her kitchen hadn't helped to sort through her emotions. If anything, she grew angrier and more confused.

She and Alex Frank had been together long enough, she thought she knew his true character and could trust him with her life. Maybe last night was a completely innocent situation, but she was still having a hard time coming up with a scenario where that would be the case. He had tried to call her twice already this morning, but she hadn't answered the calls. *If the woman hadn't been so damned good looking!*

She was sitting again in her kitchen, waiting for the coffee pot to finish. Her phone lit up. It was Sam this time. *That's all I need right now, another man!*

Reluctantly, she took the call. "Sam?"

"Good morning, Hanna." She sensed the tentativeness in his voice. "Will you have some time today to see me? We really need to talk."

She thought for a moment about their previous discussions about reuniting, about him coming back to Charleston. She sighed and shook her head. "Sam, I've got a crazy day with a case I'm working on. I need to meet with my client again this morning then we have an appointment with a judge after lunch." The nightmare that Calley and Carolyn Barbour were enduring came back to her.

"This afternoon, then?"

"I don't know, Sam..."

"My photo shoot is down by your old house on the Battery. I want you to see what we're working on."

"I just don't know. Let me call you later."

He pressed her again to meet and maybe have dinner later before they ended the call.

She thought again about Alex sitting last night with this woman, too drunk to stand and barely able to talk. Was he trying to drive her away? Hadn't he just asked her the other day why she was still with him? *Good question!*

Two hours later, the hectic chaos of her law offices had kept her distracted from thinking about the men in her life for at least a few minutes. She had hoped to talk to Alex the previous night about the Barbour sisters and bringing charges against their father for sexually assaulting the girls. Instead, she had called her friend this morning in the Prosecutor's office who specialized in these types of cases. She had everything she needed to consult with Calley and Carolyn when they came in for their ten o'clock appointment.

Alex had called two more times and she had declined both after just two rings, sending a clear message she was in no mood to talk. He had texted her, "Hanna, please call. I'm sorry. I need to explain." *You're damn right you need to explain! Do I even want to hear it?*

Calley and Carolyn arrived for their scheduled appointment and the three women were seated around Hanna's conference table. Both looked shaken and tired. They would both have some very difficult decisions to make.

"Girls, I've had a chance to speak to someone in the Prosecutor's office and ..."

Calley jumped in, panic in her eyes. "You didn't tell them about..."

"As your attorney, I'm not revealing any specifics until you tell me you're ready to proceed. We spoke only generally about a client I'm representing with no names used to this point."

Her words didn't seem to calm Calley down. She fidgeted in her seat and was obviously close to tears. Her older sister was more stoic and just looked angry if anything. "What your father has been doing is a serious crime. Sexual assault of minors, incest and I have no idea if there has been any other physical abuse."

The girls didn't answer but looked at each other for a moment.

Hanna continued. "Your mother may also be implicated if she was aware of your father's abuse and refused to intervene or report the... well, let's call it what it is, rape." She could see that Calley was visibly shaking now. Hanna reached over to take her hand to comfort her. "As your attorney, I have to advise you both to bring charges against your father. Calley, we will get you out of the house where you will be safe..."

"Oh God, Hanna!" Calley cried out. Carolyn leaned over and put her arm around her younger sister. She said, "Honey, we need to do this. We should have done it years ago."

"I have nowhere to go! What will momma do?" Calley said, the tears flowing heavily now.

Hanna let the two of them process the situation for a few moments, then said, "And we have to make a decision about the baby, Calley. I'm sorry, but we do. We have another appointment with Judge Kraft this afternoon."

Calley didn't hesitate, "I don't want this baby!"

"I understand dear and your case with the judge will be very clear. Incest is unacceptable and one of the main issues considered in these cases."

"But he'll be arrested... prison." Calley said, thinking out loud. "And what about Momma and the congregation?"

Carolyn was remaining remarkably calm and said, "This needs to end."

Judge Louise Kraft was ten minutes late for her appointment. Hanna and the girls were finally showed into her office. They all sat across the desk as the Judge finished with some paperwork and turned her attention to them.

"So, where are we?" Kraft asked.

Hanna looked at both Barbour sisters, then said, "Your Honor, new information has surfaced that puts this situation in an entirely new light. First, my client wants to apologize for not being fully truthful with us leading up to our meeting yesterday."

"I figured," Kraft said, impatiently.

"We have an even more difficult situation to deal with, Judge."

"And what is that?"

Both Calley and Carolyn have been sexually abused by their father since they were young girls." The judge's face remained impassive. "Calley's father is the father of this child. There was no intercourse on the beach with another boy.

Judge Kraft took a deep breath. "Calley, I'm very concerned that you came to me with lies about your pregnancy. How am I to believe your story now?"

Carolyn spoke first. "Judge, my father is a monster and my mother let him get away with it. We should have come forward years ago, but there are so many issues we've had to deal with. I left home when I was old enough to take care of myself. I've tried to get Calley out of there, but she kept trying to convince me things had changed. When she told me about the pregnancy, I knew we had to expose this, regardless of the consequences."

"And you're absolutely right to do so, dear," Kraft said. "You will both need to file a complaint with the police. Hanna can help you with that."

"What will happen?" Calley asked, her voice broken and shaky.

"Your parents will be brought in for questioning. Charges will likely be filed based upon how the police view the veracity of your charges. A DNA test of the embryo should certainly provide solid proof of your father's assault."

Calley looked at her sister, then the judge. "And what about the abortion. I don't want this baby, Your Honor."

"I understand completely, and if all of this proves out, I will certainly grant your waiver of parental permission to have this procedure."

"Thank you, Judge," Hanna said. "Is there anything else today?"

"No, I would strongly encourage you to go immediately to the police and file formal charges. Hanna, you might call your friend, Greta, down at the Women's Shelter for temporary living arrangements for both girls."

"Yes, I've already spoken with her."

Later that afternoon, the Barbour sisters filed formal charges against their father. He was arrested in his office at the church. The sizable staff and several congregation members there were stunned as he was led away in handcuffs. Their mother was also brought in for questioning. After hours of interrogation of both parents, Reverend Warren Barbour was charged with numerous counts of sexual assault and related charges. He was booked and later released on a sizable bail commitment. Their mother, Katherine, was released but with assurances there would be a thorough investigation of her role in enabling the reverend's crimes. The ripples of chaos for the pastor, his family and his congregation were just beginning.

Chapter Thirty-eight

The coffee did little to clear his head. He was sitting up in a bed in Beau and Amelia Richards' ranch house and he had no idea how he had ended up here. By the current state of his *undress* and Amelia's tiny and slinky robe sitting across from him in a large overstuffed chair, he could only imagine the worst. He remembered Hanna coming into the bar at *Gilly's* and seeing the two of them together. He had barely been able to speak let alone go after her to explain what was going on.

Amelia said, "Can I get you anything else?"

He looked over at her clean washed face and wet hair combed back. The guilt kept sweeping over him and the embarrassment in not knowing what was going on.

"Alex?"

"Amelia, I'm not sure what happened last night, but...."

"Nothing happened Alex, if you mean between you and me."

He stared back at her for a moment. It's not that he wasn't attracted to her, but he had never been one to chase women for one-night stands and he was in a relationship, he thought, again chastising himself for getting into this position. "Then what am I doing here?"

"We were talking about the evidence I found with recordings Beau had made. You wanted to listen to them."

Slowly, their conversation at *Gilly's Bar* was coming back to him. She had found recordings of phone conversations between her husband and Asa Dellahousaye, recordings the gangster was somehow aware of and trying to get back.

"I'm sorry. I'm sure I must have passed out when we got back here. I'm on painkillers for the neck and..."

"Yes," she said, smiling, "you were asleep in the car almost immediately and it was all I could do to get you inside."

He looked over at his clothes on the chair.

"I thought you'd sleep better," she said, following his gaze. "I've got some breakfast in the kitchen. Why don't you get dressed and come out? I've got the recordings on a laptop."

"I'll be right out."

Alex had listened to three different conversations between Amelia Richards' now incarcerated husband and the gangster, Asa Dellahousaye. All had contained damaging evidence of the two men's complicity in an organized drug ring along the coast of South Carolina. He could see why Asa D wanted to get these recordings back. The last had also included Dellahousaye's demand that Beau Richards eliminate Detective Alex Frank who was getting too close to the truth about the drug dealings as he investigated the murder charges against his father the previous year. It was unnerving to sit and listen to a man order your death sentence.

He looked up at Amelia, standing across the counter in the kitchen. Her face was troubled with concern as he clicked off the last recording. "What should I do with these, Alex?"

His first reaction was to call in the cavalry, local and Feds to go after Dellahousaye immediately, but he hesitated, thinking about the danger this would put Amelia Richards in. The evidence should be enough to get a warrant to question the man, not only on the drug network that was surely still operating, but also on any attempts Dellahousaye was making to influence upcoming legislation to expand gambling in the state. *How do I protect Amelia if we go after Asa D? He'll know the source of the evidence.*

"You were right to bring this to me," he said. "I need to think about how we go forward with this. I'm worried about your safety, frankly." He could see the fear on her face.

"Maybe it's a good time for me to go home to visit my family in Italy," she said, thinking out loud.

"That's probably a very good idea. How soon can you make arrangements?"

"I'll check," she said and then walked around the counter. As she came up, he stood, and she placed her arms around him and pulled him close. He tentatively returned her embrace. "Thank you for helping me with this, Alex. I didn't know where else to turn."

She didn't back away and he continued to hold her, smelling the wet scent of her hair and feeling the tautness of her skin under the thin robe. His senses were colliding in a jumble of lust, guilt and confusion until he finally pushed back. "As soon as we're sure you're out of the country and safe, we'll get these recordings to the proper authorities."

Amelia reached for his hands. "Thank you, Detective." She glanced away, then said, "Where can I take you?"

Amelia dropped him at his father's house just after ten in the morning. She leaned over and kissed him on the cheek from the driver's seat before he got out. He watched her drive away and tried to clear his mind on what needed to happen next. *Hanna!*

He had already left a call that had gone unanswered.

Walking up to the house, he felt the familiar ache in his neck growing. He found the bottle of pills in his pocket and, at first, hesitated and was going to put them back, but the constant pain was more than he thought he could endure through another day. *Just one more day.*

His father was in the kitchen sitting at the table with Ella Moore. Both were obviously nursing hangovers from the previous night's excess with coffee cups held in both hands in front of them. Ella was dressed only in one of Skipper's old fishing shirts. She looked up when Alex came in. "Well, good morning young man."

"Ella."

"Been wondering about you wandering off with that little Italian number last night," she said.

"Just business, Ella," he said.

"Yeah, right," she said, smiling back through tired and glossy eyes. Her hair was a jumbled mess and he could only imagine the crazy night she and her father had just had.

Skipper said, "You better call Hanna. You remember her comin' in last night, don't you."

"I remember."

"You better cut out those damn pills. They're makin' you loopy, boy. Let's not go through that whole thing again."

"I'll be all right."

His father stood and walked to the sink to rinse his cup. He was wearing a pair of old faded boxer shorts and a sleeveless white t-shirt, along with his accustomed fishing hat. He was bent over at the waist and moving slowly.

"You okay, pop?"

Standing at the sink, he said, "Think I pulled a muscle in my damn back last night."

Alex looked over at Ella Moore and she just smiled back.

"We're makin' a shrimp run this afternoon," his father said. You up to comin' along?"

He thought about it for a moment, then said, "I need to get back down to Charleston for the afternoon. Can I borrow the truck?"

"Won't be needin' it while I'm out on the water."

Ella said, "What does Amelia Richards drive, a Lamborghini?"

"That's enough, Ella," Alex said.

Chapter Thirty-nine

Phillip Holloway slammed an overhead smash and watched the yellow tennis ball find the far corner of his opponent's court. The man actually dove to save the point and rolled twice in green powdery clay before sitting up and throwing his racket in disgust. "Nice game, Phillip," he yelled back, clearly pissed at losing the match.

Holloway walked up to the net triumphantly and waited to shake the man's hand. "At least you won a game this time," he said arrogantly as they shook. He watched the man walk away to the locker room of the country club past the high fences of the tennis complex, then walked over to his tennis bag on the bench and pulled out his phone to check messages.

He was scrolling through a long series of calls when he was startled by a man walking up and sitting next to him on the bench. He was dressed in casual shorts and a fishing t-shirt with an old stained ball cap and flip flops. His face was hidden behind large black sunglasses. Hardly appropriate attire for the club, Holloway thought.

"Morning, Counselor," the man said calmly.

"Who the hell are you?"

"A friend of a friend, let's say."

"Well call my office and make an appointment, I don't have..."

"Shut-up, Counselor!" the man said quietly but firmly.

Holloway was stunned for a moment and didn't respond. He also suddenly realized this was the man Alex Frank had shown him the picture of. An icy chill of fear swept through him.

The stranger lifted his shirt to reveal a handgun in a holster on his belt.

"We need to take a ride. Don't even think about calling for anybody. Are we clear?"

Holloway drove in his long white Mercedes sedan while the man who Alex Frank had identified as Asa Dellahousaye's hired killer sat beside him, looking ahead and holding the semi-automatic handgun in his lap.

"What the hell's going on here?" Holloway finally said.

"Most people with your education, Counselor, would be smart enough to know better than threaten a man like Asa D."

Holloway felt a renewed rush of fear. In his heart, he knew the risk he'd taken in confronting Dellahousaye, but he felt he needed to play the card to ultimately protect him and the senator from any backlash. He tried to calm his shaking hands on the steering wheel, and he felt drips of sweat under his arms. "Listen, let's go talk to Asa. I think he misunderstood..."

"I don't think so, Counselor. Mr. "D" seemed clear on your intent. "Let's get one thing out of the way first. We can do this the hard way or the easy way. The easy way won't require much pain."

Holloway blanched and swallowed hard, looking over at the man who was smiling back at him. "What do you want?"

"You claim to have some files that would be an embarrassment to my employer. I want to know where they are and what's in them." The man laid the gun between his legs and pulled a long knife from a scabbard on his other hip. He held the knife an inch below Holloway's right eye as they continued down the road, out of town now with little traffic around.

The thought of some sadistic form of torture from this madman was more than he could imagine, and he immediately answered. "It's a written log of my contacts and the money involved as we've been moving to grease the skids on this gambling bill."

"And where would this 'log' be?"

The lawyer hesitated for a bit, weighing his options. If he gave up the information, what was to stop this man from killing him? On the other hand, the big knife in his face was going a long way to break down any thoughts of delay or deception. He had no stomach for the promised pain. "My bag is in the trunk."

"And that's the only copy?"

Holloway nodded. "Where are we going?"

"You know the old pier down by the commercial docks over this next bridge."

Again, Holloway nodded.

"Let's stop there and we'll check your bag."

Holloway pulled off the main road and took a turn to go under the bridge over the river, then down along the docks that held two large freighters with cranes overhead unloading cargo.

The killer indicated a place to pull over behind a small outbuilding.

"Give me the keys," the man demanded.

Holloway turned off the car and handed him the keys.

"Pop the trunk and don't move. Am I clear?" The knife hovered again in front of his face, the point of it pressed into the side of his right nostril. The man got out and walked to the back of car, coming back quickly with a leather shoulder bag. He handed it to the lawyer. "Show me the file."

Holloway unzipped a back compartment of the bag and drew out a manila envelope with no writing on it or label, then handed it to the man. He watched as he read through the information on the handwritten ledger of names, contacts and money.

"This is the only copy?" the man asked.

"Yes."

"No computer files, just this handwritten note?"

"I wouldn't keep information like this on a computer."

"Nothing at your office?"

"No, this is it, I swear."

"How much of this is your friend the Senator aware of?"

Holloway hesitated, then asked, "You mean Senator Hayes?"

"Yes, Counselor," the man said impatiently.

Holloway was struggling to keep from going into total panic. "Jordan and I have been working together to help with getting this legislation passed, but

166

he's not involved in the details I've outlined in the report I keep."

"You wouldn't be lying to me, Counselor?"

"For God's sake, no! Look, you and Asa are over-reacting to all of this. I only wanted Asa to know there were risks we were all facing, and the Senator and I were concerned about our involvement if things... got out of control."

The man continued to read, then opened his door, getting out with the file, his weapons already back in their holster and scabbard. "Come with me. We need to have a little talk."

Holloway got out and the man gestured for him to lead the way over to a long finger of a dock coming off the main pier in the shipping yard. He felt his knees wobble and he thought he might even piss his pants he was so scared. *So, this how it ends?*

He looked in both directions and there was no one in sight. The smaller boats out ahead on the pier seemed uninhabited. They were twenty yards out on the pier when he felt the stranger's breath on his neck.

"Far enough, Counselor."

Holloway was breathing heavily and felt his heart would burst out of his chest. At any moment, he expected to feel the slicing edge of the big knife in his back or across his throat. "Please!" he moaned urgently in final desperation. "I can pay you..."

Rather than a knife blade, the next thing he felt was the man's hand on the side of his face, then a savage jerk that smashed the side of his head into a tall thick piling beside him. The pain ripped through his brain and he immediately felt himself falling, unable to control his limbs or yell for help, the dark oily water of the river rushing up to swallow him.

Chapter Forty

Hanna had Calley and her sister, Carolyn, settled in at the Charleston Women's Shelter. She knew they would be safe there as the events surrounding their father's arrest played out.

She had returned to her office and was watching the small television monitor on the wall. A local news station was outside the police precinct where the girl's father had been processed and released. Someone had obviously tipped-off the media. A reporter was talking on a split screen next to another video shot of Reverend Warren Barbour leaving the station with his attorney and wife trailing behind, a dazed yet determined look on all their faces.

The reporter continued, *"... and the attorney for Barbour refuses to comment, but our sources tell us he is being charged with multiple counts of sexual assault and child endangerment linked to his two daughters and perhaps several other members of his congregation..."*

Hanna turned down the sound. She felt some pleasure in knowing the man and possibly the girl's mother would now be held to account for their frightening and disgusting behavior. She also knew the family's problems, public humiliation and ultimate criminal penalties were only just beginning. She had tried to assure Calley when she left her at the shelter, they were doing the right thing. Calley had also insisted more fervently than ever that she wanted the abortion as soon as possible. She had said she couldn't stand the thought of this baby inside her any longer. Hanna had checked with the judge's office and was told a decision and the necessary paperwork would be expedited.

She looked at her phone and saw two more messages from Alex. She was still so angry with him she was in no mood to hear his excuses. She was now more convinced than ever he was truly trying to drive her away. For what reason, she was completely baffled. His comments the other night about his crazy and dangerous career and the danger he was putting her in seemed a forced excuse. If he truly loved and cared for her, she thought, certainly they could work through all this together.

She had also reluctantly agreed to meet Sam Collins in an hour down at his photo shoot. She was still trying, unsuccessfully, to tell herself she was only curious about his work and also the chance to see her old house down on South Battery. Regardless of her current anger and frustration with Alex, she was not ready to abandon what they had built together. *But after last night, it was damned tempting.* The notion that she and Sam could suddenly find a way to come back together after 20 years apart seemed outrageous. *So why am I spending more time with the man?*

Hanna found a parking space along the curb at the park across the street from their old home she had been forced to sell after her husband's treachery plundered their finances. It had broken her heart to give up the 1700's home along the historic Battery on the river. She looked up at the towering white facade of the house showing through the tall trees along the front. Memories of her family and their time together there swept through her mind. She fought back tears as she remembered happier times there before everything fell apart and Ben was gone.

"Hanna!"

She turned to see Sam walking up on the sidewalk, his loose clothes and hair blowing in the wind off the water. She waved and walked up to meet him. He opened his arms to give her a hug and kiss on the cheek.

"Thanks for coming down. We're just moving the set to catch a new angle on one of the houses down the street with the sun moving over behind these big live oaks."

She looked where he was pointing and recognized the home of one of her old friends, a red brick three-story of similar vintage to her own. "You know this is our old house here then?" she asked, looking across the street.

"Yes, I tracked it down online. What a beautiful place," he said. "The new owners don't want to be included in the piece we're doing. My producer said they were a little *uppity*."

Hanna grimaced and shook her head. "I never met the new owners, but I do know they paid cash for the place. It was not a small number. Unfortunately, my ex-husband had led us down a path leaving a sizable mortgage to pay off when it was sold."

"Such a shame. I'd love to see the inside." He put his arm around her waist and pulled her with him away down the walk. "Let me show what we're working on."

Three doors down the crew members were setting up lights and other equipment to continue the external shots of the beautiful old house.

Sam said, "I'm working with a great writer who's doing this piece on the stories behind some of these wonderful old homes."

Hanna was impressed by the number of people on Sam's team and the incredible array of cameras, lenses, lighting and other equipment she had no clue what they would be used for.

"We have a couple more minutes," Sam said. "Let me show you the backyard. It's spectacular. We just finished-up back there."

She followed him across the street, waiting in the middle for a couple of cars to pass. They walked through an old ornate metal gate and along a brick path to the back of the house. They were surrounded by lush canopies of flowers and shrubs. In the back, there was a large brick terrace with multiple groupings of furniture, an outdoor kitchen and fireplace, a hot-tub and numerous pieces of contemporary sculpture mingled throughout the gardens. Along the back of the property, tall pines, live oaks and palm trees provided almost total privacy. Hanna was reminded of how much she had enjoyed the backyard of their own home just down the street.

"The owners are away for the week," Sam said. "Have a seat." He gestured for her to join him on a low cushioned couch. He sat a comfortable distance to her side but put his arm along the back of the couch behind her. "I wanted to ask you something."

Her senses went on alert as she tried to think what he was going to share with her now.

"I have to leave tomorrow for another job."

"You told me you were only in town for a few days," she answered.

"I have a job in the Bahamas I need to follow through with."

"Sam, you can't start canceling work," she protested. "This thing between you and me isn't even a thing," she said, awkwardly trying to make sense of what was happening.

"I know it's short notice, but I'd like you to come with me."

Chapter Forty-one

Alex had the windows down in the old truck, the wind rushing through and offering some relief to the intense heat from the sun rising above the trees to the south. He was oblivious to the sites of the historic old city of Charleston as he approached the downtown district. His thoughts were shifting through the troubles he was facing down at the department with Internal Affairs trying to build a case he was somehow connected to the shooter in Lonnie Smith's death. *Who planted that damn phone?*

Then, his night at Amelia Richard's house and the secret recordings of Asa Dellahousaye came back to him. He was relieved to know that nothing had happened between him and Amelia, but how was he going to explain ending up at the woman's house for the night to Hanna. *And what to do with the evidence against Asa Dellahousaye?*

His head was still on fire from the aftermath of the pills and too much booze the previous night at Gilly's. Another pill before he left Dugganville had dulled the throbbing pain in his neck, but it was still there as a constant reminder of the mess he found himself in. *When will the shooter decide to make another try?* he thought.

Hanna still hadn't returned his calls and he certainly couldn't blame her. He reached for his phone and pressed the number for her office. He heard the familiar voice of Hanna's assistant, Molly.

"No Alex, she had to go out with a client. I don't expect her back for a while."

"Please tell her I'm back in town and need to speak with her."

He waited for a reply, then Molly finally said, "I'll let her know."

Alex pulled into the parking lot for the police precinct and found a space in the shade near the back. As he got out, he heard a call, "Alex!"

He turned to see the detective, Nate Beatty, coming through the cars toward him. The man seemed troubled and hurried as he came up to the truck. "What in hell have you done?" he said, looking like he was ready to throw a punch.

Alex was stunned and surprised but managed to stand his ground. "What are you talking about?"

"The whole squad is on you to tipping off the shooter..."

"Nate, wait a minute! I swear to you..."

Beatty pushed him hard back against the door of the truck, then grabbed him with both hands by his shirt. "Frank, if you..."

Alex pushed his hands away. "Nate, I'm being set-up. I have no idea where that phone came from."

Beatty stared back for a few moments, breathing hard, sweat beading up on his red face. He shook his head, saying, "IA seems to think otherwise."

"You really think I would get my partner killed?"

"I don't know what to think."

"I'm godfather to his damn children, Nate!"

"Alex, you need to get this cleaned up. Half the department up there is ready to take your head off."

Alex stood outside Captain Guinness's office, waiting for the man to get off a phone call. As he looked around the large open office space, angry and hostile faces stared back at him from every direction. Guinness ended his call and waved him in, standing behind his desk.

"The Internal Affairs team wants another shot at you this morning. I'll let them know you're back."

"Captain, you know this is all bullshit," Alex said, standing across the desk from the man. "Lonnie was my best friend..."

"I really don't know what to think."

"Someone's trying to set me up."

Guinness looked down at the mess of papers and files on his desk, then back at Alex. "You better damn well find out who. IA wants to bring charges and lock you up."

Alex wasn't surprised. He knew this would be the next step in the process.

Two hours later, drained and trying to contain the panic he was feeling, Alex walked out of the interview room with the two IA officers. They had grilled him repeatedly about the events of the day of the shootings, going through every minute leading up to the attempted arrest of the hitter known as Caine and the subsequent death of four police officers. They had presented no further evidence implicating him tipping off the hit man. The phone found in his desk and call records of that morning were still all they had. Alex had pressed them on fingerprints or DNA or anything that could definitively link him to the phone, but they wouldn't or couldn't produce anything further.

In the end, the lead on the IA team had set a time for the next morning for him to come back in. While he didn't say it, Alex had the distinct impression he would be brought up on charges and arrested.

Beatty was at his desk when Alex walked past to leave. He looked away in disgust as Alex passed.

Alex walked into the bar where his best friend, Lonnie Smith had been killed along with three other officers just a few days ago. The bartender who had tipped them off to Caine being there was back behind the bar. He saw Alex come in and a look of anger flashed across his face. Obviously, Internal Affairs had talked to the man.

"You got some nerve, Frank," the bartender said, walking down behind the bar to face across him. "You could of got us all killed for chissakes!"

"Jeb, listen..."

"Get the hell outta here!"

"Just give me a minute," Alex pleaded.

The old man didn't respond, angrily wiping at the bar in front of him with a dirty towel.

"That morning," Alex began.

"I already told the damn cops ten times."

"Well, tell me. Did this guy take a call at the bar."

"He sure as hell did, about ten minutes before you all came chargin' in. Not long after I called you the asshole was here. He went back into the kitchen right after he hung up. When I went back there to shoo him out, he jumped me."

Alex could still see the lump and bruise on the side of the old man's forehead. "Did you hear him say anything during the call."

"No, I was down there, Jeb said, gesturing to the other end of the bar.

"What did he say in the kitchen?"

"Didn't say a damned thing! Just whacked me upside the head with his gun and stood over me like he was gonna take me out right there."

"Did he call anybody else while you were back there?"

The bartender shook his head no.

"Jeb, you know Lonnie and I go way back. You know I wouldn't do this."

Anger came back across the man's face. "I don't know what the hell you'd do or why, but I want you the hell outta here!"

When he walked into his front door, Alex felt the gloom of the day's events wash over him again as the quiet loneliness of the place consumed him. The blinds were all closed and there was a stale musty odor. The kitchen was cluttered with unwashed dishes and pans. Unopened mail was scattered on the dining table. He sat on a stool at the counter and checked his phone again, still nothing from Hanna.

He squeezed his eyes tight as the pain in his neck flared. His first reaction was to reach for the bottle of pills in his pocket, but he hesitated and then pushed himself to try to get by without them. He walked into the living room, scrolling down through other calls and messages on his phone. He sat on the couch and leaned back into the comfort of the deep cushions.

A phone message from his boss stared back at him. He pushed the button and listened to the call.

"Alex, it's Guinness. You need to come back in. Internal Affairs is going to bring you up on charges. They've got you in a picture with the shooter."

With Caine! Alex was shocked. *I never saw the asshole 'til that morning of the shooting.*

"*We can do this the hard way or the easy way,*" he heard Guinness say. "*Just get down here.*" The call ended.

He laid back along the long couch and stared up at the ceiling. *Where in hell would they get a picture like that? It had to be doctored.* His heart was pounding, and he struggled to contain his anger and then fear as he felt his life spinning out of control, his career... Hanna.

Chapter Forty-two

Phillip Holloway's first conscious thoughts were trying to listen to the low conversation of two people in the room with him. His eyes were closed, and his head was flaring with pain. His body felt like it was weighed down with some immovable force. He managed to blink open one eye and was blinded by a bright fluorescent light above him. He held an arm over his face to shield the glare.

"What the..." his voice was hoarse and weak.

A voice said, "Welcome back, Phillip."

"What's going on?" He tried again to open his eyes and this time he saw the white lab coat of a doctor standing beside his bed. He looked up and saw the face of a young woman with large glasses, dark hair and a clipboard in her hands. Then he heard the familiar voice of his law partner, James Molner.

"We weren't sure we were going to get you back, Phillip," Molner said.

Holloway looked over at his partner standing beside the doctor.

"Where the hell am I?" he said, the words coming tentatively.

The doctor said, "We're at the downtown hospital, Mr. Holloway. You're a very lucky man."

He tried to piece together random fragments of thoughts racing through his brain.

"Not sure what you were doing down at the docks," Molner said, "but you got a nasty bump on the head when you fell in. Probably would be at the bottom of the river right now if one of the dockworkers hadn't driven by on a forklift and seen you in the water."

"The river...?"

"Down at the commercial docks..."

The images started coming back to him... the man at the tennis courts, the drive down to the docks, the file on his gambling bill contacts...and bribes, walking out on the dock with some maniac who tried to kill him. He felt a flush of fear send chills through his body and he tried to sit up, but the pain on the side of his head intensified and he lay back on the pillows.

"Don't try to move, Mr. Holloway," the doctor said. "You have a bad concussion from whatever you hit your head on."

He quickly decided not to divulge what had really happened. "I remember now. I was down there to look at a boat a friend is thinking about buying. I must have slipped or something."

Molner patted him on the shoulder. "Just get some rest. The doc says you're going to be here for a couple of days. I'll check with the office to see if there's any work we need to bring down."

"Thank you, James." He was trying to keep calm, but thoughts of the killer sitting across from him in his car and then walking out on the dock with him kept searing into his brain. *What if he finds out I'm still alive?*

Holloway was dozing when he was startled by a hand shaking his shoulder.

"Mr. Holloway."

He opened his eyes and saw a man and a woman in business suits beside his bed. He tried to shake off the grogginess and focus on his visitors. "Who are you?"

The woman spoke first, an attractive blond with a no-nonsense expression. "Mr. Holloway, we're with the FBI. I'm Special Agent Sharron Fairfield and this is my partner, Will Foster."

Holloway felt a sick feeling in his gut and then he remembered both of these people. They had been assigned to the kidnapping case of Hanna Walsh's son over a year ago. He tried his best to sound casual and calm. "What can I help you with?"

The other agent said, "We have some questions about your association with Mr. Asa Dellahousaye."

It was all he could do to keep from throwing-up. He reached for a cup of water on the bed-stand beside him and took a long drink. He finished and looked back at the two FBI agents. "Yes, I know Mr. Dellahousaye. We have common friends. I've attended some events at his house here in South Carolina."

"Yes, we're very aware of your associations, Mr. Holloway," Foster said. "We've also learned you've been quite busy, should I call it "lobbying" on his behalf for the upcoming vote on the gambling bill in the State House."

Holloway started choking and held up a hand to gather himself.

The female agent, Fairfield, said, "Mr. Holloway, there's no need to dance around this. We have considerable evidence of your contacts, bribes and other illegal efforts to help Mr. Dellahousaye get this bill passed. He stands to make a considerable fortune developing casinos in the state as you are well aware."

He managed to stop gagging and took another drink. "I really don't know where you're getting this..."

"Please," Foster said, "we don't have time to listen to your fabrications about this. We have a solid case and are prepared to hand it over to the prosecutors today."

"You what!" Holloway felt helpless and weak, something he was totally unaccustomed to. "There must be some mistake."

Sharron Fairfield moved around to the other side of the bed. "We are also aware of your work with Senator Jordan Hayes on this matter."

Holloway started shaking his head, "No, you've got this all wrong..."

"Let me cut to the chase here, Phillip," she said. "You have one chance to make this easier on yourself."

"One chance?"

"We are authorized to provide limited immunity for you in this matter if you provide your full cooperation."

"Cooperation?"

"You have a choice, Phillip," the FBI agent said. "You can work with us on this or spend the next couple of decades in a federal prison."

Chapter Forty-three

Hanna had reluctantly agreed to have dinner with Sam Collins. His invitation to join the trip to the Bahamas for his next photo shoot was still unanswered. She had left him at the house down on the Battery with a swirl of confusion and doubt.

Back in her office, she was trying to distract herself with returning messages and sorting through files she would need for client meetings the next day. Thoughts of her afternoon with an old boyfriend she hadn't seen or heard from in over two decades kept interrupting her concentration. *There's no way I can run off with Sam,* she kept thinking. *This is crazy!*

She looked down at her phone and three pink message slips, all reminders that Alex had been trying to reach her all day. She picked up the phone and pressed the button for his latest voice mail.

"Hanna, I need to see you. I'm back in Charleston. What you saw last night is not what you think. You need to let me explain."

She clicked it off before the message finished and sat staring out the window at the trees behind her office. She was fighting the conflicting emotions of sadness and anger. *Alex seems determined to push me away and yet he wants to see me and explain his crazy behavior with that woman at the bar last night.*

She was startled when her phone buzzed. She looked down and saw it was Sam Collins.

"Hanna, I've made reservations at seven. Can I pick you up?"

She hesitated, looking down at all the messages from Alex.

"Hanna?"

Finally, she said, "Sure. I'm down at my office."

"Great, I'll pick you up in an hour."

She looked at the clock on the wall. "Sure, I'll see you then."

Hanna sat across from Sam Collins. He didn't look much older than her memories of the man when they were back in college together so many years ago. She had been thinking of their time together at school in Chapel Hill and how much she had cared for him, probably even loved him. Then, he had left her. She had aborted their baby... and twenty years had gone by without a word. Now he was back and trying to rekindle what they had been together.

"Hanna?"

She came back to the present and looked across at him.

"I've been trying to tell you about the trip to the islands for the shoot and you seem a million miles away."

"I'm sorry... Sam, I really can't get away and..."

"Of course you can."

"No, really. I have so much work and there's a case I have pending with a young girl..."

"Hanna, I know you have help down at your clinic. You can get away for a few days."

"No, actually I can't!" she said, growing angry at his naive insistence.

He poured more wine into her glass and she reached for it to take a sip. The deep flavor of the red wine was soothing, and she took another longer drink.

"We need some time together, Hanna."

She tried not to think about how she might actually enjoy a few days away in some tropical paradise with a man who she had obsessed over for so many years. And now he was back and wanted to be with her again and what, just drop everything and run off with him? There was more work than she could keep up with... and there was Alex Frank, an unresolved issue she still couldn't sort out.

Sam said, "Our client is sending his jet for us. It's going to be a marvelous trip. Have you been to the Abacos?"

"Sam, this is crazy. You come back out of nowhere after all this time and I'm supposed to just drop everything and fall into your arms and live happily ever after? It just doesn't make sense."

"We'll never know if we don't try."

She couldn't answer and looked away from his prying gaze. She took another sip from her wine. Finally, she said, "Sam, give me some time, please. I need to be in the office first thing. Let me see what I can do to make sure everything is covered. No promises!"

"That's great! We're not planning to leave until noon, so you'll have time to get things in order. Hanna, you have to come." He reached across the table and squeezed her hand. "We'll never know unless we try, Hanna."

Sam pulled his car to the curb in front of her office and apartment. In the dim light of the darkened street, Hanna looked over at Sam before opening her door. He leaned across and kissed her on the mouth, and she let her lips linger there. He kissed her again. She pulled back, trying to regain control of the situation. "I'll call you as soon as I can in the morning," she said.

She got out quickly without looking back and as she was unlocking the door to the office, she heard his car pull away. She went in, closing the door behind her.

She didn't see Alex Frank sitting in his father's old truck down the street.

Chapter Forty-four

Alex watched Hanna close the door and then the car drove away with the man who had just kissed her. If he had been feeling like his life was cascading out of control, he held on now to the steering wheel like it was the only thing that would keep him from totally free-falling into an abyss. He closed his eyes and tried not to see the scene unfold again... Hanna pulling up in the car, kissing this man goodnight.

He had been waiting over an hour for her to come home after Molly told him earlier, she was out for the night. With all that was crashing down around him, he needed her to understand how he'd been feeling after Lonnie's death, how crazy he'd been trying to deal with the grief and guilt, and then the damn pills making him act like a total idiot. He thought he could explain why he had been trying to drive her away and yet he knew for certain, up until a few moments ago, that it was the last thing he wanted. He needed her. He loved her.

He fought the urge to rush to the door, to do whatever, to say whatever it would take to help her understand, to forgive... to put her arms around him and hold him. Then, a sudden sense of clarity swept over him and he knew his life was not only in a tailspin but would likely drag Hanna down with him. He would be brought up on charges in the morning by his own department and he had little hope of proving his accusers wrong. If he was convicted of accessory to the murder of Lonnie Smith and the others, he might never see the outside of a prison again. In his heart, he couldn't ignore the clear signs he was going to have another tough climb out of the dependency of the damn pain meds... and the booze, just like he had struggled with them in the past.

Isn't she better off without all of that, without having to live with all that anguish and calamity?

At that very moment, he wasn't sure he had ever felt more hopeless, more lost, more alone.

He looked ahead at the dark street and then put the truck in gear and drove slowly away.

He pulled up to his father's house in Dugganville just past ten. Under the lights along the docks he saw that the *Maggie Mae* was back. The lights were out in the house, but he doubted his old man was asleep. He was surely down at *Gilly's* spending some of his take on the day's shrimp run. His first thought was to get some sleep and get up early to deal with Captain Guinness and the Internal Affairs Department back in Charleston. He should have turned himself in tonight but couldn't bring himself to surrender, keeping some distant hope alive that this was all just a bad dream.

Despite the sharp pain in his neck, he'd been holding off on the meds, knowing he had to get the truck back home tonight. He pulled out the bottle from his jeans and held it up to the light. He shook the bottle and saw a dozen or so pills left.

All the way back up to Dugganville, he had been trying to get his head straight about screwing up in Lonnie's death, and the other men, the sergeant from his old platoon bringing his past failures to everyone's attention on national news, and then the investigation and the very real likelihood he would be charged as an accessory to the killings of his fellow officers... and what about Hanna? It was all just too much to sort through. He looked at the pill bottle again. *What the hell!*

His father was at his usual spot at the bar when Alex walked into Gilly's. Ella Moore was hanging on him, laughing at some comment he'd just made, and she kissed him on the cheek as Alex walked up. The bar was near full as always and the music from the juke box could barely be heard over the loud talk and noise of the crowd.

Skipper and Ella were both taking long drinks from their beer bottles when they noticed him coming up behind them. Ella pushed her stool back and almost fell over. Her eyes were glazed, and her cheeks were flushed from the alcohol. With a drunken slur in her voice, she said, "Alex, honey... we been wunderin' if you was comin' down." She kissed him on the cheek now and he could smell the beer and sweat on her.

"Damn, son, you missed a helluva day out on the salt," Skipper Frank said. "More damn shrimp than we've seen in months."

"That's great, Pop."

"Pull up a stool. Ella slide that stool over here."

Alex sat down next to his ex-mother-in-law as she cozied back up to his father. He watched as Gilly brought three beers over and placed one in front of him. His head was already in a daze from the pills, but he took a long drink anyway, then leaned around Ella. "Pop, I need to talk to you. I've got some serious shit back in town I need to talk to you about."

"Nothin' can't wait 'til morning, boy," Ella said, and then clinked her beer bottle against his.

Alex stood and walked around to his father, taking him by the arm. "Really, Pop, let's go outside for a minute."

Skipper reluctantly slid back his seat and whispered something in Ella's ear before he stood. She laughed and slapped him on the rear before he followed Alex out the front door.

Alex led his father to the far end of the parking lot and a walkway along the river. The night air had cooled some and the first signs of a fog coming off the marshes drifted through the lights above them.

"What the hell's so important?" Skipper said.

Alex turned to face him and saw him holding onto a bench to steady himself. "Sit down, Pop." He joined his father on the old bench. "I wanted you to know I'm going to turn myself in to the Department in the morning."

Skipper seemed confused and didn't respond.

"Internal Affairs is building a case I tipped off the shooter in Lonnie's death."

"That's bullshit!" the old shrimper roared. "Why in hell would you do somethin' like that?"

"Pop, somebody set me up. They found a phone in my desk linked to this guy. Call records for this phone back up their case. They've got a picture of me with this killer."

"Who's tryin' to set you up?"

Alex stared back at his old man for a few moments, considering the question. He'd been asking himself the same thing ever since Guinness and IA had confronted him about the phone and now the picture. He'd thought through every scenario and the only one that fit was Beatty. Nate Beatty was the only other person who had survived that morning at the downtown bar. Who else would also have access to his desk? But why? To cover his own tracks? Asa Dellahousaye's tentacles reached deep and surely money in the right hands would provide access and information within the Department. He would deal with Beatty in the morning.

"Alex, you gotta fight this!" he heard his father say. He looked back at him and nodded slowly, continuing to think about Nathan Beatty and a confrontation in the morning with Guinness and Internal Affairs.

"You need a good lawyer, son. Can Hanna help you with this?"

His father's question startled him, and he thought again about Hanna and how it had all fallen apart between them in the past couple of days. He shook his head and looked away down the dark flow of the river. "Not sure..." He didn't finish the thought.

"What are you talkin' about?"

He looked back at his father. "Me and Hanna are through, Pop."

Skipper looked back at him for a moment, then said. "Don't know what happened, but you need to fix this."

"Nothing to fix, Pop. I blew it. I drove her away." He hesitated. "She's got someone else now."

"Sorry to hear that. She was the best thing I seen happen to you in a long time."

Alex heard what he said but didn't answer.

Chapter Forty-five

Caine was sitting on the aft deck of his boat, tied up to his slip in Charleston. The night sky had been clear with stars out all over and the first sliver of a new moon, then he'd noticed a fog blowing in. He could smell the damp air of the Low Country marshes pressing in over the city. His cell phone vibrated in his pocket and he pulled it out to check the screen. The number was blocked, but he knew it was Asa Dellahousaye.

"Yeah, boss."

"Where the hell are you?"

"Down on my boat," he answered, his senses on full alert at the tone of the gangster's voice. "What is it?"

"I thought you were going to take care of that lawyer we discussed."

"It's done."

There was silence on the phone for a few moments and Caine stood and walked to the transom of the big fishing boat.

Dellahousaye finally said, "Then why in hell did I just get off a call with the sonofabitch?"

Caine tried to remain calm, keep his voice steady. "There must be some mistake."

"There's no goddamn mistake!"

"Boss..."

"He just called me to say someone had tried to take him out, but he got fished out of the river. He threatened me again and said if anyone comes after him, he'll blow the whistle on this deal we're working."

Caine's mind was swirling. He'd seen the man go down in the water below the docks and when he came back up, he was face down. The blow he'd given him against the pier piling would have been enough to kill him. "I'll take care of this, boss."

"I want this cleared up now!"

"I said I'd take care of it," Caine spat back, his anger flaring.

"And what about the cop?" Dellahousaye asked. "Too many damn loose ends here. I want this all cleaned up by tomorrow, do you hear me?"

"Loud and clear, boss."

Phillip Holloway knew he couldn't stay in the hospital. He was a sitting duck for this madman killer to come back and finish the job he'd started down at the docks. The FBI had talked about security and protection, even relocating in the Witness Protection program, but that would take time. He was barely able to walk on his own to the bathroom, but he was certain he had to get to somewhere safe. He had just called his latest girlfriend, Ruth, to come down to pick him up. He would have her drive him to his condo down in Hilton Head. It was owned by the firm and he doubted Dellahousaye would even know about it.

The night nurse had just checked in on him and the halls outside were dark and quiet as the day wound down. He reached for his phone again and found the number he was looking for. The call rang four times before he heard, "I told you not to call me here." Senator Jordan Hayes' voice was clear and firm.

"Jordan, they tried to kill me today."

There was no response at first, then, "We're not going to talk about this on the phone. I have to be in South Carolina tomorrow. Where can we meet?"

Holloway said, "I need to get out of town tonight. I have someone taking me to the place we held the fundraiser at last month down on the coast." He didn't want to say the location over the phone. *God knows where Dellahousaye has eyes and ears.*

Hayes said, "I'll be there early afternoon tomorrow."

Chapter Forty-six

Hanna gave up trying to sleep and looked at the glaring red numbers on the digital alarm beside her bed for the tenth time... 5:15. She got up and went into the small kitchen in her apartment to put coffee on. She looked out the window over the sink across the parking area behind the house. The early morning light was just beginning to show through the heavy canopy of trees. She sat down at the table against the wall and put her head in her hands, trying to clear her mind and push the exhaustion she was feeling away to get her focused for the morning.

All night she had been thinking about Sam. When she had almost convinced herself she would leave with him today, all the doubts about their time apart, about Alex Frank, about all the responsibilities she had here in Charleston would rush back and change her mind.

She couldn't get the kiss out of her brain. *It was just a damn kiss goodnight!*

But it was more than that and she knew it. She had felt the old connection between them rushing back, all the time apart suddenly slipping away.

The coffee pot beeped, and she got up to pour her first cup. She knew she had to get matters cleared up for Calley Barbour, regardless of new men and entanglements in her own life. She would call the judge's office first thing to check on final approval of the waiver for Calley's abortion.

She still hadn't returned any of Alex's messages and all night she had been trying to think through what she was feeling, what she would say. She couldn't let this just hang between them.

Hanna showered and dressed and went down the steps to her offices. It was just past six o'clock when she turned on the lights and sat behind her desk. No one else would be in this early. Normally, they opened at eight and most of the staff would be in a few minutes early.

She tried with all her will to put thoughts of Sam and Alex aside and started sorting through the work in front of her, making piles for what was truly urgent in the next couple of days and what could wait or be handed-off. An hour passed quickly and she, thankfully, lost herself in the work.

A loud banging on the front door down the hall in the reception area startled her and she looked at the clock on the wall. Molly wouldn't be here yet to answer. She got up to go see who it was, and the pounding intensified. "Alright, already."

When she got to the front of the office, she saw the silhouette of a man through the glass in the door, his face obscured in the low morning light, still pounding. She got to the door and hesitated to open it with no one else around. The man seemed unhinged. Then she recognized the face and a sudden panic swept over her. Calley Barbour's father's face was now clear, and he was obviously enraged.

"Open the damn door!"

Hanna stepped back, trying to decide how to handle the man. "We're not open yet. Come back after eight," she yelled through the door.

"Open the damn door or I'll knock it down!"

"I'm going to call the police!" she yelled back. This got him to stop pounding and step back.

Trying to calm himself, Reverend Barbour said, "We need to talk. I don't know what you've put in my daughter's head, but this is all wrong."

Hanna's anger was growing, and she was finding little patience with this man's depravity and unthinkable behavior with his daughters. "I have nothing to say to you!" she snapped back. "I'm calling the police unless you leave immediately."

Barbour pressed his face close to the door. "What's this about my daughter being pregnant?"

Hanna had no idea how he had learned about Calley but wasn't going to offer anything.

"She wants to have an abortion and you're helping her!"

"I'm going to ask you one more time...".

"I don't know where my daughters are staying but I reached Calley's older sister on her cell. She told me everything, all the lies they've been telling you."

For just a moment, Hanna hesitated. Could she really trust Calley Barbour and her word? Hadn't she already lied the first time about her pregnancy? She reached in her pocket for her cell and held it up in front of the window in the door. "I'm calling 911 unless you're gone immediately!"

Barbour started backing away, the fury in his face returning. "I will be back, and we will get this all straightened out. You're ruining our lives!"

"It's up to the courts now and I will *not* discuss this with you. Your daughter is my client. Have your lawyer call me. And get the hell off my porch, now!"

By the time Molly and the rest of the staff arrived at eight, Hanna had mostly calmed herself from the encounter with Calley's father. She had them keep the door locked in case the man decided to come back.

Chapter Forty-Seven

Alex had stayed at his father's house in Dugganville the previous night and slept little as his mind stressed about the events of the coming day with his job, thoughts of Hanna, how he was going to handle the evidence against Asa Dellahousaye that Amelia Richards had left with him, and generally, how his life was swirling out of control. Skipper's first mate, Robbie, had agreed to drive him back to Charleston this morning and dropped him at his apartment to get showered and changed.

He was sitting in his car now in the parking lot of the Charleston Police Department precinct downtown. It was just past nine o'clock. He had managed to avoid taking any of the pain pills yet today and his head was clearing, yet still trying to shake off the lack of sleep. He watched as officers and civilians came and went through the back door of the precinct. He was parked at the back of the lot under the shade of a sprawling live oak tree.

He saw Nate Beatty pull into an empty space. Alex quickly got out and was standing next to the car when Beatty opened his door. The man looked up and was obviously surprised.

"Alex, what are you doing?"

Alex stepped back so the man could get out of the car and then stood facing him. "I have the same question for you?"

Beatty reached back into the car and grabbed a leather bag and put the strap over his shoulder. "What the hell are you talking about?"

Alex had decided to take the direct approach. "I know you planted that phone in my desk, Nate."

Beatty looked back with a confused stare, then said, "Excuse me?"

"You and I are going up to see the Captain right now," Alex said, "and I swear, you sonofabitch, if it was you who tipped off that shooter and got Lonnie and those boys killed..."

"Alex, whoa... wait a minute!"

Alex watched carefully to make sure the man didn't go for his gun or do something else stupid.

"You got this all wrong, man," Beatty said. "I lost my damned partner that morning, too, or don't you remember?"

Alex looked into the man's eyes for any sign of lying, but only saw the face of a man who looked completely bewildered and surprised by the allegation. He pressed on. "And how is it you're the only one who walked out of there without a scratch?"

"Lonnie set me as backup to cover the front of the place. You remember," Beatty insisted. "When I heard the shots fired, I came into the kitchen. The shooter was on his way out the back door."

Alex was starting to waiver on his certainty in Beatty's guilt.

"I swear to you, Alex, I didn't rat anybody out on this. I would never do that."

"Then who did?"

Beatty stood staring back at him, an empty look on his face, then said, "The whole damn department thinks it was you. So does IA. Tell me why they're wrong."

"You know I would never do anything to put Lonnie or any of you in harm's way. He was my best friend, Nate."

"Your sergeant on TV seems to have a different opinion on how you handled that deal in Afghanistan," Beatty said. "Sorry, man, but it doesn't look good."

Alex wanted to put his fist through the man's face but controlled himself enough to just say, "That was a long time ago and a very different situation."

"Look, I'm sorry," Beatty said, reaching out and holding his arm. "If I were you, I'd get my ass up there," he continued, glancing toward the precinct building, "and I'd cooperate with IA as best I could and help them find who's trying to set you up."

"They've already made up their minds, Nate. They're gonna lock me up."

"So, what are you going to do?"

"I want you to do something for me," Alex said.

"Okay."

"I want you to go up and tell the Captain we talked and that you think these charges are bullshit. I want you to tell him I'm not coming in until I figure out who's behind this."

Beatty hesitated.

"Please, I need your help."

"This is only gonna make it worse with IA, Alex."

"Let me worry about that."

Chapter Forty-eight

Hanna was sitting in the outer office of Judge Kraft. The judge had agreed to see her before her morning court session. As she waited, she thought about the earlier visit of Calley's father, Reverend Barbour. The man was clearly unhinged and a possible danger to his daughters. The Women's Shelter was secure, but Calley and Carolyn couldn't stay there forever. Their father was out on bail and would eventually find them. She planned to ask the judge about a restraining order to keep the man away from the girls. It was only a slight deterrent, but she had to try to keep them safe until the man was tried and hopefully convicted, which could take months.

Sam had called just before she left her office. He wanted her decision on leaving with him at noon. She wasn't ready for the call and she surely wasn't ready to commit to the trip. She put him off until after her meeting with the judge, assuring him she would call as soon as she could. His final words were stuck in her mind. *We have another chance here, Hanna. Let's not waste this one.*

Her phone chimed and she looked down to see another text message coming in from Alex. *Five minutes. Please!*

She hesitated, her mind swirling with Sam's invitation, Alex's behavior these past few days, the emotions of helping young Calley Barbour get approval for an abortion and the dark memories coming back of giving up her own child so many years ago... Sam's child.

Reluctantly, she typed, *Back in my office at eleven.*

She knew she had to clear the air with Alex. She couldn't just walk away without hearing him out. She certainly couldn't decide to leave with Sam later today without telling him. The thought of that discussion made her stomach churn.

The judge's assistant took a call and then said, "Miss Walsh, you can go in."

"Thank you." She put her phone away, gathered her bag and went through into the judge's office. Judge Kraft was pulling a file from a drawer in her desk.

"Have a seat, Hanna."

"Thank you for seeing me."

"I only have a few minutes," the judge said, standing and reaching for her long black robe on a coat stand behind her desk. As she was putting it on, she said, "Clearly, with the charges brought against the father in this case, I will grant the waiver of parental permission for this abortion for Calley Barbour."

"Thank you, Judge."

"Are you certain Calley has really thought through the implications of this? Adoption is another option here."

Hanna leaned forward as the judge sat back behind her desk. "I've spoken with her about it several times. She's absolutely convinced she can't take this pregnancy to term and under the circumstances, I can sympathize with her decision."

Kraft said, "And are you completely sure the father is at fault here? Calley has already lied to us on her first version of the story."

"I've thought about that a lot, Judge. I'm more confident in Calley's story now that her sister has come forward and validated the years of abuse they've suffered with their father."

"Right."

"Reverend Barbour came to my office early this morning and threatened to knock down my door. He's understandably upset, but I also fear he's a danger to his daughters. I'd like to have a restraining order issued to keep him away. They're at the shelter now but can't stay there as long as it will take to bring their father to trial."

"I'll take care of it later today," Judge Kraft said. "I also have the necessary paperwork here to grant the waiver for the abortion. I'll have it sent over to your office later today."

"Thank you, Louise," Hanna said, both relieved and yet, still troubled at the path this young girl was taking.

Calley and Carolyn Barbour came into the conference room of the Women's Shelter. Hanna stood from behind the long table and came around to give each of the girls a hug. They all took a seat and Hanna said, "I met with the judge this morning, Calley. She's going to grant permission for you to have this procedure."

"Oh, thank God!" she said. Her sister, Carolyn, reached over and put her arm around her shoulders. Calley's eyes started to well up in tears. "I know this is the right thing, Hanna. Thank you for helping me."

Hanna looked back at the two sisters, thinking how sad it was they had endured a childhood with a father who had abused and betrayed them and a mother who for, whatever reason, had enabled the outrageous behavior of her husband. "I'll have the paperwork later today. We can meet with the clinic for an initial consultation whenever you're ready." Hanna thought again about the invitation to leave town with Sam. "I may be gone for a couple of days..."

"I want to get this over with, Hanna!" Calley said, wiping at her eyes. "I want this... I want this over with."

"I understand. I've already alerted the clinic to the situation. They want to review the court documents. It could take a few days."

Carolyn said, "Please do what you can to hurry this up."

Hanna nodded. "I don't want to upset either of you anymore, but your father tried to get into my offices before we opened today. As you can imagine, he was very angry. I've asked the judge to issue a restraining order to keep him away from both of you."

"Thank you," Carolyn said. "As soon as Calley can have this procedure, we're going to leave town. Calley's going to stay with me for a while until all of this is worked out."

"Okay, good," Hanna replied, thinking this was best. She looked over at the tear-stained and flushed face of Calley Barbour. She thought back to the days, so many years ago, when she had been facing the decision to abort her own pregnancy. Certainly, the circumstances were far different. She hoped that Calley would find peace with her decision and hopefully not live with the doubt and regret that she had endured for so many years.

Hanna stood and came around the table and opened her arms to Calley. The girl laid her face on Hanna's shoulder and held her tight.

She was driving back to her office when her phone buzzed. The call screen said, "Allen".

"Good morning, father." As she said it, she had a brief thought of how fortunate she had been to have such a loving father in her own life. They'd had their differences over the years. His idiotic decision to fly his plane in bad weather with his family and the crash that had taken the lives of her mother and brother was still a barrier between them that would never be toppled, but she still loved the old fool.

"Oh, Hanna. So glad I caught you." His voice was typically hurried and official sounding. As usual, he couldn't drop his *senior law partner* demeanor.

"What is it, Allen?"

"I wanted you to hear it from me first. I know Martha tends to call you before we've had a chance to catch up."

Thoughts of her stepmother didn't help to brighten Hanna's mood. "What's going on?"

"Martha and I had dinner last night. You know we've been apart..."

"Yes, is she really having a thing with this other man?"

"We talked about all that," Allen Moss said, hurriedly. "I've been such a fool."

"What!"

"It was nothing, Hanna. They're just friends. Martha has a lot of friends and I'm a jealous old fool."

"So, you're taking her back?"

"We're flying to Paris later tonight for a second honeymoon!"

Hanna was shaking her head while she was driving, thinking whether this woman had really betrayed her father or was it all just a misunderstanding.

She had to admit she was happy for him to not be alone. He needed Martha to throttle his relentless work schedule and maybe get him a few more years before his fragile heart finally gives out. "I'm glad to hear that, Allen," she finally said.

"Life's too short, daughter."

Yes, indeed it is.

Chapter Forty-nine

Alex pulled up in front of his condo building and found a spot along the curb. He didn't plan to be there long, only stopping by to pick up enough clothes and items to be on the "loose" for a few days until he was able to sort through all that was happening to clear his name and get enough on Asa Dellahousaye to close that chapter. And then there was Caine. He was certain the man was still in town, though the body count had fortunately slowed down.

As he got out of his car, he was surprised to see two familiar faces walking toward him down the sidewalk. He hadn't seen Special Agents Foster and Fairfield since Hanna's case and the kidnapping of her son. There were no smiles or signs of recognition from the two of them, only looks of grim determination.

"What do I owe this pleasure?" Alex started.

Neither agents offered their hands in greeting. "We need a few words with you, Detective Frank," Agent Will Foster said.

Alex had put on coffee and the three of them sat around his dining table. "We understand you're having some issues down at your department," Agent Sharron Fairfield started.

"They're calling the FBI in on this?" Alex said, shaking his head, astonished.

Foster replied, "No, but we're aware of the charges being filed in your role in the shooting the other day."

Alex tensed. "I did nothing wrong..." He stopped for a moment, then continued. "My only fault that day was letting my partner get killed when my gun got knocked away."

"Yes, we've read your account," Foster said.

"I didn't tip anyone off. I didn't call that guy. It's not my phone!"

"That's not why we're here," Fairfield said.

"Then what?"

"We're investigating a corruption case linked to the gambling bill currently under consideration by the State of South Carolina."

Alex was confused by the about-face, then quickly said, "And why are you talking to me?"

"We think the man who killed your partner and those other officers is working for a man named Asa Dellahousaye."

"Yes, I know who he is."

"We know that," Foster said. "We have a source who is cooperating in the case who has revealed a long list of names involved in bribes and other persuasion to make this bill pass successfully."

"I'm not involved in any of that!" Alex protested.

"Only that Dellahousaye's hit man has already tried to kill you twice," Agent Foster said.

"I've seen his face," Alex responded. "I'm sure he's trying to clean up loose ends."

"We agree," Fairfield said. "You're a lucky man, Detective Frank. This shooter named Caine is very good at what he does. He doesn't leave many survivors. I hope you're still watching your back."

Alex nodded. The coffee pot beeped, and he went to fill three cups. When he sat back down, Foster said, "There were some interesting names on the list our source provided."

"Surely, you're not talking about me," Alex said. "I've had nothing to do with any gambling bill and..."

"No, it isn't you," Foster continued.

Alex was relieved but still on guard about the intent of the two FBI agents. He was also thinking about the thumb drive Amelia Richards had given him with damning evidence on Asa Dellahousaye and the drug ring he and Beau Richards had been involved with.

Fairfield said, "We were very surprised to see the name of your boss on this list, Alex."

He was stunned. "Captain Guinness?"

"Yes, he's been receiving money from Dellahousaye for some time, apparently providing access to police information that could be helpful not only with this gambling affair but going back several years. You know Dellahousaye is linked to drugs, prostitution and a number of other niceties."

"Yes, I'm aware." Alex was thinking fast now about the investigation down at his department, the phone planted in his desk, the fake picture of him and Caine, Beatty's response earlier this morning. "Captain Guinness?" he said again, still struggling to link his boss being on the pad to this gangster.

Foster said, "So you've had no reason to believe Guinness had any role in the tip-off to the shooter the other day?"

Fairfield continued, "Or any connection Guinness might have to Della-housaye?"

"Not a clue," Alex said, both angry and relieved at the same time. "I do have some new information I just received that is related, though."

"What is that?" Foster asked.

Alex got up and went to get his bag laying on the counter. He reached in and pulled out the small thumb drives Amelia Richards had given him. "There are recordings here of Asa Dellahousaye and a man named Beau Richards who was convicted of attempted murder and drug charges last year."

"Yes, we're aware of Mr. Richards," Foster said. "Again, you were a lucky man."

"These recorded discussions reveal both men's involvement in the drug ring along the coast as well as their plans to have me taken off the board."

Foster reached over to take the thumb drives.

Alex said, "My source needs to be protected. She would be in grave danger if Asa D finds out she's provided this information."

"You're talking about Amelia Richards then," Fairfield asked.

Alex wasn't surprised. These two seemed to know much more than he would have thought. "Yes, she's making arrangements as we speak to get out of the country. That's why I was waiting to turn this information in."

Foster said, "I'm not sure we want her leaving the country, but we'll make sure she's safe."

"There's nothing about the gambling bill on the recordings..." Alex started.

Fairfield jumped in, "This will all help to build our case."

Foster was examining one of the thumb drives, obviously thinking about next steps. He said, "Have you had any further contact or heard from this man named Caine? We need to get this asshole off the street."

"No, not since the night at the hospital when he came back for me. The department had a detail watching my back and my girlfriend... you know Hanna Walsh?"

"Of course," Fairfield said. "We are aware the two of you are a couple now."

"Well, I'm not so sure anymore," Alex responded, "but I'm still concerned for her safety. This lunatic, Caine, is obviously capable of anything."

Foster said, "Our next stop this morning is the office of Captain James Guinness down at the Charleston Police Department. There will be a series of raids and arrests today."

"So, you have enough to arrest Guinness?" Alex asked.

"Absolutely," Foster replied. "Don't be surprised when you hear some significant names being brought up on charges later today, including a prominent U. S. Senator from the State of South Carolina."

"Jordan Hayes?" Alex asked, completely surprised.

"We will speak with your Internal Affairs Department when we're down there this afternoon," Foster said. "I think this will clear things up with the charges they're considering against you."

Alex suddenly realized a tremendous weight had been lifted, but the thought triggered a rush of anger at his boss and the deadly betrayal he had perpetrated. "I want to be there when this goes down this afternoon," he insisted.

"I think that can be arranged," Special Agent Sharron Fairfield said.

Hanna's assistant, Molly, had shown Alex back to her office and told him to expect her within the next fifteen minutes. He stood looking out the back window across the row of cars along one side of the property and the thick foliage of trees and shrubs across the back. His mind was full with thoughts of the treachery of Captain James Guinness, a man he had known and trusted and respected for many years. Apparently, the money from the mobster, Asa Dellahousaye, was enough to get Guinness to risk his career and betray all who worked for him. *He needs to rot in hell,* Alex thought.

He thought of Lonnie Smith's wife, Ginny, and his now deceased partner. He would need to go see Ginny and tell her about Guinness and his role in tipping off the killer. It certainly wouldn't bring any comfort or closure, but she needed to know.

He had been trying to think who the informant was who provided the damning information on Guinness and apparently, a number of other influential people including U.S. Senator Jordan Hayes. The two FBI agents had refused to reveal their source. He had to trust the agent's word they would look out for the safety of Amelia Richards. He was certain she would have been unable to get out of the country yet, but when this all goes down, he thought, Asa D won't take long to piece everything together and start going after anyone he felt had betrayed him.

There were some bottled waters on the conference table. He reached for one and took a long drink. His head was pounding with a dull ache, likely from not taking the pain meds for over twelve hours. He knew the dependency was swift and the coming off the damn things was going to be hell as he'd found in the past. He walked back over to the window feeling a little light-headed and dizzy. His bouts with similar pain meds after wounds in Afghanistan and a gunshot wound he had taken several years ago had both resulted in serious addictions that had required professional intervention to get clean. He knew he should have been more careful after this latest episode with the neck wound.

And what was he going to say to Hanna? His behavior the past few days had been clouded with his grief and guilt with Lonnie's death and his failure to back his partner up. The damn meds had made him crazy and whatever Hanna thought she saw with him and Amelia Richards up in Dugganville was going to be hard to explain. He thought about seeing Hanna the night before with the man in the car out in front of this office. He thought, *it certainly didn't take her long to get over me.*

Chapter Fifty

Molly stood when Hanna walked into the office. She walked over to Molly's desk and took the phone messages from her.

"Alex is waiting for you in your office. I hope you don't mind. I didn't want him to have to wait out here."

Hanna knew Molly was more concerned about the possible scene of Hanna and Alex together in front of all the clients waiting for their appointments. "Thank you, that's fine." She felt a chill of apprehension, still not clear how she felt, what she was going to say... how this day could possibly end.

Alex was standing at the window in her office overlooking the back of the old house. He didn't hear her come through the door. She saw that he was dressed in jeans and an old t-shirt, his hair was a mess and the bandage on his neck stood out as a stark reminder of the gruesome events of the past few days.

"Good morning," she said softly as she went around behind her desk. He turned suddenly and she was stunned to see how tired and gaunt he looked. His face was pale and dark circles under his eyes looked like he'd been hit in the face. He started toward her and she thought he was going to come behind her desk to hug her, but then he obviously thought better of the idea and stopped across the desk from her. "Alex, I don't know..."

"Hanna, please. Let me start. I need to apologize."

She was in no mood for excuses, but offered, "Alex, I know you've been going through the worst. I can't imagine how hard this has been for you, losing Lonnie and everything else."

"It doesn't make it right for how I've treated you, Hanna, and I'm sorry.

I'm sure you think I've been trying to push you away."

"You *have* been!" she jumped in and then watched as he looked like he'd been slapped. He stepped back and looked around for a chair. He sat across from her and she pulled her chair over beneath her.

"I was hoping you would give me a chance to explain," he said.

"First, how are you feeling? I'm sorry to say it, but you look like hell." She saw a thin smile spread across his face.

"You noticed?" Alex reflexively reached up and touched the fresh dressing he'd put on his neck that morning. "I've felt better, but I'm not complaining."

"Alex, I'm still so sorry about Lonnie. I feel badly, I haven't been back over to see Ginny and the kids."

"I'm going to see them later this afternoon. There have been some new developments."

"What?"

"I'll tell you later. It's a long story, but first, I need to explain about what was going on up in Dugganville the other night."

Hanna put up a hand. "Really, there's no need," she said, but her inner voice was screaming, *you sure as hell do!*

"I don't think you ever met Beau Richard's wife, Amelia."

"The man who tried to kill you last year?"

Alex nodded.

"And that was his wife?"

"She's in some trouble. I'm trying to help."

"I'm sure you are!" she said, more sarcastically than she meant.

"Excuse me?"

Hanna stood and walked over to the bookshelves along the wall. "Alex, look, I'm sorry. I should have let you explain that night, but I show up and you're wasted and in deep conversation with this incredibly beautiful woman."

"I know, these pain pills I've been taking are making me crazy and I shouldn't be drinking."

"Are you still on them?"

"I've been trying to start cutting back, but I have some bad history with this and it's, well, it's going to take some time."

"That stuff is so dangerous, Alex."

"Trust me, I know." He looked away for a minute, then said, "I need to tell you everything."

"Okay."

"I went to Amelia Richard's house that night."

Hanna wasn't surprised by his admission, but her heart sank anyway as she listened.

"She has some evidence her husband hid away against this gangster we talked about."

"Dellahousaye?"

"Right. Amelia wanted me to get this information to the proper authorities, but she was afraid what Dellahousaye might do."

"So, you went back to her house," Hanna said, impatiently, trying to calm her instincts to just throw him out of her office.

Alex nodded. "I did. I slept there. I passed out, actually."

Sirens were going off in Hanna's brain. "I'm not surprised. You could barely make a sentence when I saw you at the bar."

"Nothing happened, Hanna, I mean between me and Amelia. You have to believe me."

She was surprised to realize she did believe him, but it didn't make her any less angry. Then, a flood of guilt washed over her as she thought about Sam and their last couple of days together. She heard him start talking again, but she was still thinking about Sam's kiss and the invitation.

"Hanna?"

She shook her head, coming back to the moment. "Alex, we need to talk about something else..." She stopped and looked up when she sensed someone standing in the open door. Alex had his back to the door and hadn't noticed anyone there.

"Sam!"

Sam Collins smiled that easy smile she was getting used to again and stepped in. "Hope I'm not interrupting anything, but we need to get going Hanna."

Hanna watched as Alex turned. The expression on his face went instantly from curious to enraged. She looked up at Sam who was suddenly moving quickly backward. He slammed the door closed. She stood speechless as he reached behind his waist and pulled out a gun from under his shirt and pointed it at Alex's head.

"Sam, what...?"

Alex yelled out, "Hanna, get down!"

She couldn't make sense of what she was seeing or hearing. Alex stood and quickly jumped between her and Sam. She watched as Sam's expression suddenly turned from his normal easy going and gracious calm to a dark anger she had never seen before.

Sam said, "Detective Frank, how inconvenient."

"You two know each other?" Hanna said, completely stunned. "Sam, put that gun down! Have you lost your mind?"

Collins moved closer to Alex and said, "Keep your hands in front where I can see them. Hanna, take his gun and put it over there on the table." His own gun was now only a few feet away from Alex's face.

Hanna pleaded, "Sam, what are you doing? Please..."

"Take his gun!"

She heard Alex say, "Hanna, I don't know who you think this is."

She couldn't respond. The scene before her was beyond comprehension.

"I'm going to ask one more time!" Sam hissed through clenched teeth.

"Sam, please stop!"

Alex kept his eyes trained on Sam Collins and said, "This man's name is Caine, Hanna. He killed Lonnie..."

"Shut up, Frank!" Caine snarled.

Hanna could see his finger pressed firmly on the trigger. She tried to calm the panic that was exploding through her. She couldn't make sense of what she'd just heard. "Caine?" She flinched when Sam suddenly rushed forward and smashed the side of his gun into Alex's temple. He fell to the ground in a heap and Hanna cried out.

"Shut up, Hanna!" Sam said as he knelt and took Alex's gun from the holster on his belt. He stood and stepped back, looking quickly at the door behind him, still closed.

"Sam, what are you doing?" She looked down and Alex was not moving, and blood was now leaking out from the blow to the side of his face. She got down on her knees to press her hand against the flow of blood. "Sam, what is he talking about?" When she looked up, the man she knew as Sam Collins was staring back, the gun now pointed at her.

"We obviously need to talk, Hanna."

Ten minutes later, Hanna was in the back seat of Sam's car, holding Alex's head in her lap, a handkerchief pressed firmly to the side of his face. Alex had regained consciousness enough to allow Hanna at Sam's insistence to help to get Alex out the back door of the office and into the car. Sam had grabbed plastic tie strips from the trunk and secured Alex's hands behind him. Sam had threatened to kill Alex on the spot if she didn't help.

She looked up at the back of Sam's head as he drove through the shaded streets of Charleston. "Where are we going?"

He didn't answer.

"Who are you?" she cried out.

"I'll explain everything, in time."

"You killed Lonnie Smith and all those other men?" Hanna said through her tears, still not understanding or believing anything that was happening.

Sam... or Caine, didn't answer.

She looked up from Alex when the car stopped. She could see boats along a long pier. Sam turned to her. "You're going to help me get him out to my boat. If you say anything or don't do exactly as I ask, I will put a bullet in the side of his head and throw him in the river. Are we clear?"

She nodded back in shock and disbelief.

Hanna sat across from Sam in the cockpit of the big boat. Alex lay on the deck behind them, his hands and feet now both secured by plastic ties. The bleeding from his head wound had slowed, but he was barely conscious. She looked back over at the man she thought she knew as Sam Collins driving the boat. His gun was now on the console in front of him. She was shaking and felt cold even though it was near eighty outside and little breeze was blowing into the closed cabin of the boat as they made their way out the river toward open water.

She listened as Sam started to speak over the dull roar of the engines. "Hanna, you need to understand a few things."

"Who are you?" she shouted.

Sam looked over at her with a grim and determined look, a frightening look. "I was brought back to Charleston to do some work. I couldn't resist looking you up again."

"You did kill those men!"

Sam didn't respond.

"This isn't possible!" she cried out, looking again at Alex, motionless on the deck of the boat.

"Hanna, years ago when I left school, I was getting some photo work in France, but barely getting by. I met some men one night in a bar. They were mercenaries working for an outfit out of Paris. It's a long story, but we became friends and they introduced me to another line of work that's become far more profitable."

"You're a killer!"

He smiled back at her and said, "Yes Hanna, I get paid to kill people... and I've become very good at it.

"And your name is Caine now?" she said.

"When I'm working, yes."

"And the photography...?"

"A convenient cover."

Chapter Fifty-one

Alex felt the low vibration of an engine through the cold hard deck of the boat against his face. He was beginning to regain some sense of where he was and what was happening. Caine had come into Hanna's office. *She knew him, for God's sake!*

He cautiously tried to move but felt his hands and legs both secured. Without lifting his head, he glanced up and saw Hanna sitting across from Caine who was steering the boat. He could just make out their conversation over the loud roar of the boat's engine.

Hanna shouted, "You need to take us back. You can't do this!"

Alex watched as Caine just grinned at her. Finally, he said, "Your friend here, Detective Frank, he and I have some unfinished business to take care of and then you and I are going to the Bahamas as planned."

"I'm not going anywhere with you!" Hanna yelled out.

"I had planned to take my client's plane and come back for the boat in a few days... but plans change, right?"

"Sam, this is crazy! You need to take us back!"

"Hanna, I'm sure this is more than you can understand right now, but this is just a job. I still want us to be together again."

"You've lost your mind!" Hanna cried.

Alex pulled at his restraints to see if there was any chance he could get free. He was held fast and remained motionless with his eyes closed. The side of his head was screaming with pain and he struggled to keep from passing out again.

Alex wasn't sure how long he had lost consciousness again. The boat's engines were throttling back and then the boat slowed and moved up and down in the swells from the big wake coming up from behind. He could smell gasoline and putrid fish from the oily deck of the boat. His head was suddenly jerked up by the hair and he saw Caine's feet beside him. He heard Hanna yell out, "Please, Sam! Don't hurt him again!

Alex watched as Caine's right foot reared back and then came crashing into his forehead, a new flash of pain searing into his brain. His last conscious thought was the sound of Hanna crying out. "Please, no!"

Chapter Fifty-two

Hanna jumped down from the tall boat seat and fell to Alex's side. He lay there, not moving, Sam's kick doing more damage to his face. "You're a monster!" she yelled as Sam walked past and opened the doors to the back deck of the boat. She looked out across a long stretch of blue water with no land in sight, no boats. She stood and looked around through all the cabin windows. The shoreline of Charleston was barely visible to the west. She saw a few boats now, but all were miles away. Sam had taken her phone and thrown it overboard with Alex's soon after they left Charleston harbor. She looked over and saw the ship's radio on the other side of the steering wheel on the console.

"Don't even think about it," Sam said, coming up from behind. He put his arm around her waist. She cringed and tried to pull away, but he held her close.

"There's no need to spoil this new chance we have, Hanna."

"Let me go!"

He let her step away and said, "We can live anywhere, go anywhere. It can be a marvelous life."

She stood there shaking her head in disbelief at what she was hearing. The man was truly deranged. *How could I not see this?*

"I know this is difficult, Hanna. I don't expect you to understand right away."

"And what if I tell you to go to hell!" she yelled out. "Will you kill me, too!"

He smiled back at her but didn't answer.

"Sam, please take us back," she pleaded.

"Much too late for that, dear. How about a little fishing."

Hanna watched in stunned silence as Sam moved about the rear of the boat, dipping bait with a small net from a live well along the side rail of the boat. With a long knife, he was cutting the bait fish into small bloody pieces and scraping them into a large white bucket. The boat drifted along on the blue swells of the ocean. The sun overhead stifling hot and only a hint of breeze blowing.

Sam opened a gate across the back transom of the boat as Hanna sat down in a folding chair on the deck next to Alex, still lying unconscious at her feet. She leaned down and stroked his hair. He felt cold and she pulled back, the fear continuing to build and blur her senses.

Sam took the bucket of cut fish and walked out on a small platform behind the boat. He threw the contents of the bucket out into the water. Hanna could see the oily bloody mess spread out across the calm surface of the water. Sam came back up on deck. He went over and scooped more fish, larger this time and continued hacking away at them with the big knife.

He had poured three buckets full of the bloody chum into the water when she saw the first gray fin sweep across the water behind the boat. The fear she was feeling now turned to sheer panic. She ran over to Sam at the back of the boat, screaming, "You have to stop this!"

"You might want to go below, Hanna," Sam said calmly. The look in his eyes was almost manic. She saw the grip of his gun in the holster under his shirt on the back of his pants.

"You can't do this!" she cried out, the tears coming again.

"This is just business, Hanna. You'll come to see this is just business."

She could tell from the crazed look on his face that this was far more than that. He was enjoying this, getting some sick pleasure from it.

Without thinking, she said, "You'll have to kill me, too, Sam. I'll never go with you!"

He just laughed and said, "Don't be ridiculous."

She lunged at him, thinking maybe she could get to the gun. He grabbed her easily and held her arms in vice-like grips. His face grew deadly serious.

"Do not get in my way."

She backed up, the terror of the moment now totally overwhelming her. She fell to the deck beside Alex and lay over him in some futile attempt to protect him. She heard Alex whisper in a hoarse and weak voice, "Hanna?"

She looked over at his face and his eyes were half open. Beyond, she could see two large sharks now, thrashing through the bloody bait behind the boat. "Oh my God!"

She felt Sam pushing her away and watched in horror as the crazed killer she thought she knew as her college lover, Sam Collins, swung a large handled hook into the thigh of Alex. Even half conscious, Alex screamed out in pain as Sam started pulling him to the back of the boat deck.

Hanna tried to breathe, to get enough strength to stand. She saw Sam pull Alex by the hook in his leg onto the back platform of the deck, the sharks only a few feet away in the bloody froth of water. Sam put his foot on Alex's leg, still bound and lifeless. He pulled hard and the hook came out in a spurt of blood. She watched in stunned horror as Sam laughed and threw the gaff up onto the rear deck.

Sam turned away and watched as the sharks raced through bloody bait now, clearly in a frenzy. Alex lay motionless on the platform beside him, moaning in a low haunting voice. Hanna saw Sam staring at the sharks, laughing.

She managed to get up and stood for a moment, staggering in the slow rolling motion of the boat. She thought she was going to be sick, but pushed the sensation down and then, on instinct, ran quickly towards the rear of the boat, reaching down to grab the long handle of the fish gaff. With all her strength, she swung the hook and felt it thud into the man's neck. Blood immediately gushed from the wound and splattered down on Alex and the deck. Sam tried to turn but she held him tight with the handle. He managed to turn his head just enough to look back at her with a twisted smile.

He started to speak, but Hanna didn't give him a chance. With her last reserve of strength, she pushed hard on the gaff handle stuck into his bleeding neck. He lost his footing and fell with arms out wide into the froth of water and blood and streaking sharks behind the boat. Hanna let the gaff go as he fell.

The man she now knew as Caine, came back to the surface quickly, his face remarkably calm. He was pulling at the hook in the side of his neck when his body shuddered and was jerked sideways and then down below the surface. Hanna fell to her knees beside Alex, still half conscious and not moving.

Caine's head burst through the surface of the water again, his eyes now showing the first sign of panic, but still, he managed to smile back at her, blood staining his teeth a bright red.

Hanna lurched back in sheer fright as the huge jaws of one of the sharks flashed up across the water and took the man's face and then his entire body down with it, down into the blue depths of the Atlantic.

Sam Collins... Caine, didn't come back up.

Hanna peered over the edge of the platform and could see the dark shapes of two large sharks tearing at the body several feet below the surface. Blood and torn limbs were coming to the surface and joined with the other bloody chum. She looked away retching and then fell to Alex's side, her arm over him, holding him close. She heard him groan, "Hanna?"

Chapter Fifty-three

Hanna lay with her arm across Alex's stomach. She'd been dozing and woke when someone came in behind her. The nurse walked to the other side of the bed and checked the readings from the monitor Alex was hooked up to. He was still sleeping. The nurse made several notes on a chart, then left without speaking.

Hanna looked down at Alex's face, still bruised from the earlier beating. She took a deep breath to clear her head.

Somehow, she had gotten the radio on the boat to work and kept screaming "911" on different channels until someone answered back. The Coast Guard had found them about an hour after she had pushed Sam into the frenzy of the big sharks. The memory of it made her shudder and she felt like she might be sick again at any moment. She was just laying her head back on Alex's chest in sheer exhaustion when she heard him whisper, "Hanna."

She sat up. "Oh, Alex!"

His eyes were glazed and only half open. She reached for his hand and squeezed it tight. She watched as he looked around the hospital room. "What the hell...?" he rasped, not finishing the thought.

She fell down into him, her arms around him, holding him close. She couldn't speak, the memory of the horror out on the ocean more than she could bare to think about. She felt Alex tense beneath her and say, "Where's Caine?"

She looked up at his battered face. "He's gone, Alex. He's gone."

Special Agents Foster and Fairfield knocked on the open hospital room door.

Hanna looked up and saw the wall clock at just past 5 pm. She hadn't seen them in over a year since their help in the safe return of her son. More than ever, she felt sure the gangster, Asa Dellahousaye, was involved in her deceased husband's failed land deal and her son's kidnapping as the mob element in the deal tried to recoup lost money they thought Hanna had squirreled away. She rose and gave both the FBI agents a warm embrace.

"How's our patient?" Will Foster asked, looking over at Alex, sleeping again under the influence of a sedative and the controlled release of pain medication for his multiple wounds.

Hanna said, "We're lucky either of us is even here."

Sharron Fairfield said, "The Coast Guard filled us in on your story as we were coming over. We were quite surprised to hear you were a former acquaintance of this hired killer."

"I still don't believe what happened. An old friend from college returns, a close friend, actually. He starts pressing me to think about getting serious again and going away with him. The next thing I know he's got a gun to Alex's head and he nearly kills both of us out on the Atlantic. If I hadn't..." She couldn't finish.

Fairfield put her arm around Hanna's shoulders. "Are you sure you're okay? That must have been terrible out there."

"To be honest, it all still seems like a really bad dream."

Foster said, "Did Alex have a chance to tell you our progress on the Dellahousaye case?

"What case?" Hanna asked, knowing Alex was looking into something about the gangster but not totally clear on all that was involved.

"An informant has led us to a huge fraud and bribery effort linked to pending legislation to broaden gambling access in the state. A number of people have also ended up dead thanks to your now departed friend."

Hanna winced at the reference to Sam Collins. "An informant?"

Foster continued, "We aren't in a position to reveal our source, but this individual is being extremely cooperative. Alex also provided some additional evidence against Dellahousaye that will be helpful in the prosecution."

A weak voice behind them said, "Who called in the cavalry?"

They all turned. Alex was awake and struggling to sit up. Hanna reached over to help him get pillows positioned. She and the two FBI agents stood around his bed.

Fairfield said, "You seem to have nine lives."

"Only about two left, I'm afraid," Alex replied.

Hanna put her hand on his shoulder. She couldn't keep it from shaking. The doctor thought she was still experiencing symptoms of shock.

Will Foster said, "Had an interesting meeting with your boss this afternoon."

"Guinness?"

Fairfield said, "Of course he denied everything, but he's being processed as we speak on charges of accessory to murder just for starters."

Hanna watched Alex close his eyes and his chest heaved in a deep breath.

Fairfield continued, "Your Internal Affairs department is not pursuing any further action against you at this point."

"Thank you," Alex said, the relief in his voice obvious.

"Our D.C. office paid a call on the Honorable Senator from South Carolina this afternoon," Foster said. "As you can imagine, he has ten excuses and alibis for every charge. I'm sure there will be a Senate Committee investigation along with our criminal case. I don't see much chance of a re-election run for the Senator."

"Jordan Hayes?" Hanna asked in surprise.

"We can't reveal the details," Fairfield said, "but Senator Hayes is closely linked to the corruption in this case with Dellahousaye."

"And when are you bringing Asa D in?" Alex asked.

Agent Fairfield said, "He was taken into custody this afternoon at his home out on the coast. The U.S. Attorney's office has a list of charges as long as your arm to pursue. We don't expect Mr. Dellahousaye to see light outside a prison cell for a very long time."

Hanna looked down at Alex. He smiled back at her through his battered and bruised face. She turned to the two agents across the bed. "And who is this informant?"

"As soon as we're sure we have this individual secure, " Foster replied, "we'll be able to talk to you about it. In the meantime, it looks pretty likely that Witness Protection will be the best option to protect our source."

Chapter Fifty-four

Alex was finishing a call with his father back in Dugganville, filling him in on the day's nearly tragic events. He looked up when he saw Lonnie Smith's wife, Ginny, standing in the doorway. Hanna was down trying to find some edible food in the cafeteria and in Alex's mind, likely trying to sort through her feelings about the death of a man she had once loved, who had somehow become a killer.

"I'll call you tomorrow, Pop." He listened for a moment while his father continued to scold him about "being safe".

"I'll be okay, Pop. Goodnight. He smiled as Ginny came into the room and over to his bed. He sat up slowly, trying not to let her see the discomfort he was in. They embraced and Ginny pulled up a chair.

"Hanna called to tell me what happened... that you'd been hurt again."

Alex didn't quite know how to respond. His guilt in the death of this woman's husband still haunted him and he was finding no path to forgive himself for how it had gone down.

Ginny said, "This man on the boat today, he's the one who killed Lonnie?"

Alex nodded and lay back in the pillows behind him. "He won't hurt anybody again, but..."

"No 'buts', Alex. He's gone and thank God for that."

Alex saw the last moments of Lonnie's life play out in his mind again; Caine throwing open a door in front of him, knocking him down and knocking his gun across the floor. Quick bursts of gunfire from the killer that ended Lonnie's life in a split second and then the gun turned back on him. Alex could not imagine a more terrifying sight than the cold cylindrical barrel of a gun pointed at your head, about to explode and end your life. His colleague, Beatty, had burst into the room just in time to disrupt the shooter's aim. The bullet had seared through his neck and fortunately not split the middle of his forehead with a lethal round.

"I was supposed to have Lonnie's back, Ginny."

"Enough, Alex! No one is holding this against you. I'm not. The kids surely aren't. They love you and they need you now that Lonnie is gone."

Alex sighed deeply, closed his eyes and let her words of comfort and assurance try to break through the wall of guilt he was unable to tear down. She leaned in and hugged him again. "You need to let this go, Alex."

If only it was that easy, he thought. How many years had he been carrying the guilt of taking his men into a situation that day in Afghanistan that had almost gotten them all killed? Despite the findings of the follow-up investigation of the incident where he was cleared of wrongdoing that could have led to charges being filed, Alex knew in his heart that Sergeant Grove from his unit was right in his accusations. A split-second decision made without sufficient intel had suddenly led his men into an ambush. His initial reaction to the chaos and death raining down on the them further exasperated the situation and ultimately got two more men under his command killed. Over the years, he had second-guessed his actions and reactions over and over and was never able to fully accept he had done all that could be expected under such sudden and deadly circumstances. He also knew there would be no relief from his guilt over losing his friend in this shootout with the killer named Caine.

He felt Ginny Smith pull back and he looked at her sad face. "Let me know what I can do to help with the boys," he said.

"They've been asking about you. I didn't want to bring the entire herd of them down here, but when you're ready."

"I'll stop by in the next day or so," he said.

"Thank you, Alex. Please get some rest and get well."

He hugged her again and watched as she walked out the door. He wondered what was keeping Hanna and then the episode earlier on Caine's boat came back to him.

Caine, he thought to himself, *or Sam Collins.* How could this monster have ever been close to Hanna? He just couldn't see a way Hanna would be attracted to such an evil force. Had the man changed that much since they were together in college? He still couldn't get the image of their kiss in the car from his mind.

Hanna walked in with two cups of coffee in her hands. She handed one to Alex.

"You just missed Ginny," he said.

"No, I saw her down the hall. She said you had a good chat."

He thought about that for a moment. *Had anything really been resolved?*

Hanna walked over and stood looking out the window to the street below. She sipped at her coffee, then turned and said, "I need to tell you something."

"Okay."

"I still can't believe what happened today with Sam. That person on the boat wasn't Sam, Alex. I don't know what's happened over the years he's been away, but that's not the man I knew."

"I have to believe that," Alex said.

"Even in the couple of days he's been back, I didn't see any sign of this in him." She paused. "You need to know he was actually trying to get us back together and quite honestly, the way things had been falling apart between you and me, I was actually giving it some serious thought."

Alex stared back at her waiting for her to continue. When she didn't go on, he said, "I saw the two of you kiss in the car last night in front of your office."

Hanna's eyes opened wide and she was obviously stunned. "You saw us?"

"I was waiting across the street for you. You wouldn't return my calls."

She walked around the bed and came up beside him. "I can't tell you I didn't have feelings for the man. He meant a lot to me many years ago and when he came back, all those emotions came, too."

"Would you have gone back with him?" Alex said, feeling a hollow emptiness in his chest.

"I don't know! Honestly, I don't know."

"Fair enough," Alex said, though thinking just the opposite.

"And by the way, *he* kissed me!"

"And your mouth just happened to get in the way," he said.

Hanna didn't reply.

Chapter Fifty-five

Two Months Later

Alex adjusted his tie and looked back over the small gathering seated on the lawn of his family's backyard in Dugganville. The familiar faces of his childhood and more recent years in this remote fishing town looked back at him. The old bartender, Gilly and his wife sat in the front row. Sheriff Pepper Stokes saw his gaze and smiled back.

The preacher's words brought him back to the moment. "We are gathered here today..."

Alex looked over at his father standing beside him, dressed in a new blue suit with a bright red silk tie, the first time he could ever remember Skipper with a tie on, let alone a suit. He was holding the hands of Ella Moore as they prepared to take their vows.

Alex had been stunned when his father called a few weeks earlier to tell him he and Ella had decided to "tie the knot". The two of them had been a train wreck together as long as Alex could remember. Skipper had assured him they had worked through all their past issues and wanted to be together as "man and wife" in the years they had left. As the date approached, Alex had finally been able to reconcile his father's decision and he was hopeful the two of them would find some sense of happiness and fulfillment. He was not particularly optimistic, knowing the full history of their tumultuous affair, but *let's hope for the best,* he thought. He also knew his father would need a companion to help with his declining memory and the likelihood of oncoming dementia.

Ella looked ten years younger with her hair beautifully arranged, her face tastefully done. She was dressed in a peach lace dress that matched the color of the flowers in her hair. She smiled back at him past his father and Alex nodded, happy now for the two of them... *and hopeful.*

Beyond Ella Moore, soon to be Mrs. Skipper Frank, stood Alex's ex-wife, Adrienne. She had come into town the night before for the wedding from Florida, but Alex hadn't seen her until a few minutes before the ceremony. She was standing as her mother's maid-of-honor. When Alex had heard she was coming back, he cringed to think about another reunion with a woman who had made his life miserable in so many ways. Her last attempts to win him back with a false claim about Alex being the father of her son, was only the latest example of the woman's treachery. He had been cordial when they met earlier before the ceremony, but it was all he could do to not just ignore her presence. He realized he had been staring at her when she smiled back at him.

"Do you Ella, take this man..." the preacher continued.

Adrienne was dressed in a surprisingly tasteful white dress, Alex thought, compared to her normal look of clothes two sizes too small revealing way too much of everything. Her hair was piled in sweeping curls on top of her head, matching her mother's and Alex had to push away thoughts of how good she looked today, past memories coming back to him of their happier times together in high school and the early days of their marriage before it quickly went all to hell with her infidelity and lies.

He looked away and turned to the preacher as he reached the end of the ceremony.

"If anyone has reason..." Alex heard the man say and of course he had twenty reasons why this marriage was a bad idea, but he would *"forever hold his peace."*

Alex stood at the bar set up in the back corner of the yard and took another cold bottle of beer from the bartender. Over the past weeks he had worked with his doctor to get help in pulling himself away from the dependence to the pain meds that had dragged him down again after the gunshot wound.

So far so good, he thought. This was the first alcohol he'd had since checking out of the hospital after nearly dying out on the salt at the hands of Asa Dellahousaye's killer, Caine.

He took a sip from the beer and looked out across the gathered reception. His father and Ella were holding court with their friends. It was a beautiful afternoon in the Low Country, despite Alex's dark mood at his ex's return and the fact he and Hanna had yet to work through their own issues.

Alex had seen Hanna twice since being released from the hospital. They had both come prepared to work out the differences that had come between them, but both times they left each other with little resolved. Hanna was, for good reasons, still terribly shaken by the violent death of Sam Collins... Caine, when she pushed him into the frenzy of sharks out on the Atlantic. She had saved Alex's life and perhaps her own, but the man had once been more than close to her, even the father of her aborted child. There was a lot for her to sort through there, and Alex knew he had to give her time.

His own reservations still lingered about getting close to any woman again with the chaotic and dangerous life he lived as a police officer. *Was it fair to pull anyone in to that craziness?*

He had invited Hanna to come to Skipper and Ella's wedding, but she had hesitantly declined, finally being open about the fact she wasn't keen on another encounter with Alex's ex-wife, Adrienne, when she found out she was planning to attend.

The old town sheriff, Pepper Stokes, walked over and touched his beer glass to Alex's. "To the happy couple," he said.

Alex nodded, remembering not that long ago the sheriff was seeing Ella Moore. *Just a little more drama for the newlyweds,* he thought.

"How you been, Alex?"

"I'm okay, Pepper," Alex replied, but it was clear in his tone he was far from it.

"Nasty stuff with Dellahousaye and how that all came down. And really sorry about your partner. He was a good man."

The mention of Lonnie Smith grabbed at Alex's gut. "Thanks Pepper."

"Heard that lawyer Holloway was the damn informant that took Asa D down. Brave sonofabitch. He better be watchin' his back."

Alex said, "My sources with the Feds tell me he's been sent away in the Witness Protection program. I hope they put his ass out in the desert somewhere."

Stokes laughed and said, "The man took down a lot of people."

"They all deserved it."

"Thought I'd get to see the beautiful Hanna today," Stokes said, looking out across the crowd.

Alex was about to reply when Adrienne walked up. She hugged the sheriff who quickly excused himself leaving the two of them alone.

"How you been, soldier?" she asked, smiling up at him as if there was no dark history between them.

"I'm not in the mood, Adrienne..." he started before she put a finger to his lips.

"Can't we put everything behind us at least for today for our parents?"

"Sure," he said, clearly not meaning it. "Where's the husband?"

Adrienne hesitated, then said, "We're working through a few things. He's back home with Scotty."

Alex thought about the young boy who for a while, Adrienne had convinced him was their son. "Scotty doing okay?"

"He's fine. Playing football now. You wouldn't believe how much he's grown."

"Look, Adrienne..." Alex started, trying to get away.

"I just want to say I'm sorry... for everything. I know there's a lot to forgive, but you need to know I feel terrible about all I've done and wish, well... I wish things would have been different."

Alex looked back at the face that had once been all he thought about. He had truly loved Adrienne Moore and still couldn't shut out the deep emotions of their early time together. He saw Ella coming toward them. "I think your mother needs you," he said and then walked away.

Alex sat in a folding chair on the aft deck of the old shrimp boat, the *Maggie Mae*, tied up at the docks along the river in front of his dad's house. The music from the wedding reception echoed through the tall trees and he could hear muffled laughter and conversation up behind him. He was staring down the river toward the west as the sun fell below the tree line. The beer in his hand was untouched and he noticed the condensation dripping onto his pants. He leaned down and placed the bottle on the wooden deck.

His thoughts were swirling from women to lost friends, to a future that remained uncertain.

He heard steps on the dock and turned, expecting to see Adrienne, but instead, it was Hanna Walsh.

Chapter Fifty-six

When Hanna pulled up to the house along the river in Dugganville, she saw Alex sitting alone out on his father's shrimp boat. She was relieved they would have some time together without Adrienne. She had been regretting her decision to decline Alex's invitation to the wedding. It was more than just the presence of his ex-wife. When Alex had asked her to attend, she still hadn't sorted out all her feelings about the events of the past weeks. The shock of her role in Sam Collins' death was haunting her days and nights. The unthinkable man he had become in their years apart was still more than she could comprehend or been ready to work through with Alex.

But, as she sat at home earlier today, stewing about whether she had made the wrong decision in not coming to the wedding, she had time to play it all out in her mind again... her feelings for Sam... the man who used to be Sam, and more importantly now, her feelings for Alex Frank. On the drive up this afternoon, she tried to convince herself she wasn't coming because she was jealous of Alex's ex and afraid of what she might try to pull to get him back again, *but of course she was.*

She watched as Alex turned when he heard her coming down the dock. She was pleased to see him smile. He stood and walked over to help her onto the boat. She was surprised when he pulled her into his arms and held her close.

"I'm sorry, I should have been here today," she said.

Alex pulled back and she saw a sad expression staring back at her. "It was quite an affair," he finally said. "I hope the two of them can have a happy life together... and not kill each other." He smiled again. "I think Ella may actually be good for him. His mind seems clearer these past weeks."

"That's great. And how is the lovely Adrienne?" she couldn't help asking.

He just shook his head, then sat on the rail of the boat and patted the space next to him for her to sit.

Hanna's mind raced with all the doubts and fears she'd been trying to process. She looked over at Alex and saw the wound on his neck was healed, though it left a nasty scar. The bruises and cuts on his face were gone.

Alex said, "Thank you for coming. I'm sure Skipper will be glad to see you."

"And how about you?" she asked, afraid of how he might respond.

He put his arm around her shoulder and kissed her cheek. "I've missed you, Hanna."

Smiling, she said, "I've missed you, too."

She watched his face stare back, uncertain, then he said, "I've had a lot of time to think about all this."

"So have I."

"How about a walk?"

Hanna walked alongside Alex through the quiet main street of little Dugganville, not much traffic or commotion on a Saturday evening. Little had been said, other than Alex's brief recap of the wedding and Adrienne's attempt to wash away past sins.

They came up to the park, heavily shaded with big live oaks and tall pines. They walked up the gently sloped lawn to a white painted gazebo on a knoll overlooking the town. They sat on a bench together and Hanna watched Alex sigh heavily and put his hands on his knees.

"I hope you didn't come up here today to break it off." He looked over at her and she could see he was serious.

In that moment, all her thoughts and doubts came together in a flood of clarity. "No, I came to apologize and..."

"You have nothing to apologize for."

"Well, yes I do. I want to get this thing about Sam behind us. I almost betrayed you and I've lost a lot of sleep trying to sort all that out. Anyway, I'm sorry, and I hope you'll forgive me." She looked over at him, her heart beating out of her chest when he didn't say anything.

A flood of relief washed over her when he pulled her close and she felt his face in her hair, and then he kissed her.

"Hanna, you are a saint to put up with all the chaos and nonsense I put you through."

This time, she kissed him. "For some crazy reason, I still think you're worth it."

She held Alex's hand as they came up the sidewalk to Skipper Frank's house, the party noise still loud from the back. They had been catching up on their past few weeks, mostly apart from each other.

"My client, the young girl whose father got her pregnant, had her abortion last month."

"Sounds like her father's going to be doing a long stretch in the penitentiary."

"The mother is facing charges for abuse, as well," Hanna said. "I went with Calley the day of her abortion and it brought back all those memories of my time..." She felt Alex squeeze her hand. "I'm still trying to convince myself it was the right thing for her. We talked again about adoption, but I understand she just couldn't go through with the pregnancy, with her father and everything."

"You and the judge helped her make the right decision," Alex said.

"Calley's sister has moved back to Charleston and she's going to be Calley's guardian and stay with her here until she finishes high school."

"Good, I hope she can get beyond all this," Alex said.

They walked out on the dock again. The sun was down now, and the last light of day filtered through the trees. A trace of the moon was showing just above the trees. A light at the end of the dock lit up the dark water of the river's slow current drifting by.

Hanna said, "I got an interesting call from an attorney in the Bahamas yesterday."

"What was that?" Alex asked, sitting beside her on a long bench at the end of the dock.

"It seems Sam had accumulated a considerable fortune over the years, including a very nice home in the hills in St. Croix and of course, the boat we got to see way too much of."

"I assume the money didn't come from the photography business."

"I wouldn't think so," Hanna said. "The thing is, this attorney informed me that he left a sizable sum to me in his will."

Alex looked over at her with an expression of total surprise. "You're kidding?"

"No, I'm afraid not. The man caught me so off guard, I didn't know how to react or what to say. I told him I would call him back on Monday."

"Collins had no family or anyone else close?" Alex asked.

"He was married once, but otherwise, I don't know. I assume his ex-wife got the bulk of the money." Hanna had already made up her mind about the inheritance. "I certainly don't want his money, Alex, particularly knowing how he earned it."

"What are you going to do?"

"I'll be donating all of it to the Women's Shelter in Charleston. They've been trying to raise money for years to add-on to their facility and bring in more help. Unfortunately, the demand for their services continues to grow."

She watched Alex processing what she'd just told him. He finally nodded his head and said, "Good for you. That just feels right. After all the death and darkness linked to that money, it's right to use it now for some good."

"I haven't told my friend, Greta the director, but she's going to be overjoyed."

"You're doing a good thing," Alex said.

Hanna caught Skipper Frank's eye as she and Alex came around the side of the house. His face lit up and he excused himself quickly from the group he was talking with and came over to them. He wrapped her in a big bear hug.

"Damn, Hanna, I'm so glad you were able to come."

"Congratulations, Skipper. I'm really happy for you." She noticed his bride coming up. They had met previously, and Hanna always felt she was a little guarded because of her daughter's former marriage to Alex. She had a big smile today and also gave Hanna a hug and kiss on the cheek.

"Hello, honey," Ella drawled. "Thanks for coming." The big woman pulled her new husband close and gave him a wet kiss on the cheek. "Finally corralled this old salty dog."

"You look beautiful, Ella," Hanna said. "Congratulations."

"Thank you, dear." Ella leaned in close. "When you gonna get this guy to settle down again?" she said, looking over at Alex.

Hanna noticed the word *again*, not surprising from Alex's ex-mother-in-law.

"One step at a time, Ella," she replied. She felt Alex put his arm around her waist.

Alex handed Hanna a glass of white wine as they stood apart from the rest of the gathering in a dark corner of the yard. A DJ was still playing dance music and half the guests were putting on their best dance moves in celebration of Skipper and Ella Frank's wedding day. She toasted Alex's beer bottle with a gentle clink. "To the happy couple," she said.

"Cheers."

They both turned when a voice from behind said, "Couldn't let the night get away without saying hello."

Adrienne walked around and held out her hand. "Hello, Hanna."

Hanna gave her a firm grip in return, trying her best to control the urge to throw the glass of wine in the woman's face. "Hello, Adrienne. We're very happy for your mother." She looked over at Alex who was obviously concerned about this little *gathering.*

"Well, that's nice of you, thanks," Adrienne said, cozying up to Alex and putting her arm around his waist. "Looks like we're family again, darlin'," she said, the effects of a long afternoon and evening of drinking evident in her slurred speech.

Alex pushed her away with a not so subtle shove. He reached for Hanna's arm to lead her away. "Goodnight, Adrienne." They left her standing there. Hanna looked back and the woman was weaving a bit and unsteady. She watched as Adrienne took a long drink and then threw the empty glass on the ground and stomped away toward the mass of dancers.

Alex led Hanna into the house and the small kitchen along the back. "Always a pleasure seeing your ex again," she said.

"Don't start," he said. "How about some coffee or..."

"I need to get back to town tonight. I've got an early morning at the office."

"When can I see you?" he asked.

"How about dinner at my place tomorrow night."

"Should I bring my toothbrush?" he asked.

"I think that would be a good idea."

Chapter Fifty-seven

The last few guests were saying their goodbyes to the bride and groom. The music had stopped, and the bartender was packing up. Alex was sitting on a chair on the back deck, nursing a cold cup of coffee. He watched as his ex-wife staggered around the side of the house in the arms of Robbie Reynolds, his father's first mate on the *Maggie Mae. Good luck, partner,* he thought and drained the rest of the coffee.

He got up and walked across the lawn to his father and new bride, Ella. Both had been drinking and celebrating for hours, which was actually a normal evening for the two of them, but Alex could see the day's events had taken their toll. Skipper was doing his best to support his new bride from slipping in the dewy grass.

"Great party, Pop," he said and then hugged them both. "You got a ride to the B&B?" They were staying at local inn just outside of town.

Skipper said, "Yeah, Gilly's droppin' us off."

"And you're off to Key West in the morning," Alex said, confirming the honeymoon plans they had shared earlier.

Skipper nodded and said, "Gonna get some sun, drink some rum, catch some fish..."

"Get naked!" Ella said, and giggled.

"Well, you two have a great trip. It was quite a wedding, Pop. Congratulations." Alex had a fleeting thought about the times shared in this backyard with his mother, now gone many years following a tragic car accident. He was happy for his dad, though. He'd been alone a long time. He wasn't sure the old man and Ella would be the best influence on each other, but who was he to judge.

Gilly came up and said, "Y'all ready to go?"

They all said their goodbyes. Ella kissed him sloppily on the lips and gave him a big hug. He watched as they disappeared inside the house.

An hour later he was just about to turn out the light to go to bed when his phone buzzed on the nightstand. He looked at the screen and didn't recognize the number. He looked at the time and it was just past 2am. He took the call. "This is Alex."

There was a pause for a moment and Alex was about to end the call when a low voice said, "We need to talk, Detective."

"Who is this?"

"You've been a thorn in my side far too long, Frank."

Alex then recognized the distinctive Cajun accent of Asa Dellahousaye. "Thought they had you locked up."

"I got good lawyers."

"What do you want?"

"The question is, what do *you* want?"

"What are you talking about?" Alex asked, sitting up on the bed now, his internal alarms flaring in his brain.

"Do you want to see your lawyer girlfriend alive again?"

Alex felt the air sucked out of his lungs. He tried to control the panic that raced through him, standing and pacing across the small bedroom in his father's house.

"Detective?" he heard Dellahousaye ask.

"I swear..."

"No time for idle threats, Frank. I'm trying to clear-up a few things, and frankly there are some people who continue to piss me off... and you're one of them."

"Where's Hanna?"

The gangster didn't reply at first and then Alex heard Hanna cry out in the background, "Alex!"

"Dellahousaye!" Alex yelled into the phone.

"You and I need to have a chat, Detective," the gangster said slowly."

"Tell me where."

"We're at your old man's fish camp. Nice wedding by the way."

"You have no reason to hurt her," Alex said, trying to control the fear in his voice.

"I have your other lovely friend, Miss Richards. She tells me you have something I need to get back."

Alex immediately realized the FBI hadn't been able to successfully secure Amelia Richards.

"I don't know what you're talking about," Alex said, trying to buy time and think through his options.

"No time for games, Detective!" Dellahousaye hissed. "You and your girlfriend took out one of my primary 'enforcers' shall we say, but I have another associate here with me who is very anxious to get his hands on these two lovely ladies."

Alex's heart was pounding through his chest and he struggled to push back the nausea rising in his gut. The phone trembled in his hand as he said. "When I know the women are safe, I'll bring you what you want." He knew the Feds already had the taped conversations, but he had to buy as much time as he could.

"You're in no position to haggle, Detective. Get your ass up here now, or we'll start feeding pieces of these ladies to the gators!"

"I'll be there... I'm coming right now," he said, his mind racing on how to handle the situation.

"Do not call anyone or bring anyone with you. If we get any indication you've called for backup, it's going to end very badly up here. Do you understand?"

"Loud and clear."

Chapter Fifty-eight

Hanna tried with all her will not to show these men the fear that was consuming her. She was tied to an old wooden chair, her hands bound painfully behind her in Alex's father's fishing camp. She and Alex had spent some weekends up here to get away. Amelia Richards sat across the table from her, also bound. She had already been at the camp when Hanna arrived. Her face was flushed and swollen with tears. The old cabin, built up on stilts over the marshes north of Dugganville, was darkly lit with two kerosene lanterns. It smelled of mildew and ash from the stone fireplace.

She had been only a few miles out of Dugganville after leaving Alex at his father's house when a large SUV had passed her on the dark two-lane road and then pulled over sharply to run her off the road onto the shoulder. Two men had rushed out and pulled her from her car. They bound her hands quickly behind her then threw her in the back of the SUV. One man followed in her car. She had recognized Skipper Frank's fish camp as they drove the final stretch of the narrow two-track through the swamp.

She had listened to Asa Dellahousaye's phone conversation with Alex. Fear and panic were nearly overwhelming her ability to think clearly. The gangster had two men with him who had abducted her. Both were tall, stocky men, dressed in dark clothes. Each had a side arm visible on their belts and one was holding a shotgun, pointed at the ceiling. Dellahousaye was dressed in a white dress shirt, open at the collar, and pressed jeans above a pair of brightly polished black leather loafers. His gray hair was swept back from his tanned face. She watched as he came over and sat beside her.

"You seem to have the worst taste in men, Miss Walsh," he said, grinning.

Hanna didn't respond, afraid her voice would reveal the terror that was pulsing through her.

"Your husband, Ben, was a stupid man. He thought he could steal from us."

Hanna's belief that Dellahousaye was involved with her husband in the disastrous land deal that had led to his death and her son's kidnapping was now confirmed. She just stared back at his face trying her best to keep from shaking.

"And now you're with this idiot detective who should be dead... and will be shortly."

The events of the past weeks, including the death of Sam Collins by her own hand, had shaken her but more recently had also given her a new strength and sense of purpose. She was determined now not to let this man see her fear.

"This will all be over soon," he said, grinning before he stood and walked over to talk to one of his men. She watched as the man with the shotgun nodded and went outside.

She was startled when Amelia Richards cried out, "Please don't hurt us! We'll give you what you want!"

Hanna looked across at the woman who was near hysteria.

"Please!" she yelled out again.

Dellahousaye's other man walked calmly over and slapped the side of Amelia's face so hard the sound almost echoed in the small cabin. Hanna flinched as she saw the woman topple over, still tied to the chair. The man left her there on her side and then glared at Hanna as he walked back to a front window to check outside.

She felt Dellahousaye's hand on her arm and looked back as he said, "Not sure how you and Frank got the best of my man, Caine. He was one of the best I ever worked with."

Hanna saw images of Dellahousaye's hit man, the man she knew as Sam Collins, being pulled under by the sharks. She cringed and looked down.

"And your friend, Holloway..." she heard him say. She looked back. "He better find a big rock to hide under."

The front door opened, and Hanna gasped as Alex walked in. Della-housaye's man had the shotgun pressed to the back of his head. She made eye contact with Alex as he quickly assessed the room. She saw him hesitate when he saw her tied at the table and Amelia Richards still lying on the floor, crying.

"Welcome, Detective," Asa D said. "Glad to see you could join us."

"Let the women go now," Alex said. "I'll give you whatever you want."

Dellahousaye walked up to Alex and threw his full weight into a punch that hit him in the gut and dropped him to his knees, gasping for air.

"I know the Feds already have the information, Frank. We'll deal with that down the road."

Alex was trying to catch his breath to speak. Dellahousaye kicked him hard in the side and Alex fell over, holding himself in almost a fetal position.

"Just cleaning up a few *loose ends* tonight," the gangster snarled.

"Stop it!" Hanna yelled out. Dellahousaye turned to her and smiled as if he was really enjoying all this.

"Pick him up, Etienne!" Asa D commanded and the other man who had stayed inside knelt down and lifted Alex to his feet. "No need to drag things out."

She saw Alex look over at her as he tried to gather himself. She could see the pain he was in. She struggled at her restraints but was held fast. In horror, she watched as Dellahousaye took a long knife from one of his men and walked over to Amelia. "Pick her up!" he shouted, then stood behind her chair and drew the knife up to her neck. "Let's stop playing around, Detective."

Hanna screamed as she watched the knife cut into the side of Amelia Richard's neck, a thin slice of skin erupting in blood as Amelia yelled out and fought to get free.

Dellahousaye just laughed and stared back at Alex. "You would think people would have learned better than to betray me."

Alex struggled to stand. "Let them go!" he demanded.

Hanna saw the blade of the knife go back to Amelia's neck and the woman stopped screaming now, trembling in anticipation of the next cut.

A loud explosion of broken glass shattered across the dark room and Hanna nearly fell back in her chair as chaos erupted all around. She watched in horror as the side of the face of Dellahousaye's man holding the shotgun on Alex was blown away in a bloody mist. He fell to the ground in a heap and Alex turned quickly to grab the long gun.

The door burst open and Hanna saw the old sheriff, Pepper Stokes, rush into the room. He had a shotgun up ready to fire. The gun thundered in a deafening blast and Hanna saw Dellahousaye's other man blown back against a counter and fall, a large bloody wound opened in his belly.

She turned as Alex yelled, "Stop!" Dellahousaye was running to the back of the cabin, a door there to the back deck. Another shotgun blast caused her to recoil again as she saw the gangster's right shoulder explode. He crashed into the wall and then fell to the floor. He still had the long knife in his other hand. He managed to stand, blood dripping from his arm. In a fury, he rushed at her with the knife coming straight for her face.

She screamed out as the sound of a shotgun echoed again behind her and Asa Dellahousaye's chest exploded as he was hurled back against the wall and then fell in a lifeless heap on the floor.

Hanna was gasping for breath. The air was heavy with smoke and the smell of gun powder. She felt Alex cutting at the ties holding her to the chair and then he was kneeling in front of her. She fell into his arms and they both tumbled down onto the floor still holding each other.

She heard Pepper Stokes say, "Holy shit!"

Chapter Fifty-nine

The long sailboat cut through the swells of the blue Atlantic. The air was cooled by a steady wind from the west, waves capping white as far as the eye could see. A school of flying fish raced along beside the big boat, slicing in and out of the ocean swells, then were gone. Hanna sat on the high side, feeling the wind and the mist of the water on her cheek, watching Alex at the wheel of the sailboat.

Skipper and Ella Frank sat across from her, Ella snuggled down into her new husband's arms, a margarita half gone in her free hand. Skipper had his old stained fishing cap on and the most joyous expression on his face. His third drink was helping with his good mood.

Hanna looked up at Alex. "Good job, Captain!"

"Thanks, we should be in Havana for lunch," he said, smiling back at her.

"Right." They had chartered the boat out of Key West for the day. She and Alex had suddenly decided to get out of town after the horror of the night at Skipper Frank's fish camp and all that had gone down in the Dellahousaye affair. She was still struggling to get the terrifying images of that night from her mind.

They had surprised Skipper and Ella, arriving in the Keys just a few days after they had come down for their honeymoon. It had taken some time for the Sheriff's Department and agents Foster and Fairfield from the FBI office to clear up all the mess linked to the death of Asa Dellahousaye and his men. Amelia Richards was recovering from the neck wound inflicted by the brutal gangster, but doctors had assured them she would be okay. In the end, the authorities had privately thanked her and Alex for saving them considerable time and expense in prosecuting and convicting the man.

In the process, Hanna had been surprised to learn that her husband's old partner, Phillip Holloway, was the informant the FBI had referred to who was to testify against Dellahousaye with plans to disappear in the Witness Protection program afterward. She had seen Phillip briefly at the FBI office in Charleston and he assured her that now with Dellahousaye gone, he planned to stay in town and continue his work at the firm. Of course, he offered to take her to dinner to celebrate the demise of Asa Dellahousaye, but she quickly put an end to his lecherous invitation.

She and Alex had caught a plane to Key West the next morning and surprised his father and new bride. The last couple of days were clouded with drink and celebration and relief at surviving the frightening ordeals in the swamps of the Low Country and offshore on the blue Atlantic.

"Where to next?" she said to Alex, standing at the helm in front of her.

"Wanted you to know," Alex said, "I called the Department this morning and quit my job."

"What!"

She watched Skipper and Ella turn in surprise as well.

"Enough already with Charleston PD," he said, a big smile spreading across his sunburned face.

Skipper said, "What do you plan to do?"

Alex looked down at Hanna. "Our friends at the FBI want me to apply for a job there."

"Are you serious?" Hanna said, standing to join him behind the big wheel of the sailboat. He placed an arm around her.

"We'll see."

Hanna said, "Special Agent Alex Frank. It has a ring to it."

"Like I said, we'll see."

Hanna looked over as two dolphins surfaced just beside them and continued along, playing in their wake. Their smooth gray shapes slipped effortlessly along, wet and shimmering in the bright sunlight and clear green water. She looked back at Alex who was smiling at her. She glanced at her watch. "Time to take us home, Agent Frank. Wouldn't want to miss happy hour at *Sloppy*

Joe's."

"I agree!" Skipper yelled out, holding up his margarita.

THE END

A note from author Michael Lindley

Thank you for reading *DEATH ON THE NEW MOON*!

You've come this far, so I trust you're enjoying the "Hanna and Alex" stories. I can't thank you enough for your time with my books.

… and there's more!

In Book #4, *THE SISTER TAKEN, the shocking disappearance of a young woman and a suspicious death put Hanna and Alex back in the cross-hairs of the ruthless Dellahousaye crime family.*

A missing twin. A wayward sister. A "jaw-dropping" twist.

To keep reading **THE SISTER TAKEN**, go to Michael Lindley's online store to buy direct at **store.michaellindleynovels.com.**

About the Author

Michael Lindley is an Amazon #1 bestselling author of mystery and suspense novels. His *"Hanna and Alex"* Low Country series has been a frequent #1 bestseller on Amazon in that genre.

His previous books include the "Troubled Waters" novels of historical mystery and suspense begins with the Amazon #1 bestseller, THE EMMALEE AFFAIRS.

"I've always been drawn to stories that are built around an idyllic time and place as much as the characters who grace these locations. As the heroes and villains come to life in my favorite stories, facing life's challenges of love and betrayal and great danger, I also enjoy coming to deeply understand the setting for the story and how it shapes the characters and the conflicts they face.

I've also loved books that combine a mix of past and present, allowing me to know a place and the people who live there in both a compelling historical context, as well as in present-day. I try to capture all of this in the books I write and the stories I bring to life."

Copy the Bookfunnel link below to sign up for my *"Behind The Scenes"* newsletter to receive announcements and special offers on new releases

and other special sales, and we will also send you a FREE eBook copy of the *"Hanna and Alex"* intro novella, *BEGIN AT THE END.*

You can connect with me on:

🌐 https://store.michaellindleynovels.com

Subscribe to my newsletter:

✉ https://dl.bookfunnel.com/syy533ngqn

Also by Michael Lindley

The "Troubled Waters" Series

THE EMMALEE AFFAIRS

THE SUMMER TOWN

BEND TO THE TEMPEST

The "Hanna Walsh and Alex Frank Low Country Mystery and Suspense" Series

LIES WE NEVER SEE

A FOLLOWING SEA

DEATH ON THE NEW MOON

THE SISTER TAKEN

THE HARBOR STORMS

THE FIRE TOWER

THE MARQUESAS DRIFT

LISTEN TO THE MARSH

THE SISTER TAKEN

Buy direct at Michael Lindley's online store at *store.michaellindleynovels.com.*